THE
DEATH
OF THE
MOON

☾

BRIAN PANHUYZEN

☾

the
Death
of the
Moon

STORIES

CORMORANT
BOOKS

© Brian Panhuyzen 1999

FIRST EDITION

The publisher gratefully acknowledges the support of the Canada Council for the Arts and the Ontario Arts Council for its publishing program. We acknowledge the financial support of the Government of Canada through the Book Publishing Industry Development Program (BPIDP) for our publishing activities.

THE CANADA COUNCIL FOR THE ARTS SINCE 1957 | LE CONSEIL DES ARTS DU CANADA DEPUIS 1957

Canadä

Some of these stories have appeared in *B+A New Fiction*, *ink magazine*, *The Malahat Review*, *Prairie Fire*, and *Smoke*.

Copyedited by Gena K. Gorrell.
Proof-read by Margaret Booth and Barbara Glen.

Typeset in Janson, created by Miklós Tótfalusi Kis (1650–1702).
Book interior design by Brian Panhuyzen.

Printed and bound in Canada.

CANADIAN CATALOGUING IN PUBLICATION DATA

Panhuyzen, Brian, 1966 –
    The death of the moon
Short stories.

ISBN 1-896951-15-5

I. Title.

PS8581.A638D42 1999   C813'.54   C99-900065-9
PR9199.3.P324D42 1999

Cormorant Books Inc.
RR 1, Dunvegan, Ontario KOC 1J0

FOR

John & Arina

AND

all the cats

Contents

Marijke and Shonny

IT IS A JULY SO HOT that it is killing the birds. Every day the corpses of pigeons and sparrows and blue jays litter the griddle-hot pavements of the city. Municipal crews in fluorescent vests and hardhats dispose of them, rolling the mottled bodies onto shovels, but they always miss a few, these carcasses reanimating a few hours later with the curdling of maggots.

Death also visits the rooms of the city, the unchilled apartments of the elderly and infirm. They sit in collapsed poses, beside mugs of copper brandy, the remote still cocked towards the television, which, oblivious, expresses the same channel throughout the brief night.

But despite death, there is also desire. The collision of moist flesh.

John is asleep on his side, nude, uncovered, lying broadside like a sail, trying to catch the fan's soft breath as it pans across the room, forever searching for something unknown. The staccato knock that rouses him from this slumber of sweat and drool is certainly from his landlady, Miss Hobarth, requesting the overdue rent. He leaps up and bolts down the carpeted stairs, unattired, knowing what will scare her off: a fit, young, naked man, varnished with sweat, asking her in for tea while he makes out the cheque.

Instead he finds himself face to face with his cousin Marijke, with her bales of chocolate hair and aquamarine eyes. She carries a suitcase and is out of breath, frostings of sweat on her neck and the pale skin above her breasts. She brushes John aside and drops her suitcase, then wipes her forehead with a handkerchief.

—*Hoi*, cousin. Are there many people coming through here? Is it safe to leave that there? she asks, pointing to a tall column of fabric propped against the wall outside his door.

John covers himself with a hand and nods.

She shuts the door and looks him up and down.

—A good idea in this heat. Not allowed on the beaches here, *nee?*

She picks up the suitcase and mounts the stairs.

John follows her and at the top of the stairs hurries towards the bathroom. He shoves open the door but she halts him by addressing him as she did when he was twelve and she was thirteen.

—Shonny.

He does not turn.

—Shonny, I was going to say I don't see enough of you, but now I think I'm seeing too much.

He continues into the bathroom and shuts the door.

When he comes out fifteen minutes later, barely relieved by the cool shower, Marijke is chattering on the phone in Dutch and scribbling frantically on a notepad.

—Is that long distance? he asks, tying the sash on his bathrobe.

She waves him away and continues to speak. It sounds like an argument. He clears the clothing and laundry from the floor and kneels into her line of sight.

—Is that long distance? he hisses.

She covers the mouthpiece with her hand.

—When does the museum open?

—I can't afford long distance.

—When is it open?

—Who will pay for this?

He reaches for the hang-up button but she seizes his wrist. Still talking, she slams her little purse on the table and cracks it open, spills a pile of guilders out and peels off a ten, its contemporary blue artwork like play money in his hand. He turns it over, looks over the thick lines and patterns, pushes it back at her.

—No. You are a guest.

She puts a finger in her ear.

—*Ja. Ja. Goede. Dag. Ja. Tot ziens.*

She hangs up and tears the page from the pad, folds it four times.

—If you have a phone book I can call the museum.

—The museum is boring. We should go to the beach.

—Boring? You are boring. I want to look at the rugs.

He provides her with a gaping yawn.

—And you should your teeth *poetsen*, she declares.

—*Poetsen?* What's *poetsen?*

—What do you think I mean when I talk about teeth? Didn't Tante Velda teach you Dutch? You have bad breath.

He closes his mouth and puts his hand over it.

—I have no toothpaste.

She picks up her suitcase and throws it down on the ragged twist of sweaty sheets on his bed. With a quick tug she unwinds both zippers and throws the top open. The case is precisely packed, each item folded and grouped with its own kind: blouses, skirts, shorts. Panties. He does not look at them, does not see their lacy decorations, does not see their translucence. She hands him a tube of toothpaste.

—Brush the teeth. And get dressed. I will phone the museum to tell them we are coming.

—So they can lay out the red carpet?

—*Nee.* So they can buy mine.

◗ It is only ten o'clock and John thinks that the sun is like the broiler in the oven whenever he makes a cheese melt, the way it feels on the back of his hand when he reaches in with the pot holder. But this heat is on his head. He spits, trying to get the chalky taste of foreign toothpaste out of his mouth.

Marijke is two metres behind him. She is holding the other end of the heavy roll. He does not look back at her but he hears her breathing, the quick gasps.

—Shonny, let's stop here.

There is a parkette in the shade of a building. They set the rug down on the grass and John goes to sit on it.

—*Niet doen!* she cries.

—What?

—Don't sit on it. It's three hundred years ago.

—Ago? You mean old.

—*Ja*, old. *Oud. Drie honderd jaar.* Sit on the grass. Here.

She takes his forearm and guides him to the ground. The grass and the soil beneath it are cool. He presses both palms to the earth and closes his eyes. He is surrounded by a corona of heat. He imagines a thermograph of his body, a blood-red aura.

Marijke, cross-legged with her back bolt-straight, dabs the sweat from her skin. She gets a compact from her tiny purse and applies lipstick, a pastel-fluorescent pink. John opens his eyes and sees her lips and she looks at him so he turns his eyes down but then is looking at the place where her thigh emerges from the violet miniskirt. He picks at the grass, plucks out a blade and stares at it. Wonders at the skin, at her skin, is it the same skin he touched twelve years ago in the loft of the red house in that little Dutch town full of red houses? He remembers Heusden, that it sat beside a river, and that this river crossed *over* a bridge. You drove under the bridge and the sail of a boat could be passing above you.

The cells of the skin replace themselves every thirty days. The physical properties of the skin cannot be emotionally important. A soldier hunched beneath the turret of his tank dreams of the skin of his wife; is he dreaming of something forever lost, the skin of their last love before his departure? No, for he is not dreaming of her skin, he is dreaming of her love and her soul as they permeate the skin. For if it is a long war and he survives the bombs and the landmines and the bayonets, and when finally he is against his wife's skin again – she who had the fairest and softest skin in creation, which has toughened and wrinkled in the sun and wind of her waiting life – it is still the same skin, her skin, the conduit to her soul, and it carries the love out of her and into his own skin, of which she too has dreamed, skin once taut and brown, now pale and thin. It is the same skin.

Marijke is jabbing down notes onto a pad.

—Would you like a drink, cousin?

—Yes, cousin, she replies, smiling. —A Spa?

—No Spa here. How about a ginger ale? Canada Dry.

—*Ja. Graag.*

◗ When he is coming back from the convenience store he sees a man talking to her. He quickens his pace.

—Here, sweetheart, he says, sitting down close to her.

—*Bedankt*, she replies, opening the can. —This is Marty.

Marty grins at the hard T and she takes a long drink.

—Hello, Marty, John says, using her accent.

—Also from Holland? Marty asks.

—*Klein beetje. Klein beetje,* John replies.

—Shonny is my Canadian cousin. I am staying with him.

—How long are you in town? Marty inquires.

—Just for one day. Just today.

—Only today! John cries.

—I am delivering this carpet to the museum. And then I go home. Is the museum far from here?

—Another ten minute walk. You should have taken a cab. Marty looks at John as he says this.

—Oh, too expensive, Marijke laughs, and also looks at John.

—We better get going, John says, standing.

—Why don't I give you a hand the rest of the way?

—That's okay.

—Yes, that would be very kind, Marijke says. She finishes the ginger ale and rises.

Now there are three people carrying a log of fabric along the street. John is at the front and Marty is at the back, with Marijke in the middle. Marty is watching the back of Marijke's legs and John, although he cannot see this, knows it.

They go to the museum's side entrance and are buzzed in. A woman in a ratty cardigan and round glasses leads them through offices which are arctic-cold and smell like the inside of a refrigerator. John shivers as the sweat on his back cools. Most of the employees are wearing sweaters.

They pass through exhibits featuring giant beetles, then purple gemstones, then Chinese pottery. Eventually they come to the textile labs.

When the door is opened they are washed over by a musky odour of canvas and wool, cotton and silk, fibre and fabric. The odour of a hundred thousand paraffin candles, the smell of incense and perfume, of food and wine, the smell of sex and sweat, the smell of animal fur, wet dogs and horse dung, the smell of earth and grass, the smell of gunpowder and blood, the smell of tears, the smell of labour and pain. In seconds these odours fill the unconscious with a thousand histories, embedded in the twists of wool and the weave of cotton in ancient cloaks, garters, shoes, mats, rugs, tapestries, tablecloths, bed covers, bags, tents.

A young woman with short brown hair snaps her head up from a workbench on which is spread a kimono of unbearable orange, her eyes gigantic behind high-powered lenses. She is introduced by their guide as Vanessa Orbel, the textile curator.

—John van Vugt.

—Marijke Zorn. I was talking on the phone with you.

—The rug! Bring it here, bring it here, Vanessa tells them, shifting the pallet with the kimono on it to make space for the carpet.

They set it on the bench. Vanessa produces a knife and cuts the strings that bind it. She places each string carefully into a drawer, then unrolls the rug, revealing a dense and intricate pattern of copper and blue and black.

—Persian, Vanessa says.

Marijke nods.

John bends down to look at the carpet.

—Late seventeenth century, Senneh knot. Silk. Look at the embroidery here! Vanessa exclaims.

—This is from the house, John cries.

Everyone turns to look at him.

—The house in Heusden, he says softly.

Marijke nods. Vanessa begins to unroll it further, her face very close to the fabric, the animals, hundreds of them, issuing from the roll like an encyclopedic scroll, wolves, deer, spiders, cats, foxes, mice, rabbits.

—I recognize the wolf, the way it's attacking that deer! This carpet was in the living room, with the harpsichord and the old chairs. I remember when we would lie on it and look up to the high ceiling with the plaster patterns. The soft carpet. . . .

John darts his hand towards it, then withdraws as a darker fringe unrolls.

—It's burned here, Vanessa reports.

He watches in horror as the geometries of soft hues, heads and legs and tails, dissolve into a jagged patchwork of charred wool and twisted filaments. A smell escapes, a desperate, humid smell. John steps back from it, expels a breath through his nose.

He meets Marijke's eyes, sees the sudden sparkle of them in the glow from the desklamp, their glint in the murky light. Her mouth is taut, a frown, an exclamation, a rebuttal, defiant.

◗ In the heat again, she tries to catch his eye but he cannot look at her, feels her gaze like a needle against the face of a balloon, some bulging emotion which he will not purge out here. He shovels change at the panhandlers young and old, doesn't wait for their liturgies, just rattles the coins into palms or paper cups.

Marty is still with them, uncomfortable but persistent, trying to engage Marijke in conversation. She is curt. They are at the storefront doorway that leads up to John's apartment.

—Why don't you two go out for a beer? There's a good bakery at the next lights. Some nice Canadian beer there. I'm going up to take a nap.

Marijke is speechless, looks to Marty, then to John. But he has already entered the building and started up the stairs. He throws a cautious glance at Miss Hobarth's door, through which he can hear a television, but it does not open.

Once inside he lowers the venetian blinds and twists them shut; the sunlight pushes through, casting acetylene bands on the floor. John avoids them as he moves through the room, peels off his clothes, the fabric clinging to his moist flesh, tosses them down on the floor and lowers himself slowly to the bed, sets himself into the path of the fan's breath. It grazes his sweaty shoulders, his chest, his neck as he lies on his side and closes his eyes. He hears a soft hum, the buzz of the heat, the traffic groaning as it ploughs through the thick air, plying the humid streets. A staccato of laughter rings through the vents. Voices whisper beyond the walls about the heat, on everyone's brows and lips and tongues there is heat, this unbearable airjam, the still tyrant.

The phone rings, muffled beneath his cast-off shirt.

—Yes.

—Marijke is there?

—Who?

—It's Allegra. Your bitchy sister? I heard that Marijke is there.

—Marijke from Holland? Marijke our cousin?

—Yes. She is supposed to be in Canada. I thought she would go there first. It was in a letter from Tante Leisha.

—I didn't know. What is she doing here? If she's here.

—I don't know. I think it's business. Leisha didn't say. Just that she would be visiting on the eighth of July and to make sure I saw her.

—How can we find her?

—Do you know that Olaf and Ellis are dead?

—What?

—Tante Ellis and Om Olaf. Dead. It says so in the letter.

—When did you get the letter? What's happened?

—The letter came today. There was a fire. The house in Heusden burned down.

—Oh my god. Did you talk to Mamma?

—She was out. I left a message.

—Saying that her sister is dead?

—No. No, saying to call. Saying to call me.

Allegra is crying now. John listens for a few seconds, sweat filling his ear against the phone, his forehead pushed into his hand.

—Allegra. Ally, don't cry.

—Maybe Marijke is here because of that.

—When did this happen?

—About six months ago. We didn't know. How could we not know? How could Mammie not know that her sister is dead?

—I don't know.

—How could she not feel it? Even if they hated one another. How could she not feel her sister's death?

—I don't know, I don't know.

—I have to go. In case she calls. If Marijke comes, phone me. Please. Or I'll phone you.

—Okay.

—Bye.

John pushes the phone into the cradle, crawls back to the bed like a crippled man. He falls asleep.

When he awakes it is dark. Thin slits of mercury light cut through the blinds. The fan continues to survey the room, rocking its head back and forth, a message, a slow-motion *no*. John rises and shaves and takes a cool shower. He pulls on a pair of briefs and begins to organize the laundry, filling the hamper and two plastic bags. He puts a single clean sheet on the little bed, flattens the futon beneath the front windows, and spreads the other sheet on it. He puts Marijke's suitcase on the floor beside the bed. He does the dishes, cleans the bathroom sink. He drinks a huge amount of water, sweats it out, drinks more. When he is done it is almost eleven. People are in the streets, hooting, bellowing to one another. He thinks about eating, instead turns out the light and lies again within the fan's sweep. The traffic murmurs, somewhere deep in the building a woman's voice sighs, "Oh yes." He strains to hear more but does not.

He falls asleep.

A bowl of change strikes the floor, scatters.

—Pardon, a voice whispers.

John opens his eyes a slit, then closes them. The floorboards creak as footsteps move around the room. He hears the click of the bathroom light, hears the door close. He drifts off again, then awakes, the sound of breathing very close to his face. He keeps his eyes closed, smelling the alcohol-rich breath.

—Stupid Canadian boys, the voice says.

The breath moves away. He hears the swish of fabric and he eases his eyelids open, sees through the cage of his eyelashes the outline of a woman undressing. She is facing away from him; she strips off her miniskirt and top, then, wearing panties only, shuffles through her suitcase. Still facing away, she pulls on a white undershirt. She patters out of view; the wedge of bathroom light strikes the ceiling, then contracts as the door shuts. Sometime in the following lull he falls asleep again.

He awakens and the apartment is in darkness. The fan drones as he looks across at the futon, which is slightly lower than his bed. He hears her breathing; it is deep and even. As his pupils swell to the darkness, he realizes that he can see just the silhouette of her form. At even intervals, however, long slits of light from the streetlamp outside shine through the blinds. One crosses her breasts; another is cast across her pelvis; a third cuts her legs just below the knee.

He dozes again but is suddenly awakened by a variation in the pitch of the air. At first he thinks that the fan speed has changed; then he realizes that Marijke's breathing has accelerated slightly. He watches her breasts as they move in the light beam. Abruptly she pulls her left arm up and wraps her fingers around the futon's steel armrest. With the other hand she tugs the undershirt up to expose her left breast. He regards the erect nipple and the nimbus of white light around it. For perhaps two minutes she lies with her hand on her throat, breathing, enjoying the touch of the light. Then she brings her hand down and takes the nipple between her fingertips, kneading it gently. A tiny moan escapes from her lips. Her head snaps towards him as she holds her breath. He closes his eyes, continues to breathe as if asleep.

Her deep breathing resumes. After a few minutes there are other sounds of motion and John cracks his eyelids again. She has pulled the undershirt completely up to her neck, exposing both breasts to the light's shaft, wriggling slowly on the mattress beneath the light's touch. John's cock is huge; he can feel the head pressing against the waistband of his briefs, threatening to emerge.

The hand is circling downwards, skimming the white flesh of her lower ribcage, her taut stomach. It glides over the top edge of her panties but retreats to her navel, back up to her breasts. Then it slides down again, passes farther south before returning. The long legs are bowing outwards; with each foray of the hand they widen more. Now the hand grazes the little swell there, flicks briskly over the mound and back up to her neck, up her chin. One finger dips between her lips before the hand starts down, over her throat, between her breasts, over her belly, over the mound and between her legs. She moans again, louder than the first time, but does not look at him. John sighs softly, looks down his own body where his cock has escaped his briefs and the head is grazed by one of the slats of light. He follows the light across his mattress, down the floor, up the futon and to Marijke's pelvis. She is slowly massaging herself between her legs. She raises her head and looks down her body, then pushes her panties aside, exposing her engorged lips. She holds them open to the light beam, moves her pelvis, allowing the lightshaft to play over the moist folds. Her body shifts in the bands of light; now she uses her fingers, they press deep between her lips as the tempo increases.

John is panicking. He knows it is irrational, but his genitals are so thick with blood that he fears permanent damage. He needs to touch himself, needs to be touched. His testicles ache, his breath is ragged and quick.

Marijke has found her rhythm; her pelvis bucks against her right hand while her left caresses her breasts, her nipples, her armpits and shoulders. Her skin is glowing with moisture, glaring in the streetlamp beams. John chews his lip, bites it hard.

The motion of Marijke's hand between her legs is slowing, becoming more intense, the thrust of her fingers deeper. John is tuned to the beat of it, senses it as a countdown, his breath synchronized with hers. For a moment he feels the vicarious pleasure, the crescendo of pressure, a force on the verge of release.

—Uh.

With horror he realizes that *he* has uttered this sound. It is unmistakably his own voice and he presses his eyes shut, clenching his jaw, trying desperately to retrieve the syllable from the air before it reaches her ears.

But it reaches her. It is like the thrust of a cock, a deep penetration that closes a circuit. She lets out a muffled cry and her body convulses, the palm of her hand pressed between her legs. John watches as she draws her legs back, her eyelids clenched shut, her mouth open. Her body quakes. John inhales, holds his breath with hers. A sharp intake; she finally breathes, her body unbending. John lets out a sob. Tears boil in his eyes, disassembling Marijke's settling body into a prismatic explosion. Slowly, slowly, her body unwinds, melts into the mattress. He watches her recovery. Her hand escapes from between her legs, crawls to her breasts, then descends to her side. She looks down at herself, blows on the wet skin of her chest. When she looks over at John he squeezes his eyes shut, feels the tears spilling out, hoping that she cannot see them.

—*Bedankt*, Shonny, she whispers. —*Bedankt*.

◗ The dawn could be called cool. It is 6:20 AM and they have found a restaurant patio and are eating fruit salad and omelettes, the shadows like retreating oases as the sun slowly mounts the hazy horizon and begins to fill every nook with heat. The awning above them shoulders against it; the air is yet fresh, sweet from the jasmine in the flower boxes.

—But I can only afford to stay this short.

—Why one day? Who crosses the sea for one day?

—I had to come to negotiate for the rug. If I only sent it anything could happen. I still didn't get what I hoped. But it is enough. And I have many things to fix in Holland. To take care of.

John bisects what remains of the omelette, bisects it again. His appetite is weak. He ladles sugar into his coffee. Marijke looks at her watch.

—How long to get to the airport?

—It can take up to an hour. You should get there two hours before the flight.

—So early?

—They always say so. You want a window seat.

—But I can get a taxi anywhere? Shonny, please look at me.

He looks up from his plate. She reaches across the table and caresses his cheek with her knuckles.

—Such a sad boy. You love your cousin, *ja*?

—*Ja*.

—Oh. Sad to see me go. Maybe it will be another twelve years before we meet again?

—Maybe. Maybe never.

—If you come to Amsterdam you can stay in my flat. You can drink Heineken and eat *poffertjes* and *haring* and *nasi goreng* all day.

The waitress swings a pot of coffee over their mugs. They both nod.

—And the check please, Marijke asks.

The waitress reaches into the pouch of her apron and pulls out the bill.

—My treat, John says, reaching for it.

—*Nee*. Mine. For letting me stay in your pension. Your little hotel. But I think I must hurry.

She stammers over the unfamiliar currency.

—Here I must leave some money for the girl, right? For a tip? How much on this bill?

—I think three dollars.

—Then I leave five. This waitress, she is in a good mood even at this time. Not like you.

She places the money among the empty glasses and plates and they stand. John picks up her suitcase from beside the table and hobbles out behind her.

A few cars flash by, windshields slinging furious pulses of sunlight into their faces. An occupied cab passes John's outstretched hand, but a cab going the opposite way sees them and u-turns. The driver, a thick-lidded man in a turban, climbs out and opens the trunk. John lowers the suitcase inside.

—I'm coming, he says as she heads for the back door.

—To Nederland?

—No. To the airport. Get in or you'll be late.

They sit at opposite ends of the back seat.

—The airport, John says. —Terminal One.

The driver nods and starts to drive. The windows are open and the morning is fragrant.

Marijke takes John's arm and pulls him towards her. He slides over the seat and presses against her. She puts her hand against the inside of his bare knee. In the mounting glare of the day, as the car negotiates thickening traffic, they kiss, deep, teenage kisses of desperation. Her hand slides up the back of his T-shirt, her fingernails draw hieroglyphs on the skin of his back, and their legs entwine. The smell of her, the smell of her scrubbed skin, the foreign soap and shampoo. Her tongue, the faintly electric press of her lips. Her lithe body twisting like a fish beneath his palms, her ribcage and breasts, the cool of the skin on the inside of her thigh. His lean shoulders, the muscular curve of his buttocks where she pushes him against her.

Then, their jawbones sore, her skin raw from the sandpaper of his cheek, he rests against her shoulder, his nose pressed to the skin of her neck, she watching the blistered city beyond the window, a hand in his hair, the other down the back of his shorts, his at the top of her thigh, not moving, just a firm pressure, a reassurance. He looks up her neck, past the blanket of hair and straight up through the side window, sees the frail undercarriage, like so many rollerskates, of a 747 as it skims the highway, hears the pitched thunder as it heads for a runway's threshold.

Out of the cab he is unsteady, he clings to her. The driver is discreet, unusually gentle, as he unloads the trunk and accepts his fare.

They are weary and silent in the throng that gathers before the KLM desk. Dutch chattering, the shuffle of the suitcase until finally it is on the scale, tagged, and sent on its way. Billets torn, a window seat is granted.

They are in a dark lounge but John can drink no more coffee. There is nothing left to say.

At the gate the kiss is deep but passionless and there are no tears. He watches as she endures the security ritual. She is soon obscured by others, baggy-pants men wearing socks with sandals, bespectacled women in cotton print dresses. The last thing he sees is her elbow as it arcs around and slides out of view.

And when he reaches for his wallet in preparation for the journey home he remembers that he has nothing. A quarter and six pennies and a breathmint.

So he goes to the asphalt roof of the parking garage, as he did as a child, his face pressed to his father's leg while he watched the taxiing clippers through the mesh. He is taller than the fence now, it reaches his chin, and the jets are like brittle models, no longer majestic, just fragile constructions of aluminum and paint. He spots a KLM jumbo, squints in the glare at the little windows. But it is an hour and a half yet before it will depart. He imagines her in the harshly-lit departure lounge among the other Dutch, sitting in a scooped-out fibreglass chair, chin in her hand.

He unexpectedly remembers a moment from the dawn when they stepped out of his apartment into the hallway, the way she twisted her shoulder beneath the carry-on bag's strap. How odd it was that he could still hear the television through Miss Hobarth's door, so early in the morning.

At this shore of the sky he bends under the ascending sun, hand shading his eyes as the loading bridge finally tips away from the jet's flank, as the last of the luggage palettes disappear into its belly and support vehicles back away like servants from their regent, as the jet rolls from the terminal and lumbers down the taxiways, the canisters of its engines whining in synchronization. It waits patiently in line behind smaller craft, and when it finally rolls onto the runway's lip and gathers speed it seems eager to depart this charred landscape; it rolls for a long time and is suddenly airborne, retreating from earth at a steep angle, wheels drawn into its gut, arching eastward, climbing away, horizon warping as she heads towards the threshold of heaven. ◑

((

The Ninth Chair

T HE NOTE WAS LEFT where we could all find it, myself, the eldest, right down to three-year-old Jeremy. Unable to read, he held the vellum close to his eyes, examining the unbearably beautiful script. It was really for our father to discover – on the white porcelain of the range, amid the polished chrome, beside the enamel kettle – when he came home from work.

"I guess you were expecting dinner," it began. Of course he was; every day for seventeen years he had come home and found dinner waiting. How could she curse him for something she had reinforced day after day, without fail, like the tick of a clock and its chiming on the hour or the familiar pop of the bathroom pipes at the issue of hot water? I watched him from my textbooks at the kitchen table. He raised the note close to his eyes to decipher the script, his face expressionless. He read it twice, then replaced it on the stove, returning it to its precise location and orientation.

I guess you were expecting dinner. I have pressed your shirts, scrubbed your sinks, disciplined your children, and entertained your clients for seventeen years. Worst of all, I have boiled your potatoes and carrots. I will no longer. You have never appreciated my efforts, you have never loved me, and I feel no guilt in saying that I have never loved you. Goodbye Walter. For the children you will now prepare Campbell's Cream of Mushroom soup. Use two cans and all milk, it's better for them. Do not wait long to find a woman who can cook for them. Hire her or marry her, it doesn't matter.

~ Carol

We all knew the note's contents by the time he came home. Brandy and Calla and Jennifer and Walter Jr. and Katy had all read it, after which I had sat Jeremy down to recite it to him.

—When will she come back, Luke? he had asked.

I felt numb and managed only to shrug. My stomach was a globe of crazed glass.

After my father had set the note down he went to the pantry cupboard and removed two cans of soup. From the refrigerator he got a pitcher of milk. From a cabinet he took a saucepan and a wooden spoon. As I watched him I thought how confidently he performed these actions, as if they were an act he had practised in private and was now performing for our benefit, like speaking a foreign language or fire-eating. All six of my siblings stood in the doorway, staring. He gazed at a can's label for several seconds before setting the can down and going to the freezer. From it he removed a large package of frozen pork chops. He put them in the microwave and punched the buttons for defrosting.

—Daddy? Jeremy called, clutching Walter Jr.'s hand.

Our father stiffened.

—Yes?

—When is Mummy coming home?

—She's not.

—Should I cry?

—If you like, he replied, then took a sack of onions from the cupboard, found a paper bag full of mushrooms in the fridge, placed a clove of garlic with them on the cutting board.

—We want to play outside Mom lets us play outside, Walter Jr. stated loudly.

Father looked at me. I nodded vigorously at the boys and they ran out. He watched them go, waited until they were gone before resuming. He started to look through the cupboards above and below, pulled out boxes of pudding and cereal, finally banged his fists down on the counter.

—Luke, do you know where the rice is?

I showed him.

● Around the rosewood table, porcelain dishes, an empty chair and Brandy sitting on her hands and rocking a little while Jennifer brushed Calla's hair. Katy clutched one of a dozen stuffed animals crowding her lap, a purple mouse among the dogs and frogs and beavers, and Walter Jr. whispered to Jeremy, illustrating with the help of a *National Geographic* the order of the planets. I watched Father, searching for signs of a wounded soul as he brought the meal to us.

He beamed as he raised the lid of the electric frying pan to reveal the mound of pork chops swimming in a sauce of mushrooms and onions and garlic. The odour went straight to my stomach and ignited my appetite. He served the meal with rice, loaded each plate, added bread and snow peas. He sat down and with uncharacteristic ceremony took a first bite which he chewed with deliberation.

—Not enough garlic, he muttered. —Chop onions more finely. He looked around at our alarmed expressions. —However, a respectable first attempt, he added. He pursed his lips with satisfaction. We stared at him, our giddy perplexity ruling the dining room. We began to eat.

For five minutes we feasted silently, looking around at one another in wonder. Katy, her mouth bulging with food, set her knife and fork down and drew a deep breath through her nose. She began to cry. I then realized that this was something we had been anticipating, for someone to break through and release us. We all began to sob, boys, girls, our father, a chorus of mourning voices which advanced Katy's wails to a higher pitch, as if her sorrow, being first, were conducting the rest.

—The food, Katy bawled, mushroom sauce and pork spilling from her mouth. —It's yummy!

◗ Our father owned a stage lighting business and also designed gobos. A gobo is a template for light. Made from a piece of sheet metal with a scene or pattern cut out of it, a gobo fits over a spotlight. Imagine that you are producing Shakespeare's *The Tempest* and you need to show a stormy sky. Instead of painting a backdrop of clouds to be rolled in and out at the appropriate times, you shine a white spotlight through the gobo, into which is cut the image of menacing storm clouds. Not only is it more manageable than a piece of stage scenery, it allows the effect to be derived through the drama of shadow and light.

Shadow and light. These words described my father, who for many years was little more than a silhouette in my bedroom doorway wishing me goodnight.

Now he atoned for his absence. He started to come home in the early evening to make dinner for us. Although these meals were derived mainly from prepackaged and convenience foods, he displayed a genuine enthusiasm for the experience of culinary preparation.

—Calla, do you like the leek soup?

—Too much pepper, she replied, fanning her mouth.

—You're absolutely right, he said, and went to her and kissed her on the head. We grew accustomed to this awkward affection.

But the food – refined, dehydrated, pulverized, predigested by machines, stuffed into cans or boxes – soon became monotonous. Our curb on trash day hosted a convention of bloated green dwarves, three, sometimes four garbage bags full of packaging. I imagined as new members of the family the common ingredients in these foods: disodium inosinate, autolyzed yeast extract, ethyl maltol.

—Good evening, Ethyl, I muttered one evening when a pasta and sauce dish arrived with fish sticks and canned peas. Our father considered our wearied expressions as he set down the tray. These expressions turned to astonishment as he retrieved the tray, dumped the steaming plates into the trash, and left the house.

He returned two hours later laden with bags of supermarket produce: tomatoes, green beans, carrots, corn, plus cuts of fresh meat in pink paper, the prices scrawled with marker in the butcher's crude hand. A bookshelf in the family room held nothing but cookbooks; from it he selected one at random and began leafing through the pages.

After this our meals arrived an hour or more later and were bland and simple, but as the months passed the cuisine became more refined. At first there were peas and carrots with an eggplant and bacon side dish and barbecued strip steaks. A month later we enjoyed Mexican garlic soup and charcoal-grilled veal with mustard herb butter. A few days later it was poached salmon with fresh basil and olive butters. He laughed like a child as he unveiled each dish, savouring every syllable of each name.

—Monterey Prawns Served in a Vol-au-Vent with an Herb Creme Sauce. Our palates kept pace with these increasingly exotic menus; even the younger children, who had never been picky anyway, became connoisseurs of fine cuisine.

One of our father's employees recommended a downtown

restaurant for its exceptional French food, so as a treat for Jeremy's fourth birthday we went there for dinner. I remember Jean-Yves, the chef, who was enthusiastically making rounds of the dining room to accept praise from the guests, how his mouth gaped like that of a dying fish when Jeremy stated, I think the chateaubriand was cooked right out of the refrigerator. It's way better if you let it warm up first. Did you know that? Our father's explosion of laughter expelled us from the restaurant.

In a supermarket that we frequented he lost his temper for the first time in public. He had been digging through a bin of green peppers for almost five minutes without success when he started to cast them with amazing precision into a display of pomegranates in the next aisle.

—What are you doing? I hissed, tugging at his arm.

—Putting these where they belong. With the other seed-stuffed produce, he replied before moving on to the next section. —This corn! he bellowed. —I wouldn't feed this corn to pigs!

I gripped his arm and began to pull him towards the exit while the astonished eyes of shoppers swivelled towards us. Before I could get him away from the display he swept his arm through the cobs, throwing them to the floor. In the car he was uncharacteristically quiet. —You are becoming an eccentric, I noted.

—To get the freshest product, he replied, we must go to the source. Where's the source? Where is it?

◗ He wore a wide-brimmed adventurer's hat, the heat of August wriggling through the air like transparent worms. He was standing with his soiled hands on his hips, surveying the furrows of plants which extended to each horizon. In the rows of iridescent green carrot tops my brothers and sisters were digging for the long orange fruits, eagerly brushing them clean and holding each aloft for his inspection.

We soon moved to a neighbouring field, this one a deeper green and speckled in red, each fat tomato a Christmas ornament dangling among the leaves, coming away with a gentle tug. We leapt from field to field, a pack of discriminating locusts, harvesting the succulent vegetables and moving on with our baskets full.

We made a final stop on the way home, at a farm where he purchased a duck, its nude skin pink and puckered where the feathers had clung. It was bound in paper and plastic and placed on

Jeremy's lap for the ride home. He held it in place with one hand, an expression of great reverence on his face.

There were letters from our mother. She was in England, then France. She visited the Ukraine where she stayed for a month with her grandmother. This was followed by Egypt. "Dear Children and Walter, we are near the pyramids tonight. They are shining against the sky." Her travelling companion, the other component of the "we" who populated every experience, was never identified. Even the sex of this person remained a mystery.

On the seventh day of September, a Tuesday, she died. "She was swimming in the Sea of Crete," the letter said, drafted presumably by this mystery companion, "and she drowned." There were meagre details of the post-mortem process, how the body would rest in the Ukraine with her family, but the letter's main intent was to assure us that everything had been handled and that grieving was our only duty in the matter. It was signed by "M.O.", who had typed it on an old typewriter with a failing ribbon. The letterhead was from the Bella Maris Hotel, Hersonissos, Crete.

September was vengeance for a hot and sunny summer. A bitter wind blew endlessly, it snowed on the tenth, the leaves brightened rapidly beneath grey skies and were thick on the wind by the end of the month. Our father's attention shifted back to gobos; the cooking diminished.

—I have a theory, I told Jennifer.

—Like always, she replied. Our school books were clustered around us, merging in the middle of the kitchen table.

—They didn't love each other. She left. It hardly hurt. He learned to cook and discovered something he loved. She died. To feel the necessary sorrow he has decided to stop doing what he loves.

—What do we do?

—Let the process of mourning take its course.

We did.

Thanksgiving brought him back. And the duck.

In October Nature atoned for the forfeiture of the warm and brilliant days I so love about September. The weather grew unusually hot. Leaves littered the backyard so we swept the flagstone patio clear and there carried the dining room table, the seven of us, while Father worked diligently inside, slicing chanterelles and boletus mushrooms for a ragoût with red wine. Calla and Brandy set the table with our mother's china and silver, constructed with surprisingly little disagreement each elaborate place setting.

When we were all assembled and the sun had set, our father presented the confit of duck, which had spent the last two months submerged in goose fat in an earthenware crock, chilled in the basement refrigerator. A dozen candles, their flames tall in the still air, illuminated the table and the limbs of our oak tree which was stubbornly withholding from the earth a few brown leaves.

—There's been a terrible mistake! I stated after I had poured a ninth glass of wine.

—Yes, our father replied. —An extra place setting. He toasted the empty chair and drank.

—Can I say the grace? I wrote it myself, Brandy said, unfolding a slip of paper.

—Please, he said, and we bowed our heads.

—For all this food, to the yellow Sun and the blue Earth and her brown Soil, we give thanks. Amen.

—Amen, we echoed and began to eat. Above us, beyond the high ramp of the house's roof and the jagged arms of the trees, twilight drained like an incandescent fluid into the west, leaving behind it a fine spray of starlight. The food left us breathless. I understood then that our father's skill had become transcendent and only at this moment had our palates managed to catch up. The effect was climactic; extraordinary flavours passed over my lips and tongue, along the length of my throat, and into my belly, where they radiated pleasure to every cell in my body.

A small wind arose and convinced the oak to surrender a handful of leaves. These fell about us with a gentle rustle and the candles flickered in the little breath of night. A final leaf fell, turned end over end before sailing through one of the candleflames and igniting. We watched through a haze of euphoria as it landed on the tablecloth. Our father leapt up and clapped it beneath his palm. It did not seem to hurt him and he sat again without comment.

At the end of the table, in the ninth chair, our mother was sitting. She gazed into the air among the candles, watching something, perhaps the lighted leaf, glimpsed through what was to her the transparent progression of time. One by one we became aware of her, our father last of all because he was looking at his watch to determine the best time to start the poached pears in Zinfandel and cassis cream. He looked up.

Gradually her eyes shifted to focus on him, to his startled expression beyond the candleflames.

—Carol? he said softly. Her body shimmered like a reflection in a still pool suddenly rippled by the pebble of his voice. —Carol, you look thin. Why are you so thin?

He was right; shadows filled her eye sockets and cheeks; her hands trembled on brittle wrists. He stood up and walked around the table. She watched him pick up her plate and heap it with food. He set it down before her and she stared at it without comprehension. —Of course it's cold now. You will not experience the full effect.

She looked at him and then at the food, hands balled in her lap.

—Maybe you're too weak, he whispered, and knelt beside her. He pushed the fork through the pieces of duck breast and onions and mushrooms, stacking it high with the fragrant food. Her expression remained puzzled until he raised it to her face. She opened her mouth and he guided the fork there.

—Take it, he whispered. —Swallow!

She closed her mouth over it and he pulled the fork away. The food fell to the embroidered chair and she looked down at it, surprised to see the mess there, surprised at her own translucence.

He fell back on his heels and rubbed his chin, watching her in thought. He brought the empty fork up and prodded her experimentally with it. The fork and his hand passed through her shoulder. She looked to where it had penetrated, then back at him. When his eyes met hers his expression was filled with deep sorrow.

—You are hungry. Where you are, there's nothing but hunger.

She nodded, her frown deepening the cavities of her eyes and cheeks. She bowed her head and pressed her face into her hands.

High in the treetops a wind started, a cold wind which extinguished the candles and drove us indoors. ◗

☽

Hotter

SHIT IF IT WASN'T A BEAUT.

And I still couldn't believe Andy coulda brought that whole bass fiddle over the tracks and down the slope without scratchin it or nothin. It sure glowed in the firelight, like the wood itself was on fire.

Sure he played like crap at first. Only natural. But out on the beach every night of the summer slappin the mother wasn't subtractin from Andy's talent. Pretty soon he sounds like . . . well, like some famous guy who's really good at playin stand-up. If I knew names, I'd tell ya. You look em up. You can read, cantcha?

After a while he makes it look so easy, you think you can just take it from him and do as good yerself. Sure, if you want everyone to howl. Tommy with his hand over his mouth, blowin a booger out of his nose, he's laughin so hard.

Then Nils figures the bass sound no good by itself, even with Andy shoutin, I just found my baby with-a somebody new! (Then we shout: I guess that means your baby ain't a baby that is true!) He learn that from a Tom and Jerry cartoon. So Nils gets a gueetar. Shit, he never said "guitar" like normal folks. Always guee-tar, guee-tar! Nice fuckin guee-tar, Pop! And it's a Yamee-ha, like the Japs can make somethin for cookin the blues. We all said we hated it. (Hey, Kyle, we's outta wood. Wonder if that crappy-Jappy axe will burn, or's it too much plastic?) If you really wanna know, I loved that guitar. It sounded just fine, and I even learned a chord or two on it. What do them fucks know?

Well, Nils sucked too, then he gets better. We got a rock'n roll band on our own beach! Then everyone starts bringin some noisemaker, mostly blues-harps and kazoos, pots and pans to rap on, and the racket booms from the Pickering nuke plant (Christ, them lights bugged me some nights!) right to the Skyway out west.

Yeh, but it was okay. Fuck, after half a two-four who was listenin? You're too busy shoutin "Be-Bop-A-Lula" to give.

(That night the cops come down on accounta the racket. Ha! I
say that like it happened once! Well, Blister's chick sees the flash-
lights first, little white dots bobbin across the sand towards us, so
we ditch the suds in a hole Tommy was diggin in the sand for no
particular reason, then Tommy buries them. Fine, except most
was open. Well, Blister sweet-talks the cops and Nils plays somethin soft and sucky.

—Can't have a fire here, boys.

—Sorry, sir, we was cold.

—What about home? Might be nice and warm there.

—Colder an death at home, sir. Cold as death since Mindy
died. (Mindy is Blister's pet rat, so there! And she wasn't dead
neither!)

Other cop puts a light on Blister's face, makin him all white and
corpse-like, and there's fuckin tears in his eyes! I see it and nudge
Johnny in the ribs. He nearly sucks his ciggie down the pipe, but
we cover okay and the cops don't notice. Well, those officers
musta been havin a banner day, cause they just tucks their head-
batters back in the holders, tips their hats, and leaves us alone. I
see Al shove his blade back and give him a swat. Who wants to
fuck with cops? (Tommy: Their wives? Har har.) So we're quiet
for a spell, hopin they're gone, and laugh like goddamn hyenas.
Then we dig up the beer, and sonofabitch it's half sand, so you
chew and drink and scream when you shit the next day.)

Yeh, we played rock'n roll, but only on the beach. Andy
thumpin on the upright, Nils twangin the six, the rest of us hol-
lerin and whoopin like banshees. Fuck it was fun.

Yeh, we did kill a guy, too. I mean, I guess you could say we
killed him. I mean, he's dead, ya know.

◐ It was summer, pissin hot July and a smell like thunder in the
air, like the whole world is endin. Sky's black as death over the
lake, still miles off but you can see the blue forks jumpin and
pumpin in these clouds. You stare for an hour, you can't hear
nothin and the air as thick as tears; I'm wearin a undershirt and it's
soaked. Just all that light flickerin in the belly of them clouds. It'll
be okay if it rains, but it might not. Like this last night, and the
night before, but no rain. Shit, you figure when it's like this maybe

God'll let it rain and cool ya off for yer troubles, but he just sits up there, turns up the gas, and laughs his goddamn teeth out.

Sun's gone behind the clouds and I don't think she's down yet but it's gettin dark. Just me and Andy on the beach. He's playin Sandy, that's his bass, but not like you should, twackin the strings. He's got this bow, like he should be in a fuckin symphony or somethin. I want to put my ciggie out in his ear, and I tell him so.

—You just don't have no culture, he says, then plays the "Popeye the Sailor Man" song.

—Well why you playin with that thing? What's wrong with twackin?

—Look, my granpappy plays with this bow, and I owe him it that I can do it too.

Then he plays that thing, what is it? Bom bom bom *bummm.* Beethoven? I almost piss myself laughin, and he laughs too, but it's kinda a sad laugh, like it's funny but you wanna cry? I think it's his granpappy, he died last year. Played Sandy in Chicago with a orchestra. Then he dies and that's how Andy gets it. First it got all fixed up, though. Andy says it was rough, like it got played lots and banged more than some whores, but after granpap croaks the will says to fix Sandy up, then give it to Andy. So Andy, as a gift to granpap, learns to play it.

—That's a fine gift yer givin him, Andy, I say, sittin back and smokin and listenin. It ain't so bad when you get used to the bow. Christ, if it's for Andy's granpap, who musta been a swell guy the way he talks bout him, then that's okay.

Pretty soon John, Al, Tommy, Blister, and a whole load of girls come over the tracks and down the slope, with a couple a coolers too, full of the brew. My mouth waters for a cool one, but the object of my drool-u-lation swerves left when I get a gander at these chicks. Jeez, they're fine, specially this hot little brunette with eyes green as trees. She flutters em at me, and man I thought I couldn't sweat no more, but I do.

The coolers are cracked and we start drinkin while splashin melted ice on us. Fuck that's nice.

I get Johnny aside and ask him bout the ladies. He harps it off until I give him a cig, then explains.

—They's friends of Blister's chick. Christ if I can ever remember her name. Debbie? Dana?

—Her name's Diana. Shit, I think Johnny forgets his own name sometimes.

—Yeh, so she says she knows some ladies who like parties, and Blister tells her to bring em. Ain't this a party every night? I'm swimmin. Still suckin on the smoke, he peels off his shirt and dives into Lake O. If you guessed the cig went out, here's a fuckin A-plus to yer brain.

I'm always too shy to talk to ladies, so I sit by Andy again, gulpin suds.

—Hey, where's Nils? Andy yells.

—He'll be by later, Tommy says. —Mumma said he gotta adjust that ratty choke on her Mazda. Yes Mazda, no Mazda. Tommy's a laugh a second. Too bad only he thinks so.

All these girls are grouped opposite the firepit. Blister goes lookin for wood, but too bad we used most around here for other nights so he's gotta go far.

I peek at the babes while pretendin to watch the flashin clouds and Johnny, who's strokin up and down in the lake and won't shut the fuck up about how nice it is, "can't you swim you stinkin Kyle?" Sometimes he don't shut up.

God, I love the summer, this crazy heat that makes girls wear next to nothin and feel okay bout it! The brunette's got on a mini and this nice sleeveless thing that shows her sweet little shoulders, and that sweat on her! She's got them heavy, soft lips, the kind you like to lick over slow, then slip between. . . .

I nearly choke a swallow up my nose and cough like a Pinto, and I see the brunette chucklin and whisperin. Shit, I should go over.

—Hi, I'm Kyle. I was just thinkin how really nice you look in this stormlight. Maybe you'd like to. . . . No way. No fuckin way. Empty bloody stomach and half a brew and I'm goddamn Casanova. I think about layin easy on the stuff tonight, then suck back the whole thing in one gulp. Gotta stop thinkin like that. Gotta stop thinkin and keep drinkin.

I snag another beer and then Nils appears up on the train tracks at the same time there's a boom of thunder. He looks worried. I know he's scared shitless of thunder, but don't say nothin. Why make his life shit? He comes right to the cooler and sets down his guitar case. I hand him a brew with nothin but a nod that means, "It's okay, man, heights bug me," and he sorta nods back, like, "Thanks, chum." He ain't even seen the honeys yet.

His bottle's done in two secs, and I get the feelin he's been swallowin somethin stronger over the last couple hours. He's okay when the guitar's on his lap and he'n Andy twang at some tune. The girls are squealin with delight and I'm wishin I could play somethin too. Banjo or harp, or guee-tar. Christ, he's got me sayin it too!

The booze'n thunder are chargin me pretty good and maybe I'm findin the confidence to say hi to Shoulders. Eight'r nine more o'these, maybe!

Blister's back with some wood, nice bits of sawed and split stuff, so I wonder where he got it. Probably up at Mulgan's again, so the old geeze'll be pissed off and come down to stick that shotgun in our faces again. Dangerous sonofabitch.

Yeh, I know, who wants a fire when it's already hell on a hot day, but it's traditional. I mean, we just gonna sit on the beach in the dark? Fire's like a beacon, like home almost, if yer home's okay. It was good for the cavemen, right? They woulda been nothin without fire. It's just a thing that keeps ya together, almost what love'd be like if you could see it. See, you always need it, but it can burn ya, and you gotta keep feedin it, and it can make you relax, or be scared, or anything. Just like love, right?

It's really goin soon and I sit close, even though I'm sweatin like three horses, stuff pourin down my face, into my eyes. The undershirt's drenched. Wouldn't be wetter if you stuck it in Lake O. Thunder booms and isn't it gettin cooler? Can almost smell rain over my own stink. Maybe tonight'll be different and it'll rain.

—You're Kyle?

—Hmmm? Suddenly I'm lookin into those deadly green eyes, and, yup, I'm jello. Her giggle almost kills me, it's like a knife in the belly, then this bit of beer drips out my mouth and down my chin, down my chest. She touches the drop with a finger, then sucks on it in a way there's no mistakin.

—Oooh, you're salty, she coos. Firelight on one side of her face, lightnin flickerin all over the other side. She keeps those eyes stuck on me and I gotta look away, but I look down and there's them shoulders and her neck, wet and tanned and slidin down to the curves of her breasts, not *tits* like all the other guys'd say, breasts, roundin out over the fringe of her little top, and my body's startin to hum.

33

—How'd ya know . . . I mean, who told my name? I blubber, her eyes in mine again, our bodies havin a deep conversation.

—Diana told me. I'm Molly. She sticks out her hand all businesslike, but when I touch it I get a shock that knocks my guts out, and there's only one business this is like.

The world is real close around me, fire on my left, thunderheads on my right, and I feel like I'm up to my chest in the sand, music thumpin around me, thunder boomin really loud and deep, feel it inside, booze in my blood and I'm dizzy and so hot, so why the fuck am I shiverin? And Molly fillin everything else out, surroundin me like cool water, the breeze toyin with her hair.

A drop of rain, cold and it makes her quiver, spirals outta the sky and strikes her neck, right where it's at her shoulder, then rolls down towards her breast. I catch it with my mouth before it gets there, and slide up to where it first hit. Her palms glide over my shoulders, under the loops of my undershirt. She looks up to the lightnin sky, my tongue comin up her sweet throat, over her jaw, into her open mouth.

This is nuts.

She pulls me forward, on top of her, our lips and tongues all over each other's, my hands grippin her shoulders and hers pullin my undershirt up, slippin and strokin my back.

Rains starts to fall harder, cold on me, but who cares? You don't or you woulda stopped readin probably.

She wraps her legs round me, the mini ridin up, me all hard through my shorts and rubbin there, my hand runnin up her leg, under her little panties, and over her smooth cheek.

And then I'm thinkin where I am.

I bolt my head up, ready to see a whole packa grins around us, already feelin my face gettin flushed and me ready to say, Aw, shucks.

But there ain't a soul. Rain's really comin down now, but Tommy, Al, Nils, Blister, Johnny, Andy, the girls? They buggered out. Fire's startin to die in the rain but it's big enough to stay on for a while. Coolers're still there, bottles all around. Where the fuck they get to?

I look down at Molly. Thunder's crashin just everywhere, rain sweepin down in sheets. Her face is soaked in rain. She looks up at me through little slit eyes, then rides the tip of her tongue over her lips, then wiggles her pelvis, her mouth curlin into the kinda smile girls only do when they're feelin one way. I melt into her, the whole damn world takin off like a flocka scared birds. I slowly start to ride up'n down between her legs. She locks around me, her hands slippin into my shorts and pushin me harder against her. I run off the buttons of her top an push it away, rain fallin all over her chest, slide my hands over the skin, over her hard nipples. I lift the front of my undershirt, I wanna feel those breasts against mine, she bucks against me, I wrap my arms all around her and she moans right in my ear. It feels so damn good I'm goin all dizzy and wanna black out. Don't matter if we're not really doin it, don't matter cause it feels so good this way. I gotta be careful. You know. I hardly know her anyways.

Then, just when everything's gettin really good, and the whole world with all its shit'n problems is a million miles away, a voice, and it goes right for my soul, shouts from far away, a voice hysterical and scared.

—Gimme back my bass, you asshole!

Andy.

I never heard his voice like that before. I push myself up, listenin, but there's just rain and thunder and the wind rippin off the lake, like the whole fuckin world's tearin itself apart. Molly's lookin at me and I think she's gonna be mad but then I see she's scared.

—Did you hear that? I yell over the noise.

She nods and I roll off her. She wraps her shirt around and pulls up her panties, straightens her skirt, and she's soaked, and for a second in a burst of lightnin, with her makeup streakin her face black and her wet hair all tussled, I feel real bad, like I did that to her, like I made her ugly. Then it's dark again and she's just a silhouette. I rise to my feet, the wind's like it'll knock me right over, and the rain's hard, cold, stingin.

Lightnin shows Molly buttonin her top, shit I'm feelin real bad now, I'm forgettin all about Andy screamin.

—Sorry, I mutter, really quiet, like just to me cause in this racket there ain't no chance no one could hear it, but there's a lull, like God hits the storm's mute button for a sec, the rain lightens, thunder hushes, wind's gone, and the word's like I shouted it.

Then there's lightnin and thunder right on its tail, but Molly's noddin. What it means, search me, like maybe, "Yeh, you should

35

be, Pike," or, "No problems, okay," or maybe somethin I ain't figured on. Chicks can puzzle ya.

I look up the slope to the tracks, the whole sky behind goes
blue-white and I see shapes. Looks like Al punchin the shit outta
some chubby guy. Then I'm lookin east, towards the trestle over
the Rouge River, which winds outta this big, beautiful valley in
the north. Comes down to like a swamp or pond (rushes and lily
pads and everything) where sometimes we fish, then slides under
the trestle, cuts through the beach, and spills into Lake O.

More lightnin, and I see something on the bridge that crushes
my guts. Flash on red wood, and two guys, looks like Andy'n
some little guy, are fightin over his bass, Sandy. Where the fuck's
everybody, I'm thinkin while runnin up the slope to the tracks. Al
gives the chubby guy one last slug and the guy falls like a sacka
shit. Al pulls him off the tracks and crumples him on the gravel
beside.

—Fuckin fashie, Al says.

I see the guy's haircut, shaved in one part but another bit
hangin over an eye. Pretty clothes, long flowery shorts and whaddaya call em, polo shirt? Shades on a goddamn string round his
neck, cracked and smacked by Al. Fuckin fashie is right.

Spoiled assholes from out west, fashies start comin into our
area by the tracks. See, these morons do whatever seems like it's
"in", and now "in" is walkin on train tracks and gettin into fights.
And gettin the crap kicked out of em.

West along the tracks, Tommy, Nils, Johnny, Blister, and the
ladies are walkin back this way. Probably chased a loada the shits
back home. I see Nils has his guee-tar case, then remember Andy.
Shit, the train signal light is green, too.

—Hey, you guys! I yell, wavin my arm. They pick up the pace
and I turn.

Andy and the little fashie are on the trestle, a place I ain't goin
in a zillion years. Remember me'n heights? I start headin that way
anyways, maybe just to shout at the little bastard. Al's just reachin
the bridge, fists clenched and ready to do some rearrangin. You'd
never see me toss with big Al.

The storm starts to swell again and I'm beginnin to think that
up here on the tracks we're some of the highest things around.
That's a spooky feelin, makes ya wanna turn around so you can
see the lightnin comin to getcha.

The trestle gets lost in the foggy rain, then the wind nearly whips me off the side. Christ, I think, crouchin, my hands snapped to the greasy rail, my body shiverin, and my nose startin to run. The wind shifts, slashin rain into my face so I can hardly look up, but I do anyways.

Deep in all this greyness something appears. It's white-hot, a little speck down the east tracks. Shit, I know it. It's a goddamn train. Last I saw, Andy, the fashie, and Al were on the eastbound track, and this one's a westy, so it's okay as long's they're stayin where they are. Goddamn, I think, gettin up and ploughin into the rain, I gotta warn em.

Between thunderclaps I hear the whistle moanin, watch that white speck gettin fatter and hotter every second. Goddamn!

The other guys are still way back, at least I can't see em. All alone up here, seems. The idea really gets my blood pumpin, I can almost hear my own heart over the wind and rain and thunder.

—Al! Andy! Train's comin! Al! Andy! I got my hands cupped and I'm shoutin, but even I can hardly hear me. Is somethin movin up there?

I start sprintin, pound pound pound, runnin shoes on slick railroad ties, if I fall I'm baked!

—*Oowwwww!* Up ahead, closer'n I thought, someone's shoutin in pain.

—Train! Train! I yell.

—Bejees! a voice yells. That's gotta be Al cursin.

I look down and all my guts fall out. No more gravel between the ties, ain't nothin but air. I'm on the damn trestle. I stop dead, can see the muddy Rouge below, fast and thick.

—Let go the goddamn bass and he'll let go of you! Andy screams.

—No way. You're gonna throw me off if I let go. I won't let – *aaaahhhh!*

—Shit, you guys! What's happenin? I scream.

—This little crud won't drop Sandy, so he's gonna die.

—Jeez, don't joke like that, Al, Andy cries.

—*Woooooooooo! Woooooooooooooooo!* Right through the storm the train's tellin us to watch it.

Then Johnny and Nils are behind me. —What the fuck?

—Johnny. Get me off the bridge quick, before the train gets here.

—It's on the other rail, Kyle. Don't worry. Don't you wanna watch this?

—Get me off the goddamn bridge!

Nils, his eyes lookin all round and breathin hard so I don't feel like such a suck, puts his hand under my elbow and turns me slowly. —Come on, buddy. Let's turn round and walk off this thing. S'not far, take it easy.

Johnny catches on that it's serious, helps out. God, there's nothin like friends. I'm back on solid in no time and slump beside the tracks, eager to see what'll come down with Al and this fashie and Andy and Sandy.

The train's light is as big as the moon now, and ten times brighter, bearin down fast. You can feel it in the earth, shakin and quakin.

Al's got the fashie in a nelson, I think that's whatcha call it, and he's bendin the guy's head forward like to snap it right off. The prep's sayin stuff like, "Yow, ow, oooh, shit," but he don't let go of Sandy. His arms're wrapped round it like it was his mamma or somethin. Andy's jumpin around in a panic, sometimes tuggin on Sandy, sometimes yellin, sometimes slappin the kid in the face.

Now Johnny and Blister are on the bridge. Nils and Tommy take the ladies under the trestle, for their protection, right? Fraidies. But Molly's there, she waves before they go under, and I smile at her.

The fashie sees the other guys, looks at the train. Whistle screams. Yeh, he's gotta give up now. He's gotta! Andy gives him a clap in the snoot, and the guy starts bleedin, all red and mixed with rain, down his shirt and over Sandy, onto Al's arms, through the ties and into the Rouge, then floatin out into Lake O.

I stand up. I'm feelin real sorry for this little guy now, why's he such a dork? They'll let him go if he just gives Sandy back. Why don't he let go?

—Here's your goddamn bass! he screams, and he's cryin too, but he pushes Sandy out, and she falls – *thunk!* – across the other track.

—Sandy! screams Andy, but you know what's gonna happen. All everyone can think to do is duck, coverin their faces, even Andy ain't so crazy to try'n save her.

Everything shakes hard as the train, engine boomin, flies onto the trestle. Andy lets go and the fashie starts runnin this way, all in the open.

I get one look at the front of the train smashin through Sandy like she's balsa wood, then duck my head from the flyin splinters. I hear the fashie scream over the roar of the engine. I look up while the cars rock past. Andy's cryin now, Al's got his arm around him. The train rolls by.

Where's the fashie? Then I see him halfway down the bridge, between my end and the other guys, and there's red, shiny wood all around. He's layin on his belly, crawlin and sobbin. Poor bastard, then I see why. Blood everywhere and it ain't from his nose. A big hunka wood is stabbed in his left shoulder, deep. My knees go all wobbly, it looks so bad. I find my hand stuck to my mouth, but I can't look away.

Al comes up, leans over the guy. I see he's talkin but the little guy's just shakin his head and cryin. Then John and Blister are there, leanin over, talkin, but this guys just keeps shakin his head. Pretty soon he's on his hands'n knees, crawlin a bit. Andy walks past and don't even look, he just walks my way, tears'n rain all over.

Al gives up and the other guys follow as he comes this way.

—He's all fucked up, Johnny says.

—Jeez, we can't just leave him, I say.

—He don't want our help, Andy sneers, his voice all cryin. Nobody blames him.

Blister looks at his watch. —That train was a 10:05. Ain't another due for a hour. He'll get off there okay.

—But he's really hurt, I say.

—It ain't so bad. Not so deep, John tells me. —Looks bad from here, but close up it's okay.

—Blister, what's that? I ask, pointin east. Another light there.

—Could be freight. Don't worry, she's on the other rail.

I guess he's right. Thunder begins to sound more distant, but sometimes there's a fork real close and then a loud bang, and the rain's still hard. Can't get no wetter, so why worry?

Andy walks close as he heads down the slope, and I pat him on the arm. He looks into my eyes and I feel my heart breakin. He sure loved Sandy. Poor Sandy. Andy holds something up, the headpiece from the top, where the knobs are? I see it and I'm cryin, but lucky no one can tell from the rain. Christ, for all I know everyone else's bawlin too.

They all go under the bridge where Nils and Tommy and the ladies are and it's probably drier. Hey, is that smoke? Them guys got a fire goin under there? Musta found some dry wood, covered by the trestle. I bet it's warm but don't go down yet, just let the rain wash over me, like not drinkin for a while so it's good later, or not kissin any girls in a long time, it's real nice when you do.

I watch the fashie. He's on his hands'n knees, trying to get up. I almost think bout goin over but there's no way.

—Hey, you all right? I yell.

He don't look up or nothin, just sits there like a sick dog, head hung. Wish he'd pull out that hunka wood.

I take a quick look west, seein if a train's comin on his track, but there ain't nothin.

Train from east is comin real fast, and for a second, I don't know how, I know it's on *his* track. It's the goddamn turbo express! They put it on the other track to pass the GO-train that just went! The realization's like a tonna bricks in my belly.

—Hey, get up, a train's comin, I say, but I know it's way too quiet. —Get up!

He staggers real badly to his feet and almost falls over the side, but rights himself.

—You guys! Al, Johnny, help!

Blister pops his head from under the bridge. —What's that?

—Jeez, Blister, a train's comin, on his track!

It's comin real fast. Christ, I never seen a light grow that fast.

That bastard Blister ain't satisfied with my word and gotta come up and have a look-see. He turns west.

—There ain't nothin, he says, poundin my shoulder.

—There, you fuckup! I scream, turnin him round.

He squints his eyes like, and I know there's only seconds. Can already hear the big turbine; sounds like a goddamn jet!

—That's not on his track. It's a westy.

Forget it, I think, and leap up on the track, grit my teeth and take a step on the bridge. Don't think. Don't think. I look straight ahead and there's just this light, the Cyclops comin to break me into bits and eat me. I can't move. I can't move, goddamn!

Al comes up and sees it instantly. He don't say nothin, just jumps on the bridge and slams me outta the way, onto the other rail. The whistle screams, the turbine shrieks, and I get one last look at the little fashie as he turns.

Al, always tryin to protect me, tries to slap a hand to my eyes so I won't see it. He misses.

The big yellow locomotive, two storeys high and movin at a real clip, busts outta the fog.

It's just too fast for a guy to be alive, then dead. Way too fast. The loco's big prow sweeps his body, spinnin and spittin, off the side of the trestle. Then the train's between us'n him, rollin by like it just splatted a bug, like nothin's happened. *Clunk-clunk, clunk-clunk.* It goes on for ever, and I'm really bawlin – there ain't no mistakin it – and Al just holds me, mutterin, Bejees, over'n over.

Then I don't know what happens, cause suddenly I'm standin on the other side of the tracks, still cryin, watchin this broken body twirlin in the eddies, twirlin out into the lake, a rag doll all muddied and like so much junk, like the tires and shoppin carts and branches that are rollin out with him.

◗ And then again I don't know nothin, but here I am, layin on the far end of the beach, right by where the fire was, the sun all really warm and nice on me, sand in my shorts and in my mouth, in my hair, but I'm so relaxed. Then I see my arm's around some-body, yup, it's Molly, but I don't remember doin nothin, except my eyes sure feel puffy.

She's real close, eyes closed, her arm on me too. I look at her a long time, then kiss her real softly on the nose, but she don't stir.

As I lay there, watchin her slow, easy breathin, I can't help thinkin how nice that sun is, and that today'll probably be hot, hotter'n yesterday or the day before. ◗

☾

The Intoxication of Thought

"What did you do in the summer?" asked the Ant.
"I played and sang," groaned the Grasshopper.

Aesop's Fables,
"The Grasshopper and the Ant"

B RADY WINCES each time Helen uses the microwave oven. She is precise about it, knows the times well, fifty seconds to warm a coffee, a minute forty for hot chocolate, three twenty for a bowl of pasta. Brady thinks that she may be using it more often than usual, then retracts the thought guiltily. He is being oversensitive because of the contest. He and Henry are competing to achieve the lowest electric bill.

Helen reheats a coffee she doesn't want because it annoys Brady. She can see him from the corner of her eye, sees his vexed stare as she takes the coffee out of the oven and sniffs it, frowning.

Brady's head follows her around the kitchen. She sits down at the table, letting her eyes fall on the newspaper's front page. It's a local paper, full of gossip and outrage at events that would be trivial in the city. A convenience store is going to offer adult videos; the bridge is to be painted green. Brady stands paralyzed, trapped in an equilibrium of desires. He wants to avoid conflict with Helen; he wants to go back to the hockey game; he wants to win the contest. For a moment he can feel these forces distinctly, like wires, suspending him at the kitchen door. Then one force overcomes the others and he reels forward barking, Make a new one! Make a new one! The candles cast shadows on his unshaven face, deepen the craters of his eyes. He turns fast and stomps into the living room where he has been listening to the game on a tiny pocket radio. In the light of a single candle he clamps his eyes shut and escapes into the battery-powered hiss.

Helen boils the kettle, smiling. The steam rolls up, homemade clouds, fiery gold in the candlelight, and she inhales, feeling them glaze her dry throat. The wood stove is a desert sun, roasting the air so that it crackles when she moves. They should run the

Bionaire. She pours water through the coffee basket, her face in the steam and fragrance, and is overwhelmed by a deep euphoria, like a helium balloon suddenly liberated.

This is Helen's ESP. She cannot predict the future but she can sense, over a great distance, one aspect of the present: she knows when someone dear to her is dying. The knowledge affects her as a contradiction, a period of intense euphoria, a wave of well-being and elation.

Three summers ago Brady's grandmother died. She was an ancient, thin-boned woman, and a great fan of science fiction. She had read nothing outside the genre in thirty years, and passed away the day she began reading *The Grapes of Wrath*.

Helen and Brady were at the cottage. Helen was sitting on the dock, legs dangling in the lake, the sun near zenith and Brady thirty metres out in the rowboat, gazing at the end of his fishing rod as if at a sophisticated machine that had ceased to function. A sense of exaltation filled her belly like warm liquor. She gasped at first, surprised at its intensity, then slipped into the water until her feet touched the sand and the surface was just beneath her nose. The aromatic water pressed against her, accepting her slow dance, limbs untangling like the tendrils of an aquatic plant.

That night the phone's ring cut through the evening murmur, silencing the cricket hidden in the magazine rack. Brady answered, and Helen could hear the frantic chipmunk chatter of his sister, broken by his chirped replies: Yep. Nope. Yep.

Last year Helen's brother died of a massive heart attack while performing a coronary bypass. Helen was on the highway, and when the ecstasy overcame her she had to pull onto the shoulder and rest her head on the steering wheel while trucks thundered past, shaking the car with their giant breath.

This clairvoyant rapture accompanied the death of her father an ocean away. After that another episode sent her to the obituaries, where she learned of the passing of a favourite professor. She finally experienced it directly as the veterinarian withdrew the needle and Lupo sighed beneath her palms.

Was it their spirits, suddenly liberated, passing through her, reassuring her?

Now, as she runs her hand through the kettle's steam, the feeling billows through her like a cloud, inflating her with euphoria. For several seconds she savours the drunkenness, this warm glow, while dread throbs in the background, until in a sudden fit of desperation she throws open the kitchen door and pitches herself into the snow.

It is thirty-one degrees below zero Celsius. Helen lies face down, cold stabbing at her skin but evaded by the delight in her gut. She rolls onto her back, the air stinging her face, and gazes up at the little cottage, the curve of a snowdrift as elegant as a swan's neck against the log wall. There is no wind, and fat snowflakes fall in slow motion through the rectangle of light cast by the open door. The air is silent, gagged by the cold.

Brady appears at the open door, draws back.

—Helen? he calls, then, Jesus! and hauls her limp body up the steps and into the living room. He coils her onto the sofa and rushes back to shut the kitchen door. Helen is panting, feeling the snow in her hair becoming pearls of water.

—What were you . . . I mean why did you . . . ? Brady was once very articulate.

Helen lies on her side and doesn't look up, knows that she looks possessed, staring unblinking at the coasters on the coffee table. The radio is hissing. It is in the kitchen where Brady dropped it. He strains to hear it, takes a step towards the kitchen door. Helen watches him. She notes his sense of duty wrestling with his desire to investigate the excitement, and decides to release him. —I think I'll go to bed, she whispers, then rises unsteadily and heads upstairs.

—You're okay? Helen, you're okay, right? I'll be up pretty soon. He follows her to the bottom of the stairs, watches her climb a few steps before retreating to the kitchen.

Helen lights the candle at the top of the stairs, tucks it beneath the glass shade. She moves to the bathroom, her shadow rippling across black-and-white photographs of Brady's family, 1922, 1936, 1943, a chronology of summer vacations and Christmas visits, of the cottage's changing façade, of the generations of his family that have vacationed here. The silence outside permeates the walls, mingles with the dry air. The wooden floors creak under her feet, muffled here and there by a throw rug.

She closes the bathroom door and splashes her face with hot water. Her skin stings and she wonders about frostbite.

The bedroom is cozy, antique wood, the brass bed arching like a fat loaf of bread beneath its down quilt. Helen undresses slowly

47

and moves naked through the room, enjoying the view of her candlelit body in the mirror. The euphoric feeling is there but muted; she touches her belly and breasts, the mane of red hair, her bottom lip, then backs towards the bed, reaches behind her and clutches the white quilt with each hand, makes a little dance of pulling it back, continuing to face her reflection.

A tiny blade of cold air cuts across her shoulder and she recoils, pressing her skin there. The cottage shudders as a gust of wind flings off the frozen lake. Helen blows out the candle and buries herself in the quilt. There is a leak in the room, a split in the window frame through which the wind sometimes trespasses.

Lying in a fetal curl she listens for more wind, but it is gone; the cold has resumed its grip. Intoxication coils around her like a vapour, spreads her flat on the bed. She feels the texture of the linen pressing against her skin, on her shoulders and nipples and hips; she pushes her hands into her hair and squirms to feel the sheets' caress.

Sometime in the night Brady arrives, groggy and grumpy, and climbs under the covers, his feet like cold steel. Helen rolls out of bed and goes to the bathroom, finding the route through touch. It is utterly silent beyond the stream of urine and the toilet's flush. She goes downstairs to sit at the kitchen table. Her breathing is deep and even. She puts on trackpants and a sweater, climbs into her snowmobile suit, collects her helmet, and slips outside.

It is moonless and overcast, but snow blue-bright, the trees a jagged cage in every direction but one: on the east spreads the lake, an enormous plain of blue fenced in by pine. Helen brushes off the snowmobile's vinyl cover and peels it back, watches the flakes as they salt the black seat. She mounts the machine and glances once at the bedroom window before starting the engine. It is like a great voice, the man of the land clearing his throat, but she knows that Brady has been drinking beer and his sleep is as thick as the night. She twists the throttle and the machine lurches forward. A wedge of light cuts before her and as she accelerates onto the lake's white surface she imagines the sound as heard in the cottage, a burst fading rapidly into a distant drone, smothered by the falling snow.

The snowflakes are stars, illuminated by the halogen beam, the snowmobile a spacecraft carrying her away from this world. The throttle twists under her palm; she knows the danger of buckled ice and phantom ridges but cannot resist. The wind coils under her chin and bites through her scarf.

She must circle the island, now just an outcropping of rock and vegetation in an otherwise flat land, to get to the level area on its north side. A black crater in the snow, the rolling waves of snow-mobile prints muted by the fresh fall, three rough logs, two metres long each, arranged around the meeting pit. Embers, still warm from the party, extinguish the falling flakes and burn a gap-ing wound in the snow. A little steam still rises in the headlamp.

Helen steps off the machine and shuts it down. The headlamp fades with the engine but the expected silence and darkness don't come. Helen, her senses vivified by the night, hears the whisper of falling snow and sees the gentle radiation glow of the landscape. She sits on one of the logs with her ankles crossed, as she sat here with the others just seven hours ago. . . .

49

◑ Across the fire Gail and Beck, who have been married thirteen years, are separated by centimetres, by thoughts, as they stare into the flames. There is a telepathic link there, and Helen imagines it as a crisscross of light between them, shafts connecting their brains and bodies. Henry is there, talking as usual.

—The Red Delicious is the weakest apple of all. There are the Spartans, the Ida Reds, the McIntoshes. All much stronger, tastier. But marketing has made the Red Delicious a big seller. Red Delicious are red, yes, that's obvious from their appearance. Well, people think, "delicious" is also in their name, so they must be.

—But why make such a fuss? Brady asks, leaning forward, his breath an orange fog around his face. —If people want to buy Red Delicious, let 'em.

—Think of all the other apples that could be grown. The good ones. The Empires, Henry replies. —Think! He touches his tem-ple with the mouth of the mickey, drinks.

Henry's rants irritate Helen. He tries to catch her eye during them; she looks away, sees the fire, her mitten, a snowflake. He wants to gauge her reaction but she gives him none. She has examined her expressions in the mirror, knows how each feels, has exquisite control over them. She gives him nothing.

He watches the flames and is inspired by a new topic. —Earth has always been saturated with background radiation, whether

cosmic or domestic in nature. When the Earth was young everything exuded a lethal glow of radioactivity. This had to subside
before life could evolve, before primordial organisms would hold
together. That radiation has been dropping ever since, but it's
important to note its positive effects. Ionizing radiation causes
mutation, which is the cornerstone of evolution. Without it we
would never have evolved.

—Creativity is like evolution. It is caused by mutation, by
imperfections in the thought process. Neuroses of various kinds
are the source of this mutation, whether they are generated by
chemical or emotional imbalance. Why are so many artists crazy?
Van Gogh and Mozart? It's the background radiation. What
makes them nuts makes them creative. The artist's brain is like a
young Earth, gamma rays saturating its surface, bringing new
organisms into being. . . .

This theory excites Helen, reminds her of the kinds of things
Brady used to say, the way he once was: cerebral, contemplative.

Now she looks at Henry, but he has his head tilted back, the
mouth of the bottle at his chin, and is studying the waves and con-
tours of the overcast sky. Brady is usually silent after these dia-
tribes. Helen wonders, wants to ask him if he still has such
thoughts, but she knows his answer to such things. A snicker,
then, Why? Do you? Always turning it back to her. He hasn't
answered a question in years.

—Has either of yous guys looked at your hydro meters lately?
Beck asks. —I got some cash riding on you, Henry.

—Mmm. I haven't looked yet.

—Brady checks every hour, Helen reports. —He would drag a
deck chair up to it and sit there with a beer if it were warmer.

—I'd never let Beck play along. I love my electric blanket, Gail
says.

—Well, Brady gets mad if I get a bright idea! Helen cries.
Everyone laughs, including Brady. It reminds Helen of the trio of
them at university: Henry the Geographer, Brady the Anthro-
pologist, Helen the Psychologist. None pursued their interest
after graduation. Brady became a schoolteacher. Helen took a job
as a veterinarian's assistant. Helen and Brady married. Henry
moved two hours north to the rickety cabin he still occupies.

On the ice there in the middle of a lake, with her friends
packed into the warmth of snowsuits and Scotch, Helen stares

50

THE INTOXICATION OF THOUGHT

into the fire's heart and tries to trace the path of her life. It was once a thread that banked around obstacles, bent and twisted where necessary, the lifeline of Theseus after slaying the Minotaur, the way to freedom. Now it is fragments, useless bits of string, unrelated instances split by tiny disasters, insignificant occurrences that conspire to ravage the path, leave it unnavigable.

She wonders why Brady changed, then considers the possibility that it wasn't him at all. She has always been self-critical to a fault. She knows this, has read about it in the psychology texts, has decided it is the best way to be.

Two years ago there was an opportunity to change paths. . . .

◗ She was driving him to town. Late August, autumn a tiny kindling of fire in the tips of the trees. Henry was and always would be poor.

—This year I will have a warm winter, he said. —I'm going to seal every wall with plastic. Then I'm going to put up some fibreglass insulation. Then inside walls. If you yuppies ever give up on woodburning stoves I might be able to afford one myself. Instead of the exorbitant cost of electric heat. But first, the walls. It'll be a huge improvement.

—Over what?

—Over what I have now. I will be a warmer person.

—I thought you liked being cold.

—Being cold or feeling cold?

—Yes.

He was silent, watching the highway roll under the car. He twisted and sat sideways in his seat to face Helen and said, Do you remember in university, you used to insist that you never lie. Is that still true?

—Yes. I don't lie. Why should I?

—I have a theory. Now, don't roll your eyes. Just listen. Let the thought intoxicate you for once. There's this depth. The depth of lies.

—Look, Henry, you won't be able to impress me with any of your tall tales. I have worked with emotionally disturbed people, some who haven't told the truth in a decade. They lie about everything. Their name. Age. The time of day.

—Truth is the opposite of lies. Truth is what is. But think about what *isn't*. Your car is blue, but what isn't it? Red. Green.

Brown. Purple. There is a dimension to lies. The truth is planar, a featureless two-dimensional landscape. But untruth. That is everywhere else. How can you limit yourself to such a tiny range of experience?

—So you're saying lies will enrich my life? Make me a better person?

—Better person. Why does everyone want to be a better person? It's not like the pay goes up. He pulled a tape from his breast pocket, slid it into the tape machine. —Voodoo drums, he said, adjusting the volume, sending the thundering rhythm through the car, beating away at the wind from the windows. —Turn here.

She signalled the left, still a kilometre from the exit to town. They entered the provincial park; she drove dangerously fast on the winding road cut between birch and aspen. At the park office she bought a day pass; it was midweek and the park was empty. She drove deep into the park, past the open sites, into one on a secluded roadway. When she pulled the car in she turned off the engine. The drums cut out briefly and her eyelids fluttered, the spell subsiding. His hand was on hers, turning the key backwards. The drums exploded again, then his hands were on her shoulders, she gripped his head, pulled his mouth towards hers, and they fell into a struggle to possess the other's body, the kiss and lick and bite of flesh, the flutter of sunlight on skin.

On the drive home he insisted on preserving the drums, flipped the tape. They reached his cabin; with its sinking roof and sad windows it looked as if it were melting in the afternoon sun. After a kiss, after a squeeze of her breast, the music was the last thing he took.

As she was heading back along the gravel road to her own cottage, left with a distant country music station bitten by static, a fox darted out from the foliage leaning in from the shoulder of the single-lane road. There was a thump and she stomped on the brake. She got out and stood, listening to the mumbling of the engine and the hiss of the wind through the tall trees, then walked around the vehicle, looked cautiously underneath, and finally tried to peer into the thick underbrush. Nothing. Satisfied that the noise had come from a bump on the rough road, she climbed back in the car and drove on, but couldn't help the nagging thought that the animal may have been mortally injured and crawled off to die somewhere in the forest.

By the time she returned to the cottage the guilt of her liaison had obscured the incident.

—Did Henry get his insulation? Brady asked.

—No, he forgot his wallet, she responded.

The world expanded and for a week it held new dimensions. In Brady's universe she was the sullen thinker, setting out each dawn in the canoe for a secluded bay across the lake. In her own she became the ecstatic lover who filled Henry's cabin with the creak of the door, the floorboards, the bed.

◗ Motion startles her. Silhouettes of dogs scamper around her, maintaining a radius of curiosity. Long legs, thick coats, they trot past, turn, pass again. Wolves. Helen watches them, doesn't move. How many are there? She takes two swift steps, straddles the snowmobile, and guns the engine. The sound slams across the lake and the headlight casts a beam on a grey wolf that is standing directly in front of the machine. The wolf's eyes turn into the light and its retinas erupt in gold. Helen looks into the animal's eyes and they stare at each other for several seconds before the wolf swings a great jaw skyward and howls. The other wolves cease their pacing and join in. As a chorus of voices ignites the air Helen wrenches the throttle and swerves around the lead wolf, heading for home.

Suddenly they are all around her, seven or eight of them, running beside the snowmobile. They cut in front of her so she has to bank away. She thinks she will run one down if necessary, but cannot, continues to turn the machine as they race before her, until she is on a new bearing that will take her directly across the lake. Towards Henry's cabin. Once she is aligned, once she recognizes the hill on which his cabin hunches, the animals dissolve into the night.

The snowmobile bites its way up the slope towards the cottage, and as she pulls in beside Henry's own rusting machine and turns off the engine, the silence, undamaged by the scream of her journey, flows in like water. She can see slits of light between the cabin's cracks. He must be reading.

The creak of her snowsuit, her boots through the drifts. There is a telephone pole with a blue mercury lamp, white-blue like actinic snow. Her eyes follow the conduit from the pole to the side of the cabin. She veers away from the door, walks to where

53

the power line and the cabin meet, at the hydro meter. The disk that spins to reflect power consumption is still. There must be candles or a hurricane lamp inside.

She stands before the frozen meter, knows that Henry has won the contest. Brady, unscrewing lightbulbs and shutting down the water heater at night, never stood a chance. Henry has turned off his electricity.

Helen knows that Henry would appreciate the two worlds that exist for her in this moment.

In the first he is alive.

A silence deeper than the air and snow, deeper than this night, seeps out through the cracks of his cabin. ◑

☾

Rose Pagoda

A GEEK. That's what Clive thinks, looking at the flat-faced man in grey overcoat and salted shoes staring glumly straight ahead, a tube of lipstick clutched in his right hand. A pity that the reflection in the shop window is his own. With his left hand he kneads the top button of his coat out of the hole and extracts his shirt collar. It hangs from his neck like a fin, a genetic mutation; on it he draws a little red mouth which he buffs with a fingertip into a blurry oval.

He zigzagged through the aisles of the drugstore before finding the lipstick racks with their gooey and creamy and metallic pinks, corals, magentas, garnets, burgundies, cinnabars, carmines, alizarins, solferinos, rosanilines, ochres, blushes. He had thought to snatch one quickly and pay for it along with hemorrhoid ointment or a box of condoms, but when he saw the variety it became important that his mate be constructed from lips of the correct hue.

The lipstick labels slid beneath the jagged nail of Clive's index finger, each projecting a potential wearer into his brain so vividly that he could almost feel the quickness of flesh. Here was Pink Jewel, tall, small-breasted, with bobbed hair and great misty eyes. She liked to do it against the wall while wearing most of her clothing. Satinspun Rose raked fingers through a mop of dark hair as she straddled him, her fleshy curves illuminated by sunlight through drawn blinds. Frosted Pumpkin had fiery red hair and ice-blue eyes; the skin on her belly was as translucent as ocean foam. Silk Champagne was a cheerleader blonde, muscularly braced and sexually dexterous. Bronzed Peach, Shimmering Shell, Honeyplum Glow, Bistro Burgundy. These lips, these women, flicked past him like a slide show, a menu of desserts, exciting him, making his heart thrash, forcing him to slouch inside his trenchcoat to conceal the erection.

A short plain woman in a worn parka snarled at him to move, then plucked a colour called Rose Pagoda from the rack.

Clive also selected Rose Pagoda, cleverly accompanying it with a box of tampons which he soon after disposed of in a garbage bin beside a construction site. He hurled the pastel pink and green box into the flow of smashed concrete issuing from a pipe above the bin. Then he hurried on, the lipstick in the tube turning to mush from the heat of his sweaty palm.

He senses motion within his reflection, as if a ghost has occupied his body and is struggling to escape. He adjusts his depth of focus from the glass to the figure behind it, a young woman in a yellow dress who is pantomiming a series of actions: surfing, scuba diving, swimming, and volleyball. Clive juts his head forward and the woman steps back and with a grand gesture presents the office's interior. It is a travel agency, and posters of tropical landscapes gild the walls. She waves him inside and he smiles absently before setting off east along St. Clair towards the bridge. He nudges the collar back into his coat.

He halts at the foot of the bridge. Cars ply the wet snow, launching waves of brown slush against the sidewalk and railing like a hurricane sea lashing the beach. Clive's feet are already squishing in his shoes but he can see no way to cross the bridge without getting soaked. The air is scented with salt, which is eating the concrete, melting it just as it dissolves the snow. Clive is on a low-sodium diet; he curses salt, ally of entropy, consuming hearts and stone alike.

A lull in the traffic sends him striding onto the bridge. When he reaches the centre he slings the lipstick over the edge, watches Rose Pagoda twist through the air before puncturing the river a hundred metres below. The flow, fuelled by the vernal melt, boils over the spot like chocolate milkshake, and Clive wonders if his body would be similarly absorbed.

He has almost reached the opposite side unscathed when a milk tanker sloshes past and soaks him to his waist.

—I hate spring, he mutters, realizing that as a Canadian he has uttered blasphemy, that spring is the fetus of summer, our most revered period, when beer consumption soars and humans emerge from parkas and anoraks to assume their natural morphology. Autumn is crisp and dry, bathed in waning sunlight with fire in the trees. Winter preserves the world from decay, holds it suspended in crystal beauty. Spring is birth, with all the obstetric connotations: ruptured membranes, spilled fluids, and the labour and screams of awakening.

The city retreats as he walks east. He turns down a side street of muted bungalows and follows the sidewalk, circumnavigating miniature lakes by plumping through the wet snow on boulevards. A fine rain is falling.

Suddenly he is standing before his house, with its doleful blinds and frowning basement window. Christmas lights dangle from the eavestroughs and everything is dripping. The world is a bog; in four thousand years archaeologists will dig up the whole mess, expend a few minutes determining the find's era, then promptly restore the peat to its place and pack it down with the backs of their shovels.

Clive stands at the end of the walk and looks at the front door of his house, his grey coat and countenance like camouflage in the misty rain. Before he can muse about the implications of what he's about to do, a woman's eyes, black-lined, the lids smudged with blue eyeshadow, appear at the bottom of the door's high window and look out at him, twin orbs of inquiry. His wife, Cally. He takes a step and she backs away, then disappears.

With alarm Clive realizes that he has always underestimated female instinct. He acknowledges its existence, but is utterly uninformed as to its depth. The lipstick on his collar which she has yet to see . . . does the instinct sense infidelity, or the attempted illusion of infidelity? Or does it probe deeper, into Clive's mushy soul, into his fear of her fanatical passion? Mulling over these apprehensions he manages, for an instant, to perceive himself through her eyes: a man bold in public but terrified in the bedroom, the total opposite of herself.

Succumbing to desire invites destruction. If this were America she'd be fetching the family revolver.

He starts to move towards the door, grains of salt grinding under his shoes, begins to mount the steps, pulls the door open.

—Cally?

No answer. Perhaps in the kitchen. Suddenly he regrets stocking the household with the finest vanadium blades. He rubs his bottom lip with the heel of his hand. But the kitchen is empty.

He hears a giggle, then sees a flash of white and peach. She scoots out of the bathroom and into the bedroom, and his first

59

inclination is to run away. He is astonished by his terror. He presses his chest, concerned for the quaking gelatin of his heart. The responses for fear and sexual excitement are so similar that some people are sexually motivated by fear. Could he be the opposite? Panting and sweating, he goes to the doorway of the bedroom. The shades are drawn and he can see nothing, but her voice comes from the direction of the bed.

—Who's there? Are you a burglar?

—Oh, Cally, I'm afraid you don't know me at all, he says, immediately regretting the stiltedness of his delivery. He moves towards the voice, liberating the collar from his coat. She pounces. Although tiny, she is like a jaguar and he instantly finds himself pinned to the bed. There go the buttons on his coat. Her mouth is close to his ear.

—Then I had better find out more about you, she whispers, and the kisses come, a hundred of them, a thousand, across his face and then his body, clothing now shed, her skin hot, feverish as they tangle and claw at one another. Clive finds himself wavering between the two peaks of fear and desire; he tries to fuse them, tries to translate himself into the prey of this feral erotic mammal.

—You're crazy! You're an animal, he pants, his fingertips skimming the hardness of her collarbone, then pinching the muscles along the top of her shoulder. She howls softly.

—I want some light, she hisses. —I want to see us together.

—No. No! No! he cries as she reaches for the bedside lamp. He is rolling and groping for his shirt which is somewhere on the bed or the floor, but she pins him with her forearm. She hits the switch and he shields his eyes with one hand while snagging the shirt with the other.

—What's the matter? What's with the shirt? she demands, her voice foreign at its normal pitch. She snatches the shirt from him and examines it.

—Nothing, he whispers. In the light he sees that she has made herself up for him: mascara, eyeliner, eyeshadow, and lipstick. The lipstick is smudged around her mouth like a corona of blood. He imagines that the barrage of kisses has left marks all over his clothes and body, and he has no problem identifying the colour of her lipstick. It is Rose Pagoda. ◑

(

Long Exposure

The investigator will be enormously displeased with the kid's testimony. He will sit with his left elbow propped on the desk's tattooed blotter, his ribs pressed hard against the desk's edge and his back askew on the wooden chair, eyes returning again and again to the swell of the warrior-princess's breasts on the novel's creased cover, at the glass sword which slices across a pink sky.

THE KID DOES NOT hear the door open, continues to read the clumsy typeface from cheap, greying paper, even fails at first to detect the icy draft, a sting of snow crystals on the greasy flesh of his face, mistaking it for a chill at the turn of events in the plot. Then he perceives motion beyond the book's traumatized spine and reluctantly looks up. She is standing in the little coil of snow that has accompanied her entrance, each flake melting into a black speck on the worn boards. Destroyed boots, round-nosed, calf-high, leather sundered and peeling but ushered back into shape with string, tape, and glue. The kid follows the boots to snowpants, manufactured white but now stained with mud and soot. Above them is a coat once covered by animal fur, raccoon or beaver, but now worn down to an abrasive shell of bristles. Above the coat's drawstring and enclosed deep within a hood, a pair of silver eyes. Cracked lips turn up into a smile.

—Grocery store? the voice croaks.

—Ya-huh, the kid replies. —More like convenience store, but we got groceries. For sale.

— I got money. The little form shuffles to the cash and a hand as chapped and scaly as snakeskin rises and opens atop the counter, spilling out a small mound of silver coins. —How much you see?

He pokes through the collection. —I make it five dollar forty.

—Me too. Got a pack of crackers that might cover?

—Ya-huh, the boy says, turning back to his book. —Second aisle, near the back.

The figure stands, rocking minutely, the dry leather of the boots creaking.

—I got a problem, mister, grinds the voice. —I can't see. See?

He looks up.

—What?

—I can't see. Well barely. Just about blind as a bat.

The mouth opens into a cavernous smile, and the boy wonders how the smashed stumps of teeth could handle anything but babyfood.

—So maybe you could just pick me out your cheapest box of crackers, and if there's money left for cheese I'd be obliged if you put some up too. Then it'd be nice if you'd not gyp me off and gimme whatever change is my due. I know that's not a lot to ask but I've asked for less before and not got it.

The boy stares at her, at the silvered pupils that look at a spot beyond his left shoulder. He laughs through his nose, a quick snort, then folds over his page and sets the book down on the counter. At the back of the store he selects a box of crackers, the kind that he himself likes, with sesame seeds. He checks the dairy fridge, locates the cheapest stick of cheese, a bar of Monterey Jack. He heads back to the cash where he rings up the items. His eyebrows rise when the price appears on the display. He collects the coins from the counter and fills a plastic bag, then holds it out.

—Here, he says, and the hand rises again. He loops the handle over it and the fingers close.

—Any change?

—No. Two ninety-nine for the crackers. Two forty-one for cheese. Five forty.

—Funny that it was the exact right amount, eh?

—Ya. Funny. He picks up his book and begins to read. A moment later he stops and looks up. —Somethin else I can help with?

—Just thinking how it's funny. About the amount in my pocket being just the same as what the crackers and cheese is.

—Well. Funny things happen.

—Funny things happen. We should thank the Lord for everything, so I thank him for funny things as much as serious things.

—Ya.

—And I thank you too, mister. Good eve.

She turns quickly to the door and moves forward, one hand outstretched. When it connects with the handle she pulls the door open and steps outside. Then the door closes and it is quiet once again in the store, the coolers and fluorescent lights buzzing. He stands up and looks out through the glass to the woman standing there. She is pulling on a pair of brown gloves, they are made from animal hide. She turns and puts her hands out, runs them along the storefront glass until she reaches a cane, a gnarled branch, propped there. Once it's in her grasp she turns away from the window and pauses for a few seconds in the blowing snow. Then the staff is thrust forward and like a snout probes the ground ahead of her as she begins to walk. Almost immediately she encounters the gas pumps, which she circumnavigates without hesitation. Once clear, she returns to her original trajectory, straight off from the store and into the deepening blue, crossing the empty highway with its tracks of cinnamon sand and salt, and sets out across the field on the opposite side. He watches her for a long time, until the darkness and the snow and the distance have consumed her. Then he lets the book claim him once again and until the end of his shift at 11:00 PM receives no other customers.

◐ The snow crunches. Variations in the weather over the last few days have frozen and thawed the top to form a shell of ice four millimetres thick. She counts her steps, counts how many times she breaks through the crust and how many times she does not. The result is exactly fifty percent. This is a mathematically unique evening, she muses. First the price of cheese and crackers, now this. A downy snow is falling, light soft flakes that due to their insignificant mass move without regard to gravity, upwards, downwards, horizontally, as if they have precipitated not out of the blue-black clouds but spontaneously from the freezing air itself. She sucks these particles into her nose and lungs where they tickle and sting before evaporating in the warm cavity of her chest.

The stick skates along ahead of her, moving through the wind-borne eddies of snowcrystals that race over the ice. Replenishing the shallow cisterns of footprints her boots have created, erasing the world's memory of her. Without a reminder, without some sort of extraordinary occurrence, even the kid in the store will forget her.

But he will not forget her.

The terrain is flat. The alternating injections of her boots through the ice keep her from falling. The trees are sparse and mature, with few low branches. She walks west and makes good time.

◖ The cold barely reaches her beneath the strata of clothing. The coat, boots, and snowpants form a peripheral membrane of protection. Beneath the coat are two sweaters, the outer of grey acrylic and fraying at the cuffs and neck, the inner, the one against her skin, handknit from brown and white and pink wool, filthy and congealing into balls that dangle from her torso like an array of hirsute nipples.

Her half-sister, Mary, knit the sweater, a final act before she and her boyfriend Graham had been swallowed into the grey belly of Superior. A need for privacy had driven them onto the lake in a blue rowboat that was swamped by a summer squall. They had gone out to make love. It was thirty years ago.

She and Mary were both half-bloods, their white fathers unknown to them.

On her feet she wears two pairs of unmatched socks plus thick stockings. Even her face remains warm, assailed by cold only when the wind stabs down the tunnel of the hood.

The hunger she has been bearing in her stomach suddenly calls out. Here is a grove of sparsely spaced trees. Little penetrates the jellied haze of her vision. She moves through the trees slowly, poking at each, until she finds one with a hard base beneath it, a place where a rock is partially submerged and glazed with snow and ice. There she sits, and sets the plastic bag between her feet and peels off one and then the other glove. The skin of her hands is like rawhide, and though she can barely feel the cold, she is wary of it, wary of the danger of frostbite, of black fingers that must be amputated. Her older brother Denny passed out drunk under his Chev, replacing the clutch in early February. The upper half of his body protected by heat from the still-warm engine. At the hospital his toeless feet wrapped in heavy gauze, but the first time he wept for them it was late spring. He put his feet into sandals and they wouldn't stay on.

She pauses to breathe heat onto the cheese, which is hard and cold. The crackers are dry. She soaks one in her mouth before mashing it against the roof with her tongue. Its edges abrade her throat anyway.

The landscape, its tones and variations, gradually begins to take shape. Her retinas are like slow photographic paper, useless in bright light, but capable through long exposure of accumulating the impression of a diminutive scene. The ground is brightest, snow zealously reflecting what little starlight soaks through the deep blue filter of the sky. Wedged between earth and cloud are the cragged configurations of birch and sugar maple, sometimes the rotund cone of balsam vaguely settled among those silhouettes. Little more than variations of viscous blue light.

This emergence of vision startles her and she looks at it for a long time, a cracker between her fingers and halted halfway to her mouth, studying the architecture of the land.

Abruptly the cracker is snatched from her grasp and she turns, but darkness spills back into her eyes.

—Who's there? she calls.

From her right comes a shallow snort and the sound of chewing. She pushes her hands between her knees to warm them and a snout butts into her lap, seeking another treat. She lifts one from the package and holds it out, trembling, and it is seized and chewed and swallowed. She feels on her knuckles the hot sap from the deer's lips.

As she feeds a consecutive stream of crackers to the creature, she recalls a pineboard church she once entered after travelling through the forest and coming unexpectedly upon a logging town. The smell of woodsmoke and bacon in the air had given her such a yen for warmth and company that she sought guidance in reaching one place she might find these. After several minutes of polite solicitation of passersby, a girl who smelled of cigarettes and rancid perfume offered up her arm.

—Where do you want to go?

—Thank you, dear. You got a place of worship here?

—Oh ya. Temple of the Little Flower. It's sorta United but mostly Catholic.

—Lead on.

The girl was silent except for sudden exclamations.

—Main and Lemon Street. Here's the CIBC and Feeney's Hardware.

—Legion over there. My Aunt Cotton and her new husband up about seven houses.

— Go right here and you'd be at Cheenie's Kitchen.

—Temple Street. Little Flower is just this way.

The girl led her up the granite steps and held open the door.

—God bless for your help, dear.

She moved inside and paused, listening to the door close

67

slowly on its greased piston, shutting out the sounds of the street. She stepped forward, her hands grazing the tops of the pews. Before she could abase herself beneath she knew not what – a nativity scene or the crucified Jesus, or maybe a statue of the pale Virgin with outstretched arms – she heard from a side door a radio, and on the radio a guest, a scientist of some renown, discussing extraterrestrial life. No, not discussing, simply asking: Is there life on other planets? If so, how did it evolve? How is it like and unlike us? Will it exhibit intelligence? Will it communicate with us?

These questions, juxtaposed in that place of faith and worship, had stuck with her, for of course this scientist did not know the answers to his own questions, and in the ensuing interview seemed only to dismiss each with proof upon proof. Despite his skepticism, however, she could hear from his voice and manner that he wanted to believe, had in fact decided to believe. That day she had thought him foolish and contradictory, yet the questions still suffused the tributaries of her mind.

● Submersed in this bitter cold that seems to squeeze into the earth all that moves through it, still there is life. A deer seeking food where there is none, or perhaps dead scrub and freezedried berries or by chance a cracker in the deep of the night. Life persists. It will grow where it can. It may not flourish, but it will begin and it will persevere, sparsely perhaps, in esoteric and eccentric forms, anywhere. To her there is suddenly no question about its existence on other worlds. It is everywhere. The revelation will occur not as discovery, but as recognition.

She feeds a few more crackers to the doe, feels the jets of steam from its nostrils, smells its humic odour. She reaches the bottom of the box and scatters the crumbs onto the ground. The beast retreats and she hears its snout grazing the snow, the lap of its tongue on the ice. When the crumbs are gone the nose presses between her knees again and she pushes it away. —Go on now.

The creature persists and she gives it a little shove. Again the muzzle crowds into her and she pushes harder. Her hands are starting to ache. As she begins to pull on her gloves the huge head returns and slams into her chest, knocking her from the rock and into the snow. The head follows her down and with both hands she presses it back, shouting at it to scram. When the head swings back she balls up her hand and punches the deer hard, striking it on the ear. She hears a grunt as it staggers sideways. As she clambers to her feet, crouching in anticipation of another blow, she hears the rapid retreating patter of its hoofs breaking through the snow.

Above the blue landscape she notes a thin stroke of light etching itself into her vision. It moves from south to north, a hot fast comet hurtling across the sky, descending rapidly until the forest obscures it. A moment later a peal of thunder punctuated by a concussion reaches not just her ears but her feet, a heavy moan like the earth's exclamation at a violation. An echo reports back from the escarpment six kilometres to the south and then like water filling a wake there is quiet again, the sullen creak of frozen branches and the rattle of dead leaves still clinging to them, the hiss of snow over ice. She stands and begins to walk, banking slightly northward, to the point where the light has vanished.

The wind subsides and stillness deepens, becomes more pure, as if the night were fine cheesecloth through which the world is draining, leaving nothing but rich, distilled silence. Her modified vector, towards her estimation of the landing spot of the descending light, carries her through denser forest, over a fence made from stone, and her pace slows as she negotiates the obstacles. The snowfall has thickened into marble-sized flakes that further dampen the quiet.

Once she runs into a low branch that has escaped detection of her cane; another time she reaches the top of a little slope only to fall forward on the ice and slide all the way back to the bottom, an inert toboggan that stops at the base of the slope and without frustration or embarrassment rises and reascends. She walks for perhaps two hours before noting a change in the scent of the cold air. It is the smell of raw pine, a Christmas-tree smell that brings back memories both delightful and traumatic. The gift of a stuffed frog, its bulbous eyes jiggling, the tongue in its enormous mouth a tiny crescent of felt. A man hacking at brittle glass ornaments, scattering them from the tree into little beartraps of broken glass, as his words hammered away at the apparent misdeeds of her mother.

She steps suddenly into a current. It is not of liquid or even air, it is more like the after-effect of a current, like a dry riverbed swept wide and smooth by water. She continues to move forward, more slowly, turning with her face tilted upwards, sensing the sweep of trees, feeling beneath her boots the snow and, below that, the earth gouged and stripped by the passage of something heavy and unyielding. The direction of the sweep not readily apparent. Tucking the cane beneath her arm, she approaches a tree, senses its thick base before her, touches it low on the trunk, and runs her gloves upwards. At waist level her hands encounter shards of bark, the scent of raw wood sweet and peppery, where the tree has been sheared off by a tremendous impact. She moves around the base of the tree, feeling the open bole, until her shins connect with the trunk, here laid out flat and like the filament of a compass pointing north.

She turns back in the direction from where she has come, sees in her mind the phosphorescent trail of her passage, then rotates and begins to walk along her original vector. The sky above her is clear. After a few steps her cane connects with another felled tree.

She climbs over the trunk and moves forward again along the scraped and uneven ground before she encounters another tree, this time the crown of it, naked branches also swept northwards. She works her way around it and continues west, navigating through a forest made horizontal. It takes perhaps fifteen minutes of slow progress before she finds the first of the untouched trees, a white pine by the silky feel of its needles on her cheek.

She turns and starts to make her way slowly northward along the cut, between and over the trunks of smashed trees, along scooped troughs that smell of fresh earth. Her cane dips into craters, then encounters the objects that occupied them, rocks and boulders, uprooted, tumbled north like supplicants suddenly halted during their pilgrimage to the object that unearthed them, which must lie ahead.

Her staff meets something that makes a hollow metallic sound. She bangs it several times, the sonority like a gong, then takes off a glove and runs her palm over the cold curve. She works her way around it, trying to find detail on the smooth surface, but the cold is so intense that her hand is immediately numb. She moves around the object, feeling its general contour until she has determined that it is a large canister that tapers at one end. The opposite side is smashed and misshapen from the impact.

She works her way around it and continues forward, discovers more debris among the busted oak and birch. Nothing is uniform.

Some chunks are rectangles a few centimetres thick; she leans on them and they yield to her weight. Others are large arcs of metal that curve above her. The detritus thickens, impeding her steps. She tucks the staff under her arm and starts to pick her way forward with gloved hands, heaving objects aside, strips of metal, heavy, hard shapes geometrical or once so before the collision. Her outstretched hands connect with a long, smooth piece at head level. She runs a glove along it and steps through and now atop more wreckage, leery of the hazards of sharp metal, razor edges cutting at her coat and legs, but she works her way deeper into it, compelled by a growing sense of horror to explore further.

A squeal startles her. She halts, head up, listening. She hears it again, a tortured animal sound reverberating within a partially enclosed space, just ahead. A deer, trapped?

—Who's there? she calls.

She listens to the wind and the snow pattering on the metal around her. She moves towards the noise until she feels a ceiling slide over her, cutting off the downy cascade of snow. She pauses and listens to her own breathing, then begins to move again. Tendrils of plastic and metal graze her hood and she keeps her head low as she progresses. Her knees strike a rigid object but there is passage to both left and right.

—Noise again! she calls.

A thin moan directs her to the left. She is walking down an aisle, her hands out, grasping soft square shapes on each side. Her breath is fast and shallow.

—Keep your hands high, she whispers to herself. Then she stops again.

—Heya heya! Her voice recoils in the low space.

Then the cry, behind her. She whirls and reaches forward, feels the limp form in the chair.

She sets her cane aside, removes her gloves, feels her way down the body to where it is belted in. The cry again, and she withdraws her hand at the sudden heat, like a blowtorch, on her skin. A breath. Then crying. A long, hard, drawn-out wail, uncorked by the end of solitude. She reaches forward again, this time with both hands, and unbinds the child from her mother's grasp. The woman's body slumps forward before she can retrieve the child, and it is against the jaw, an open mouth and cold teeth, that she must push back.

71

The child is lifted, screaming. The skin clammy and gelid. She yanks the zipper of her coat downward and stuffs the baby inside, against the soft curl of the grey sweater, then pulls the zipper back up so just the wailing mouth is exposed. Then she picks up her cane and pokes her way slowly up the aisle.

As she gingerly backtracks out of the wreck, debris unsteady below her boots, the baby subsides to a quiet whimpering, its wet face against her chin.

—Chik chik chik, she tells it. —Sa sa sa.

She feels the snow and earth beneath her feet and begins to move towards the rear of the wreckage. Once well back from the major debris, she turns towards the west. It doesn't take long before she reaches the wall of the forest where the wrack ceases. She pauses there and turns around and stands facing the destruction from which she has emerged.

—Look, she says to the child as the image begins to resolve itself on her retinas. The three points of the tailsection against the blue-black sky. The sweptback wings, the cylinder of one engine standing on end. And far down, at the front of the aircraft, the high hump and the first-class section abaft the cockpit. A long wound along the fuselage allowing access to the passenger compartment. A diorama exhibiting the dead in poses of astonished deceleration.

She turns quickly away and begins to walk, her cane outstretched. Snowflakes strike and melt on her face and she moves her jaw over the child's forehead to protect it. An hour later she hears the beat of helicopter blades, far off to the east. ◖

(*Enormous Attraction*

You and I dance through the fabric of spacetime, embedded in its subtle weave. Somewhere the warp is unravelling, strings of matter twitching out of phase and facing annihilation in pools of hungry entropy which tremble with their repast, consuming the chaotic variety that is our being, sentencing all to homogeneity, converting the subtle features of existence, the nuance of your smile or the stellar furnace of a quasar, into featureless background.

I AM DESCENDING a subway staircase, romanticizing this journey by allying myself with the orphans of the sky, the nickel miners and spelunkers, frail creatures hunkered down beneath a billion tonnes of Earth, arches of rock glazed in the mucus of the planet's viscera.

This morning a New Age mechanic named Zaph, while slurping espresso from a grease-stained paper cup, convinced me that my car was suffering from "temporal relaxation", claiming that as a vehicle ages it manifests characteristics of infancy.

—The bolts, the screws. They turn anticlockwise, like a time-piece running backwards. Regressing to a state of disassembly, towards the fetal automobile. Our job now involves temporal adjustment; we advance the fasteners clockwise, fixing the car in the stasis established at the precise moment of final assembly. He gulped espresso and nodded until I returned the gesture. I was three blocks away, still absorbing this theory, when I realized I had neglected to inquire about another variable, one of greater import to me: the monetary compensation for a "temporal adjustment".

Navigating the mint-green tunnels of the subway station, I feel the pangs of age dampen my step as I approach the collector's booth. I am out of touch with the basic commuter knowledge and skills. How much is the subway these days? Students and executives move swiftly past, flashing passes and dropping tickets and tokens into the receptacle, unacknowledged by the stare of the collector in her light-brown shirt. I step into her line of sight and her eyes make reluctant contact.

—One, please, I say.

—One what? she snorts, and I am disoriented to hear her voice issuing from a speaker at the level of my belly. I bend at the waist and speak directly into the microphone.

—Ride. To Museum station?

—It's the same.

—I beg your pardon?

—The same. No matter where you're going.

—Do you mean that in a philosophical sense?

She rolls her eyes and taps the glass above a card listing fares, laid out to defy easy interpretation. A glance behind me reveals a lineup of agitated commuters.

—It's two dollars, a voice murmurs in my ear, and I meet the eyes of a young woman. She nods towards the fare box. I dig into my pocket and excavate a pile of coins, draw out two loonies, and cast them in. I tangle with the turnstile and the woman rushes past me. —Hurry if you're heading north, she cries as the thunder of a subway rises from the staircase. I two-step down behind her and duck through the doors on the last note of the warning chimes. The car is crowded and I have to clutch at a chrome railing as the train accelerates into the tunnel.

—You're still quick, the woman says, looking into my eyes a moment longer than is necessary. I am an unreasonably tall man and tilting her head clearly causes her some discomfort, but she persists. With dread I realize that she's sympathizing (*still* quick?), that in some way I embody the image of a flustered fool, a kind of absent-minded professor attempting to navigate the mundane obstacles of the masses. Dreading several stops of flirtatious pity, I excuse myself with a nod and make my way through the throng to the rear of the car. I look back once and she continues to watch me, smiling brightly.

I browse the faces of the other passengers. They are neutral, fixated on points situated past the subway's windows, beyond the tunnel's sooty walls. Sometimes one gaze collides with another, an inexplicable recognition bonding each for several seconds before one or the other breaks away, seeking greater significance in a bubblegum ad or warning sign.

As my line of sight is relayed from eye to eye, a bolt of staggering pain strikes my gut just below the navel, its intensity evoking the image of an amniocentesis needle piercing my stomach. I twitch forward, my palm pressed to the spot, as I wonder where I'm going to direct the inevitable stream of vomit. I begin to fold, my knuckles white on the bar, and I moan softly. I look at the floor and watch as a tear escapes from my eye and plummets in slow motion towards the running shoes and pumps, towards the pointed toes of my cowboy boots, striking directly between them. I clamp my jaw to defeat what can only be a wail, and the sound fibrillates inside my mouth. I look to the woman standing next to me, she is reading a newspaper and she turns her eyes to me and smiles, and I think that perhaps I'm going to die, I will collapse on the scuffed acrylic floor and have to rely on these people to assist me or comfort me or administer my last rites, and I know that they will not, that a circle will open around me, an isolation zone, a ring of riders engrossed in their thoughts and their magazines, within which I will be asked, through their oblivion, to cease my disturbance and hasten upon my mortal journey.

The attack ends abruptly. A moment later I am hunched, clutching my belly, sweating and panting as the train continues to burrow its way towards the next stop. Gallstones? Appendicitis? Cancer? The cessation of pain grants me a sudden euphoria. I wipe my soaked brow and straighten up. I notice that the newspaper of the woman beside me is Vietnamese, and for some reason I am relieved.

◑ Two months ago Ilyria and I were at dinner.

It was a trendy restaurant in the Eaton Centre, small tables tipped into dark corners, the music broadcast so loudly that everyone appeared to be bickering, the menus unwieldy tomes displaying a broad range of quasi-cultural dishes, most served with a pickle and fries. Ilyria and I were not eating, we were drinking cocktails, which instead of quenching her anxiety appeared to be augmenting it. After numerous failed attempts to soothe her through light conversation, my eyes settled on hers and I sighed deeply.

—Don't stare at me, she whispered, shifting in her chair.

—I'm not.

—You are.

—I am not.

—Stop it!

—Ilyria, do you even know what's bothering you?

—Nothing is bothering me.

—Look, can I help it if I'm your friend and I care very much about you? I hate to see you like this.

—Stop worrying, Raymond. My anxiety is strictly professional.

—Professional agitation? Of an astrophysical nature? Is a comet going to strike the Earth? If you have the scoop, I'd appreciate the warning so I can run my credit cards through the roof.

—Nothing so dramatic. But just as important. I was in Arizona last week. That's why I didn't get back to you for a few days.

—I didn't know. A secret mission?

—You know about the Gindilis Anomaly?

—Of course, although we, the bewildered public, refer to it as "the alien transmission". Am I actually going to get some inside information about this thing?

She opened her purse and rummaged through it for half a minute before casting its considerable contents onto the table. From the pile that included receipts, cosmetics, and playbills, she exhumed a three-and-a-half-inch floppy disk and passed it to me with a flourish. —Welcome to the camarilla.

I turned it in the light, examined the handwritten label which read "Message Back-up" in Ilyria's perfect script. —What exactly is this?

—Binary, it's a Mac format disk. You'll find the transmission in one file.

—The entire message?

—This is one of the early iterations. We are currently receiving the transmission almost four times every second, with each broadcast identical to the preceding one – except for a string of bits in the middle, which may be some sort of counter. I'll try to get you a later version of the message so you can compare the strings.

—But what can I do? You and your people are the experts with the advanced hardware and software. What do you want from me?

—Ray, listen. Public interest is waning, and you know that puts our funding in jeopardy. We're certain that this is an intelligent message, but without knowing its content it may as well be static noise. If we could just find out what it says! The best decryption software out there – and you know that means yours – has turned up nothing. But we only have access to the latest commercial release, which is, as you know, CiphCracker 13.02. What's the progress with your beta test of version 14?

—The front end needs work. But the decryption engine has been totally rewritten in native G4 code. I lowered my voice. —And it's staggering. Ilyria, it chews through parameterized algorithms like RC5 – even with 128-bit blocks – in minutes. I wonder if there's a code out there it can't crack. *I'm* afraid to keep secrets from it. The NSA and CSIS and every other security agency in the world are going to be very interested in CiphCracker version 14.

—Is it ready to tackle something like this? She taps the disk in my hand.

—Absolutely.

—Well. This could do well for you. Publicity.

—It's true, it would really improve CiphCracker's image. So many people think of it as little more than an enemy of privacy.

—This is more important. We could be a team, Raymond. Proof of intelligent extraterrestrial life! Can you imagine?

Beneath the table something touched my knee and gently squeezed. I tried to remain impassive while avoiding any action that might dislodge it.

Ilyria and I had always enjoyed a crisply platonic relationship. I had expected – or rather, hoped for – some kind of advance after Sharon and I split, but had lately explained away her quiescence as either abstinence or disinclination. Either way I was disappointed. At that moment, however, the world altered, as if the barometric pressure had suddenly plummeted. I braced myself for a storm.

—What should I know? I gulped, shifting experimentally in the chair. The hand remained.

—The signal was first detected on the eighth of August. The Gindilis radiotelescope was collecting pulsar data, attempting to determine the neutron star's mass, when this signal suddenly appears using the pulsar's radio beam as a carrier. Everything you need is on the disk. No, just the check, please, she said to the waiter, who fished a grease-stained bill from his apron pouch and dropped it between us. Ilyria snapped it up, spilled a handful of bills atop it, gathered her things, and stood. —My treat. Share a cab?

—We're going different directions.

—No we're not.

Initially I refused to accept the situation, even with the interlock of our fingers, her golden hair piled beneath my nose and rich with the scent of her, while our shadows flashed about the interior of the taxi, even as we rushed up the walk to her front door and she fumbled with the keys in one hand because she wouldn't let go of me with the other, while she lit a single candle on her bedside table and pressed me back onto the bed, my body's questions answered by her open mouth upon my own, her small hands unfastening my buttons, the essential weight of her atop me, still I couldn't accept this as anything more than a friendly gesture, a wave or a peck on the cheek, each doing the other a favour in the night, allies against the loneliness of the dark.

And somewhere in that nocturnal sea I awoke in the disorientation of unfamiliarity, a floating clock dial exclaiming the quarter hour remaining before 3:00 AM, and as my eyes adjusted, other objects resolved around me: Ilyria's bookshelf, Ilyria's pictures, Ilyria's plants. I spent thirty seconds in terror of turning over and seeing, on the pillow beside me, the owner of all these objects. I could hear her breathing, feel her warmth, and I raised my head to look down the length of the bed to where my clothes had been cast. A streetlamp rectangle of cupreous light from the window illuminated the comforter, its hard edges distorted by the topography of our bodies. She was facing away. I turned slowly and lowered my head to the warmth of her skin, my lips to her shoulder, the fragrance of her body in my nose. She had always claimed to be a light sleeper but she did not stir and her breathing remained slow and even. I felt relief and then guilt at the relief and then confusion over the motive for the relief. I feared her awakening because it would give her the opportunity to apologize, to ask me to leave, to expel me into the night. I wanted to capture this conjunction of her shoulder and my nose, to struggle against time, which would inevitably bring on the morning and rescind my visitor's pass to this coterie, this place of belonging.

I puzzled over the tranquillity I experienced, then astonished myself with the thought that I had come *home*, that here I had found *home*, not in the bed or in the room or in the house, but in this sleepy heat beneath the thick dome of the comforter, my skin in contact with Ilyria's.

A few years ago I boasted to her about my freedom: I live, sleep, eat, work, drive, walk, read, and bathe alone, for me, for nobody else. I rely on me and depend on me and worry about no one but me.

—You're an isolationist, she'd said, looking out the café window at a man struggling to pluck a piece of tape from his shoe. *Isolationist.* Like a clinical disorder. The pride I'd felt seconds before dissolved. I responded with defiance and reinforcement, disappearing into my house for two weeks, venturing out only for essentials, fielding calls through the answering machine. And then one day a message from Ilyria: Raymond, I bet you're right there, hunched over the phone with four days' growth on your face, sweating in your bathrobe, drinking a cup of black coffee spiked with too much Scotch –

I plucked up the phone and growled, Nice guess but it's rye. She informed me that one of her colleagues had discovered a supernova and that I was her date at the celebration that evening.

—So get shaved, put on a blazer, and pick me up in two hours, at which point she hung up and refused to answer her phone when I called back to protest. I did not want to spend an evening with a bunch of staid professors in celebration of some cryptic phenomenon represented by a smudge on a photographic plate. But I went and had all my expectations dismantled. Not only was the supernova impressive enough to be reported in the popular media, but the lucky professor, a young, bearded fellow who was drinking too much, showed slides of the exploding star taken with an ordinary camera at twilight. A brilliant crystal of light. And Ilyria, instead of abandoning me to the esoteric dialogue of her peers, escorted me throughout the evening and steered discourse towards the vernacular, admitting me into the celebration.

◗ In the weeks after she gave me the disk, we struggled to feed the appetite of infatuation, abandoning ourselves to hunger for the other's flesh, for sustained contact, a kiss, a caress, a motion. Each evening the scene replayed itself, a greeting at the front door of her house, a little banter to reaffirm our human origins, then a blind moment when the space between our bodies was eradicated.

—What's wrong?

—Nothing. I . . . I feel dizzy.

—You're hyperventilating. Breathe easy, my love.

Skimming the surface of sleep like a heron, her breath soft against my ear: We dance through the fabric of spacetime, embedded in its subtle weave. Then she sighed lightly and the incantation swept me into a dream, long bands of fabric embroidered with a billion integers running endlessly from the loom of the universe.

—Let me visit the Secret Laboratory, she begged, meaning my house, where the computer was struggling with the message. I spent my days there, watching more than working, but it was always within her space, her home, that we convened. —I want to see where history is fermenting.

—No.

—Can't I even come in and have a look?

—There's nothing to see.

—Is it a mess? Just tell me it's a mess; I can handle that.

—It's not a mess. It's very neat. *I'm* very neat.

—Avocado, coconut, lemon, peach. Raymond, is it coincidence that my bathsoaps have been organized alphabetically?

—It's coincidence that you noticed.

It took CiphCracker eleven weeks to decrypt the message from space, exactly what Ilyria and I needed to descramble our passion and affirm that the relationship extended beyond our bodies.

CiphCracker version 1.00 appeared eight years ago, originally intended to port computer programs between platforms: Macintosh to Windows to Atari and so on. A year later I discovered chaos theory and the study of apparently random systems and, recalling the linguistics unit of an anthropology course, saw how it could be applied to the formation and interpretation of language.

Two versions later, with the implementation of an Intelligent Experimenting Reverse-Engineering Fractal Cascade Algorithm, or IEREFCA, CiphCracker evolved into a highly efficient and intelligent translation program. IEREFCA, simplified, is a system for examining fragments of language and exploring combinations until they form intelligible expressions.

Initially the software translated French and Spanish into English using an appurtenant dictionary. One day I inputted a page of Italian, which it interpreted based on its experience with the other languages. Though the Italian lexicon contained no cross-reference to English, it still rendered a perfect translation. I was astonished.

Using similar logic it could also crack encryptions. A password-protected file named "thanx" appeared on my computer's hard disk. I didn't know it was Sharon's.

In just under eighteen seconds CiphCracker dissolved the encryption and our marriage.

The file contained a letter for Robert, one of her graduate students. I won't describe why he deserved thanks. It sickened me, not that he was younger than me or more attractive, but that the sacred educator-student relationship had been violated. It was like pedophilia.

Perhaps CiphCracker is my guiding angel. It ended my marriage with Sharon; it brought me home to Ilyria.

◖ I awaken from my thoughts as the yellow walls of Museum station slide out of the darkness. I squeeze through the crowded car and onto the platform, where I set my satchel down on a bench and straighten my jacket. The subway powers up and thunders into the tunnel, leaving me alone in the station but for a hunchbacked man who moves with agonizing slowness towards the escalator. I pass him, the heels of my boots banging dents into the silence. Up the escalator and onto the street, where I find myself before the bald cranium of the planetarium. I consult a sign with a map of the university's vast territory, then make my way towards the southwest.

◖ Ilyria refused to provide more information about the signal than was publicly accessible, fearing that unsubstantiated conclusions drawn by her colleagues might colour my interpretation and send me down dead ends already explored. I begged for more data but in the end garnered more satisfaction from my independent progress. Cultural conditioning also exerted its influence, however, and I almost missed a crucial key. While steering CiphCracker along the assumption that the senders of the message had wanted it interpretable by alien societies, I first examined potential references to universal constants: mass ratios of quantum and atomic particles, the natural base, the wavelength emitted by hydrogen atoms. The ratio of a circle's circumference to its radius is pi, or, as a rounded real number, 3.141592. The signal's leader included zeroes and ones in a ratio of 1.570796 to one. It took far too long for me to realize that this was half of pi, and the ratio of the circle's circumference to its *diameter* – as opposed to its radius. The revelation came to me while I was eating a plate of pancakes.

This insight provided a patch of hospitable soil in which to plant CiphCracker's seed algorithm.

◗ I am on Hoskin Avenue, beneath the spires and patinaed roofs of Trinity College. Across the street and beyond a narrow parking lot the clock in Hart House's bell tower reads 4:35. Ilyria's class ends in less than half an hour. I head south, towards the tower.

The snow fences are up on the playing field behind University College, but within their perimeter some severely underdressed young men are shouting and grappling in the mud with a rugger ball. I am so engrossed in their enthusiasm that I almost run into her.

Sharon teaches Chaucer and Elizabethan Drama at University College, and the danger of meeting her here has always been high. My first visit after the divorce was like expecting sniper fire. But many incidentless journeys to the libraries or to meet Ilyria had relaxed my guard.

Now the shots ring out.

She has just exited the college and has not seen me. I imagine it would be easy to approach her, apply a cool kiss to her cheek, and inquire about the condition of my goldfish, except that she is with a student. A male student. I take a step which puts a shrub into our line of sight, then peer through the thinning foliage. They are a metre apart, talking and walking, and then they pause at the arch that leads to the front of Hart House. I'm suddenly aware of the scent of mud from the fields, and the faintly caustic odour of car exhaust. The city is a dirty place, I think, trying to repress the tide of cruel words I once said which are again filling the cavity below my larynx.

—If your intention in becoming a professor was the seduction of young male students, engineering should've been your field of study.

—I suppose you are such a bad teacher that your students must sleep with you if they hope for a passing grade.

And the cruellest, the most crude: I guess your name is Sharon because you always are.

My anger melts then and is replaced by pity. Her hair, chemically plundered of all colour, frames a clown face of excessive foundation and brilliant red lipstick. Poor Sharon. Battling entropy with her creams and waxes and gelatins. Older and more bitter.

I blink and she's kissing him, this student, this boy, kissing him hard and long on the mouth, their hands groping at places already familiar. A second later it's over, they're parting. Did she see me, was this a display? I fluctuate between two scenarios, unable to choose the more painful. Either she saw me and meant to hurt me with her behaviour, or she always kisses her lovers this way. I turn, I retreat, not sure if I am now exposed to her gaze, imagining her glare like heat from a burning building, but I don't care, I make for the college's back entrance and the sanctuary of the courtyard.

I feel a drop of sweat roll past my ear as I enter the quadrangle and seat myself on a bench. I take a few deep breaths, absorbing the neo-Gothic architecture and the maple trees which stand in pools of brilliant yellow leaves, their branches still half stocked. Even as I watch, a few are falling and twitching in the air. I keep my eyes away from the courtyard entrance, fearing Sharon's smug-lipped entrance.

I reflect on these two women I have loved; the essential differences between them are substantial. I smile at myself, synthesizing Ilyria's reaction to such comparisons: "Such a male thing to do. As if we're pickup trucks or gas barbecues!"

And speaking of comparisons, here's one: instead of highlighting my folly with analogies, Sharon's tack would be to beat me at it: "Bob's shoulders are definitely broader than yours."

Ilyria's precise diction and pronunciation. Sharon's soft consonants and overwrought words. The astrophysics professor versus the English professor. I can almost hear Sharon commenting on the fact that "English" is capitalized while "astrophysics" is not.

And how Ilyria would lovingly chastise me. Bite my fingers too hard, then soothe them with her lips.

Gentle Ilyria, her room filled with the honey light and scent of beeswax candles, rising from a kiss to record a sudden thought, a computational error in the formula predicting the chromatic aberration of background light as it passes through a quasar's gravity lens. Sitting naked at the little oak desk, candlelight shadows caressing her spine and shoulderblades, she scribbles for fifteen minutes without stopping, abruptly drops the pencil, and returns, still aroused, to the bed.

One day, driving through the late summer countryside, the highway framed by tall stands of corn awaiting the pickers, she declares that without science she would have succumbed to lunacy. —Astrophysics is my soporific. Some people need Valium.

I am calmed by ten-billion-year-old red giants, or two-dimensional cosmic strings threading through the cosmos like an essential weave. At the moments when these miracles escape my mind I am suicidal, I am lost and terrified. On such days I could die or I could kill.

I am afraid and astounded by such confessions.

I even like her mother, who is a small and energetic Czech woman with a fanatical interest in Canadian trivia: Gretzky's total points, the advantages of CANDU nuclear reactors, Algonquin's area in hectares. Her living room, where we spend Wednesday evenings after dinner, is best described as anti-Swedish. The furniture is of the type that ends the careers of movers, and is upholstered in lush green fabric that resembles a benign moss. A thousand leatherbound books line the shelves, all with titles like *Joan's Adventures at the North Pole* and *Elsewhere: The Adventures of Mrs. Wishing-to-Be*. Stained-glass portals frame a blazing hearth; the room is too hot and you are very full; the aroma of a baked pie thickens the air. Soon you will have to eat a piece. And then you will explode.

86

◗ I am deep-breathing beneath the golden maples, my eyes closed, attempting to chase the tension from my shoulders. I stretch my arms out before me, swing them back like a pair of wings, then drop them. My right hand lands on the satchel and my eyes open. I crack the clasp and extract a fat folder.

"Gindilis Anomaly: key words," I've scrawled across it in marker.

This is the fruit of CiphCracker's labour. After eleven weeks the computer issued a soft tone and excreted 300 pages of text from the printer: not a translation, not even sentences. Phrases. Words. Semantic concepts. The document reads like a novel in which the author, fearful of misinterpretation, has presented each expression as a thesaurus citation, listing every possible synonym in all parts of speech: noun, adjective, verb, adverb. The message itself contains no more than 250 discrete packets of information. Because precise translation – even between terrestrial languages – is impossible, I instructed CiphCracker to supply every conceivable English word for each of those 250 alien ideas.

Last night I read the output like a stream of consciousness, from page one (*self, ego, id, identity, we, ourselves, yourself, himself, themselves, us*) to the end (*death, extinction, transient, dying, decease, mortality, perish, pass away*), in an attempt to surmise its meaning in a way CiphCracker could not: through intuition.

I flip to a random page and read: *decoy, bond, hasp, trap, clutch.* . . . These don't sound like expressions from a message of greeting. I initially investigated the possibility that this was a dictionary or portion thereof, broadcast in advance of a greeting, but the statistical analysis of its semantic content, the inadequate disparity, the redundancy of what were likely conjunctions, defeated that theory.

My next step was to question motive. Why broadcast a message to the stars? In addition to six decades of stray radio and television broadcasting, humanity has been transmitting into space deliberate signals declaring our existence for twenty years. Why? Our motive, simply, is to elicit a reply. We want someone out there to indicate that we are not alone in the universe.

This bulky document did not project the impression of beings conveying news of their existence. Ominous diction like *doom* and *mortality* and *extinction* cast the image of a fading civilization proclaiming its death throes to the galaxy. But my nature is to retreat from such melodrama.

I am baffled by several of the terms, *neutrons* and *protons*, for instance. Components of the atom, to be sure, but what function could they perform in such a brief monologue?

A chill possesses me in the fading light. Autumn claimed dawn and dusk weeks ago and it has been eating its way into the day's heart ever since. A leaf settles on the page, a small yellow star, and I pick it off to cast it away. I halt, struck momentarily by a sensation like flesh, a radiating warmth, and I suddenly see, quite clearly, the trees' autumnal expression of colour as an explosion of vanity before death. *Trees speak loudest before they die.* It sounds like a quote from a famous naturalist poet, but I don't know who. Maybe it's my own. I snort at the idea of creativity, of *my* creativity, the imagination of one who winds and unwinds assembler code (08F7:0170 4D FF 07 A4) like yarn, binding it into smaller and tighter balls.

A commotion of voices rouses me at one minute to five. Beneath the ornate cloister a group of female students shuffles towards Diablo's Coffee House. For a few seconds I watch them, their animated expressions, their optimistic gaits, before they disappear behind a wooden door papered with notices about essay workshops, homosexual dances, and Third World atrocities.

I walk briskly within the thickening flow of students, through an arched tunnel, and into a larger quad behind the residences. Another tunnel takes me out onto St. George Street, where the university buildings are new and ugly. Across the street, past the chemical building, up the long walk to the McLennan Physical Labs. I'm moving against the river of faces, more male and Asian than those around the humanities colleges.

On the *Toronto Sun*'s front page, above a photograph of a woman wearing a bikini, is a headline that reads, SPACE MESSAGE CEASES. Details are promised on page three. One dime short, I tug uselessly on the newspaper box's door.

Ilyria has lost track of time. I slip in the door and note the fidget of students nudging her towards a conclusion. She is beautiful, passionate, her small body dancing rhapsodically across the vast chalkboards and screens, her golden hair bound in a perfect braid.

She sees me.

I can't imagine how I appear because she halts in mid-sentence, something about stellar classes and white dwarves, and blinks.

A few students take this as a cue. They scramble out of their seats and the rest immediately follow, snapping notebooks shut, collecting jackets.

—Don't forget tonight on PBS, *Nova* is about Venus, she adds, sweeping papers into her briefcase. I stride down the steps to the front. A group of students has accumulated around the desk, asking questions, addressing her as "Professor Rehak", "Doctor Rehak". She utters a few responses, then brushes past me. I follow.

We reach the elevator and she asks, You all right? She is tiny beside me, childlike, and her brilliant eyes give me hope.

—Fine. Why? I push the "up" button and move out of her scrutiny to examine the display cases here. They are full of intricate instruments that I suddenly realize have something to do with music. I admire their workmanship, the fine coils, brass tubes and bellows, pedestals of dark wood.

In the elevator, she continues to stare. —You look like somebody died.

—I think somebody did, I say. —You know the message ended? She nods. I want to hold her but I don't move. The elevator is rickety; it shudders and whooshes, and it's some time before we reach the thirteenth floor.

She collects some objects from her office and I know by her silence that she is irritated. Her voice, a floor-to-ceiling window into her emotions, will unmask it. She is a self-declared enemy of ambiguity. If I have something to say I had better damn well say it. We head back to the elevator.

—How's your car? she asks as we descend.

—Loose bolts, I mutter. —Some things fell off. I should've taken it to the dealer.

—How'd you get here?

—I took a cab for that meeting on Bay Street, then rode the subway up.

—*You* took the subway? Where'd you get off?

—Museum.

—Should've gone to Queen's Park and taken the streetcar to St. George. You wouldn't have had to walk so far.

—I liked it.

—It's a lot closer.

—But I liked it. I like walking.

—Museum's pretty far to go.

—But I liked the walk.

Outside I say, I might know what the message says. This softens her. She is breathing deeply, in through her nose, out through her mouth. She has decided to be patient.

We cross St. George and walk through an empty parking lot. Neither of us is leading, but she is following.

It's getting dark, cooling off. I can see little puffs of steam, our moist breaths. Streetlamps ignite, cascading through the campus like a chain of rubies, each flickering uncertainly before illuminating.

We head straight out from the parking lot. I have a destination in mind and my pace has quickened.

We walk onto the playing field of King's College Circle. It is a sanctuary in the city; on the north stands University College, with its arched entrance and asymmetric towers. To the east is another old building and, attached to it like an artificial limb, the newer Sigmund Samuel Library. Continuing clockwise, the Medical Arts Building to the southeast is newer still, then olive-domed Convocation Hall behind Doric pillars, then more administrative buildings, and finally, on the west, Knox College, square and majestic, exhaling incandescent light through leaded windows. The sky beyond is pink and fragile.

—Stars! I whisper, and she looks up. Orange light dusts the thin cloud above, but in the blue ether beyond them a handful of stars are shivering. —Ilyria, where did the message come from?

—It was collected at the L.M. Gindilis dish near Lethbridge. Its source was PSR 1313 +18, a pulsar in globular cluster NGC 5024, about seventy thousand light-years distant.

—Okay. I've heard of pulsars before, but . . .

—A pulsar is like a lighthouse in space. It is a rapidly-spinning neutron star, and from each pole it broadcasts an intense beam of electromagnetic energy. When this beam sweeps over the Earth, it is detected by radiotelescopes as a pulse of radio waves. Like the flash of a lighthouse's beacon.

—So a pulsar is a neutron star? What's a neutron star?

—You should take one of my classes, she laughs.

—Tutor me.

—A neutron star is a black hole that didn't quite make it. A black hole, you probably know, is an object of extreme density, with a gravitational field so intense that even light cannot escape it. It's likely a collapsed star. A neutron star, unlike a black hole, doesn't contain enough mass to overcome proton-electron repulsion and compress below its Schwarzschild radius. Sorry, that means it isn't heavy enough to compact into a singularity with an escape velocity greater than the speed of light. Still, a neutron star is impressive. Small, with a radius of maybe fifteen kilometres, but very dense, in the order of many millions of tonnes per cubic centimetre.

—And very gravitational. Very . . . attractive?

—Oh yes.

—Okay. Okay, this is starting to make sense. Would . . . I start, and here I pause for a long time. I look at her face, at her little nose and glowing eyes, the anticipation trembling on her lips. —Could a spaceship get trapped in orbit around a neutron star?

—A . . . *spaceship?* Her tone is skeptical, but then she notes my sober expression. —A spaceship. Well, yes, if one strayed too near. It would need a large outward centrifugal acceleration to maintain its orbit. The real problems would be tidal forces and radiation. You'd have an accretion disk, too, so there'd be the danger of fast-moving debris. . . .

—Okay, okay. But ignoring those factors for a moment. *Is it possible?*

—Sure. It's possible.

—Then let me tell you a story, I begin, looking into the sky.

—Seventy thousand years ago, a research ship, a spaceship carrying a crew of scientists, is searching for life in the galaxy. They approach a pulsar and there's an accident. They become trapped in orbit. They can't escape. So they invent something to broadcast a signal on the pulsar's radio beam. And they send a message.

—What's the message? Ilyria asks quietly, her face serious. —Help?

—No. Not help. There's no chance of help. More like "goodbye". No, more like "Hello, this is who we are, goodbye."

—But what would be the point? Her irritation returns instantly. —I mean, why? Isn't that irresponsible? Isn't that cruel? Like approaching someone at random and describing your terminal illness. How is the person supposed to feel?

I'm shaking my head. —No, no. I had insight into it on the subway. I'm not sure what it was. Stress perhaps, but something intense. A staggering pain here, and I stab my belly, and there is no memory of the pain itself, only of my reaction to it. —I wanted to declare this pain to everyone. But there was no thought about assistance or relief. I experienced mortal agony and simply wanted everyone to know this. Nothing could have helped me at that moment. I didn't want their help, I didn't want their guilt. I wanted to unburden myself, to express myself. If I had been able to do that, I would have been . . . I almost want to use the word "content". Yes, I would have been content to die. I wanted the other passengers to know that I am a person, I am not anonymous, this is not a nobody dying before them, I am me, I exist, but soon I will not. Can you understand that? Can you see?

She suddenly wraps her arms around me, clutching me.

—Stop, Raymond, stop crying.

—I can't stop thinking about it, I whisper. —About those scientists spiralling towards that star but still reporting to the universe about it, about themselves, their doom. Wanting nothing more than to be heard. I didn't really understand the message until I told you the story. It's clear now.

We stand there for minutes, our arms wrapped around each other. Ilyria says softly, You should know they've done bystander experiments on the subway. Irving Piliavin did, a few years ago. Over ninety percent of the time, people helped. They helped the victim. They would have helped you.

—Really? Me? If I'd fallen, screaming, someone would've done something?

—Ninety percent. Nine times out of . . . nine times. . . . Ilyria abruptly releases me and asks, Raymond, is there a numerical reference in the message? Does it mention a number?

—What . . . what kind of number?

—A big one. In the tens of millions.

—Um, yes. I don't remember how big. . . . I open the flap of my satchel and extract the fat folder. She snatches it from me, drops to her knees, and starts spilling pages onto the crisp grass.

—Where? Do you know where?

I kneel on the cold earth and guide her hands through the pages. It takes a long time, my teeth begin to chatter, but Ilyria is frantic, oblivious.

—Here. Twenty-one million. Is that right? Help me, Raymond, I can hardly see.

—Yes, that's right. Twenty-one million. It's represented by multi-digit bits which were meant to be multiplied. And the preceding modifier suggests an approximation, so it's rounded.

Ilyria punches numbers into a pocket calculator she has extracted from her briefcase. Hyperventilating, she runs several calculations. She punches up a final function, examines the answer, and does the computation again. After a third time she states, I must make a telephone call.

We are in Hart House, breathing hard, sweating beside a hot radiator. Ilyria is feeding nickels into the phone, dialling. —Hello. Hello? Professor Major, please? Oh. Do you know when he'll be in? No, thank you. I'll try back later. More coins. She dials, then waits. —Stupid answering machine, she hisses. —David! This is Ilyria. God, sorry, I'm out of breath. I have something important to tell you. Listen, we have a translation. Of the Gindilis message. But not only that, we have *mathematical* authentication of the translation's veracity. There can be no doubt that the transmission came from an advanced civilization. I will call back later with the details. She is scrambling for coins. —Raymond, I have to tell somebody. Why isn't anyone home? Where is everybody?

—Ilyria, stop it. Stop. I take her hands in my own, still them. —You can tell *me*. What's happening?

She is staring at the brick, she looks back at me, begins to answer, loses focus again, then meets my eyes. —The version of the message I gave you, the one you decoded, was received sixty-eight days ago, on August eighth. PSR 1313 has a rotational period of 0.28 seconds. Between that date and early today there have been approximately twenty-one million radio pulses from the pulsar.

—Twenty-one million? The same number as in the message?

—It's in the math. They knew how long they had left. And they told us, in the only way we'd understand. The period of PSR 1313's rotation is the one reference these aliens could be sure we would understand and corroborate. Although our time systems must be entirely different, they managed to tell us how long they had left – in pulsar beats. She picks up the phone, slams it down. —I need coins! she cries.

We are being drawn; I feel it like gravity, an intrinsic force; it is compelling us toward the ground zero of this blossoming explosion, this revelation that will change the world. All I can think is that it's absurd that she has not stepped there, breathed there, the place where I live, the place where this vital information was extracted. The Secret Laboratory.

I take her hand and lead her out to the street.

We are members of a race of beings who call ourselves the [propername#001]. Our vessel is named the [propername#002], and I am [propername#003], her chief scientist. This is a ship of exploration. We have been on a mission, seeking life in the galaxy, life which we have concluded must exist.

Our ship is doomed. We have become trapped in orbit around a neutron star (to the best of our knowledge, the second-to-final stage of collapse of a large star, when the repulsion of protons and electrons is overcome), which is sending out powerful streams of electromagnetic energy.

In approximately twenty-one million rotations of this neutron star, our energy systems will be depleted and our orbit will decay. We will be annihilated by the star's gravity.

I give high commendations to [propername#004] and [propername#005] for their design of the dynamic wave reformer, the device that makes this transmission possible. It follows one of the pulsar's poles, tuning the electromagnetic energy into the wavelength patterns that you are receiving. It derives its power from the star itself.

Regrettably, we do not have the resources to engage the pulsar's power to aid in our escape. And so here, we die.

We are members of a race of beings who call ourselves the [propername#001]. . . . ◗

The Crowding Forest

TOM BRACED the wheel as another sinister-faced truck thundered past in the opposite direction, its trailer stacked to the sky with logs. At that moment a geyser of steam erupted from the car's radiator cap and Tom swung the Packard onto the gravel shoulder. A hail of pebbles stung the black fenders and he let up on the gas.

—Christ, with less than twenty miles left! he muttered. —I told you she was ready to blow. What the hell, I'm hungry anyway. This looks as good a place as any. What do you say, Tip?

Tippy hunched lower in his seat and grunted as Tom steered the car into the little parking area, where they pulled alongside a rusting pickup truck. He shut off the engine but the radiator continued to sputter.

—Tippy, does this look okay? If you want we could top off the water and eat when we get there.

Tippy looked up at the rusting Texaco sign and the hand-painted board beneath it which read "Johnny's Eats". —Looks okay, he replied and opened the door. Tom got out and handed him his hat; Tippy smoothed back his white hair before putting it on. Tom's own hair was just silvering around the edges, despite the fact that he was the elder. Another truck roared past on the highway but when it was gone the buzzing and clicking of the forest resumed.

—It's hot, Tom said.

—Yes.

—Well, let's go in.

They crunched along the oil-soaked gravel to the door. A boy of sixteen in a Texaco uniform was fanning himself in the shade of the awning.

—You want anything, mister? he asked Tom.

—Ya, Tom replied, tossing him the keys. —Gas her up and top up the water. We're going in for a bite.

—I gotta recommend the apple pie, the boy said before trudging off to the Packard.

Tom held the door for Tippy and followed him in. Except for a waitress who was leafing through the latest *Life* magazine with a picture on the cover of two American warships engaging a Jap destroyer, the diner was empty. A fan swept the room with a light breeze and the brothers seated themselves at the counter.

—Hi, the waitress said, approaching them with a silver carafe. —Coffee?

—Yes, Tom said, turning his cup over. She filled it.

—Coffee, sir?

Tippy had removed his hat and was sitting bolt upright, staring at the malt machine. His eyes turned very slowly towards her and he twitched his head from side to side.

—You want a malt? We only got chocolate.

Tippy nodded.

—I'll get you menus while I make it.

She handed them each a small card and Tom looked his over. It was handwritten and brief: grilled cheese, club sandwich, fish on Fridays, steak. —I'm gonna get a steak. Hey, can I get a steak or is it too early?

—You can get a steak, they ain't been rationed yet, the waitress replied over the sound of the malt mixer. She poured the mixture into a tall glass and placed it before Tippy. Then she dropped in a straw and rotated the glass until the straw faced him. —Chocolate malt, she said, smiling for the first time. Tippy picked it up and sipped.

—So, she said, turning to Tom. —How do you want it?

—Well done. Really well done, so it's almost black. Can you do that?

—I'll ask. Johnny, you don't mind burning a steak for this guy, do ya?

A fat face appeared at the kitchen window, a face so round and thick that the eyes looked as if they were hidden deep within the cutouts of a mask. —It's what I do best, he said, and grinned. He disappeared from the window and the sound of activity started up in the kitchen.

—What about you, mister? Steak?

—No, Tippy replied, and sipped his malt.

—You want some pie, Tippy? The kid said the pie's good. Is that true?

—It's the best. The waitress beamed. —He's my brother and it's our mom who makes the pies. We bring fresh ones every day. Hey, I could cut you a extra big hunk. And we got ice cream too. How's that sound?

—No thank you, Tippy responded, and slurped his malt again before setting it down. He picked up a serviette and dabbed his brow and cheeks.

—It gets hot here all right. That fan hardly helps except when it's on you. And I can bet those suits don't help much. She pushed her index finger through a drop of malt on the counter, then stuck the finger in her mouth. —Where you from?

—Toronto, Tom said, nodding southwards. —We're on our way to Chapleau.

—Business or pleasure? The way you're dressed I'd say you're going to a funeral.

—We are, Tippy spat.

—Okay, okay, don't get sore. If it's not my business I won't inquire. Who died?

—A mutual friend, Tom said. —We've known her since we were kids.

—What happened?

—Pneumonia. She had it most of the spring and it looked like she was going to get better. Then, one day. . . . Tom looked up at her and shrugged.

—That's too bad. Seems to be the way of things nowadays, though. It always looks like things will get better, but they don't. More coffee?

—Sure.

Tom turned to watch another truck burdened with logs sweep past. The trees across the highway trembled. Tom thought about the drive, how as they had come farther north the forest had thickened and pressed closer to the edge of the highway, like a crowd spilling through its perimeter. It made him feel as if he had disappeared deep within the continent, like a mysterious explorer, or a fugitive. These thoughts of escape were disturbed, however, by tremors of sadness.

—Your steak, mister, the waitress said, startling him. He turned and looked at his plate, smiled at the charred meat nestled among potatoes and peas.

—Perfect, he noted as the knife crunched through its shell. She topped up his coffee as he started to eat. He was hungry.

A logging truck pulled onto the gravel of the service station and a clean-cut young man in canvas pants and a work shirt came in.

—Hello, Martha. Pie and coffee, like always, he said, seating himself two chairs from Tippy. He nodded at the brothers and eagerly started in on his pie.

—Say, you drive one of those big trucks, eh? Tom said to him, nodding out the window.

—Yup. Haul around fifty-six of those logs every trip. Two trips a day.

—That's a lot of trees, isn't it? Tom said.

—Uh-huh. Take them down to the mill in Thessalon. Usually the stuff from here goes to Chapleau but these are special logs.

—Special?

—Yup. White spruce. They're going to be Mosquito fighter-bombers. The kind they're flying against the Nazis.

—No kidding?

—That's a secret, by the way, the man said, poking at him with his fork. —You mind who you tell that to.

—Oh, I won't tell anyone, Tom said, then continued eating. After a few minutes he said, It's sort of a pity.

—What is? the man asked.

—About all those trees. You look out there and see trees for as far as the eye can see. It's too bad they have to cut them down.

—Ya, but trees get used for everything. Without trees you wouldn't have any newspapers or houses or anything. No telegraph poles or railroad tracks or fenceposts. No bombers.

—Of course, but it's too bad they have to use trees for those things. Trees are so majestic.

—Mister, if I hauled a hundred and twelve trees every day for a million years we wouldn't get through half of them. Have you ever been up there in an airplane? Once I had to fly to Winnipeg. The trees go on right to the horizon and farther. It's endless.

—I suppose you're right, Tom replied, cleaning off his plate and pushing it forward. Martha picked it up and passed it to Johnny through the kitchen window.

—How was that? Huh? Johnny asked.

—Perfect. Just the way I like it.

—Thank you. Thank you kindly, he said, and retreated out of sight.

—My name's Dan, said the truck driver.

—Tom. And this is Tippy.

—Good to know ya. Where you fellas headed?

—We're going up to Chapleau.

—They're going to a funeral. That's why they're all in black, Martha said, hovering over Dan's cup with the coffee pot. He nodded and she filled it up.

—Who died?

—A friend. An old girlfriend of Tippy's, Tom said, wiping his mouth.

—That's too bad, eh? You never married her I guess.

Tippy turned to him for the first time. —What do you mean by that?

—Well nothing. Just an observation. You meet a girl and you marry her. Or you don't. I'm getting married in August.

—Congratulations, Tom said, feeling his pockets for his cigarette case.

—Whyn't you never marry that girl? Martha asked.

Tippy twisted to face her. —I just didn't, he said firmly.

—Hey, you got a light? Tom asked through the cigarette in his lips.

—No. What I mean is, could you smoke that outside? Her voice hastened at Tom's stunned expression. —It's just that I have an allergy. The doctor told me a few days ago. If I inhale smoke I get nosebleeds. I'm sorry. Look, I'm really sorry but that's what happens. If you want I'll go outside when you smoke. Then I'll wait half an hour for the smoke to clear out and then come back in. I don't want to stop you from having a cigarette if you really want one. Just let me know so's I can step outside. Okay?

—That won't be necessary. We're done here anyway, right Tip? What do I owe you?

—Sure, that's swell, mister. Let's see. The steak and the coffee, and your friend there had the malt –

—I'm his brother, Tippy said.

—Oh. I didn't know. You had the chocolate malt, right? She banged the amounts into the cash register. —That's one dollar and thirty cents.

Tom pulled a dollar and two quarters from his wallet and placed them on the counter. —Keep the change, he said, and he and Tippy put on their hats and headed for the door.

—Hey, let me settle up and I'll come have a smoke with you fellas. Johnny! Come on out for a cigarette!

The giant face appeared in the window. —Be right out, he called, twisting a towel in his hands.

The heat outside was powerful on the black suits, and the smell of gasoline burdened the air. Dan led them out towards his truck and sat down on the runningboard.

—It's not really my truck of course, but you get to feeling that way about it. It belongs to the company but I'm responsible. There's a big White powerhouse under the hood. Can haul ten thousand pounds. That your Packard over there?

—Yes, Tom replied.

—Nice. What you do? For a living, I mean.

—I'm a medical doctor.

—No kidding? Hmm. Dr. Tom!

The three men smoked in silence until Johnny waddled over from the building, a lit cigarette in his mouth. —This is nuts. Can't even smoke in my own restaurant. I should let her go.

—Why dontcha? Dan asked.

—She's a good waitress. And I'd have to boot her brother too, and he does a good job. They all looked over at the boy, who was snoozing under the awning. —When he's awake, that is, he added, and Johnny and Dan and Tom laughed. Tippy was looking towards the restaurant where Martha was standing at the glass, watching them. They looked directly at one another for five seconds before Tippy turned to examine the truck's bug-spattered grille.

Another logging truck roared past and Dan squinted after it. —That's Cal Koski's rig. All dented on the front fender. I'll tell ya, the Finns can chop but they sure shouldn't drive!

Soon they had each ground their cigarettes into the gravel. Dan climbed into his truck and fired up the big engine, over-revving it and sending a cloud of mean smoke into the sky. He waved as he steered onto the paved highway and rumbled away.

Johnny returned to the restaurant and the brothers headed towards their car, which the boy had parked near the pumps, close to the highway. Beads of water glittered on the windshield.

—Hey, get in. I'm going to pay the kid and we can get going. I'd say we got half an hour to go, Tom said, taking out his wallet.

Tippy headed to the Packard and found the doors locked. He stood at the passenger side with one hand on the car and leaned a little against it, watching as Tom paid for the service and retrieved his keys. Tippy looked up to the sky, which was brilliant and blue. A deer fly entered orbit around his head, then flew away. He looked down at his feet, at the shape of his shadow among the gravel and weeds, at his shoes, polished to a shimmering black.

—Hey, why didn't you get in? Tom asked and Tippy snapped his head up.

—Locked, Tippy replied.

Tom unlocked his door and was about to climb in when Tippy spoke, his voice suddenly urgent. —Tom? Can I ask you something, Tom?

—What? Tom asked across the roof of the car, then noticed the rough furrow of his brother's brow. —Tippy, are you all right?

—I was . . . I was wondering if you could tell me something. Just sort of clear something up.

—What?

—Why the promise?

—I beg your pardon?

—I was just standing here and trying to figure out what you wanted to achieve. What was the real motive for that promise?

—Tippy, you're not making sense. What are you asking me? What promise?

—The promise you made me make about Jayne. The promise. You remember?

—Tippy, I'm afraid I don't.

—You made me promise that I wouldn't marry her. You made me promise.

—What?

—You came to me and made me promise, as your brother, that I would not marry Jayne.

—I did no such thing. Why would I ask something like that?

—You did. You said it would hurt you too much. You said you loved her too and you couldn't bear to see her married to me.

—I didn't.

—You did! We were at the cottage, remember? It was fall. We were in the boathouse, hoisting up Dad's motorboat for the winter. You made me promise not to marry her.

—Tippy, I don't remember that. I can't imagine myself ever saying that.

—You said it. You did. And I promised. I promised as your brother, as your blood, that I would not marry Jayne, that I would never marry her.

—I don't remember. I could never have said such a thing!

—You did, Tom. You did! Tippy's voice was folding, his face crumpling. He turned his head down, his expression eclipsed by the hat. Tom watched his brother across the black shell of the car's roof.

—Tippy, it was thirty years ago. I can't remember something thirty years ago. If I asked you that then I'm sorry, but I honestly don't remember it. Tippy. Tippy!

His brother's head came up, a thin, glittering trail cutting down one cheek.

—Open this door, he said evenly, clicking the handle.

Tom climbed in and unlocked the passenger door. Tippy opened it and sat down, placing his hat gently on the dashboard. Tom rolled down his window. He started the engine and pulled out onto the highway, where he stepped hard on the accelerator. The wind howled through the window.

Another truck rattled past, heading south. Tom glanced out at the trees that crowded against the highway. He suddenly realized that beyond the first twenty or thirty feet of forest there was nothing, that the trees behind had been chopped down and were now heading for the mill, or already made into desks, or houses, or newspapers, or maybe a squadron of bombers in the flak-filled skies over Europe. ◖

Super Nova

☾

UM ZUM ZUM ZUM ZUM ZUM.

Along with a shaft of sunlight the thrummin sound of somethin big poured in my window. I felt all sticky and stretchy, and the taste of paste in my chops wasn't makin the day look all that appetizin, but that noise was buggin me. I dug up through the rumply sheets and mounted my chin on the windowsill, squintin out at the street.

Ain't nothin out there but a little green Nova in my drive, looks like bout a '74. Too small to be makin that racket.

Then the window rolls and that's Johnny wavin at me.

—Hey, shit-fer-brains, come on!

I roll from the bed and put a robe over naked me, burn out past Mum (Where are you going so early?) and through the door.

—What the fuck? I ask.

Johnny just laughs and says, Boom boom boom, to the engine's pulse.

I look her over. Body looks nice, cept the green sucks. I tell Johnny that green's not so fast like a red one.

Tommy pops his head from the other seat, laughin.

—Fastest thing ever is green!

—Yeh, what? Johnny asks an's sorry for it, cause Tommy snorts up his nose.

—Supersonic boogers! Tommy yells, then falls back in the seat, all laughin and hootin.

—Whose is it? I ask John, who just keeps grinnin, then nods like I'm supposed to get in.

—Tommy, back seat! he yells.

—Why do I gotta back-seat it? Let Kyle, I was here first, he moans in that baby voice he uses whenever he don't get his way.

—Back fuckin seat! John shouts, and *floop!*, Tommy rolls over into the rear, then starts some serious poutin.

—Johnny, look, I'm just in this, I say, raisin the housecoat and
showin my knees.

—Just a spin, he says, revvin the horses. It's like fuckin thunder,
fuckin scary thunder, and I step back.

—What the hell's in there? I ask, pointing at the hood.

—Four-oh-two fuckin turbo 400. Would ya get in?

Dumb dumb dumb, I think, slippin in the passenger side,
gropin for the belt, of which there ain't none. I wanna say somethin, but we're out on the street and screamin away. I always wear
a belt; it's like I'm naked without it, and my heart's all pumpin
suddenly. The engine's growl don't help me none, and I think I
gotta piss. I look at John, who's Mr. Smiles, the wind tossin his
long hair like a horse's mane.

The speedo says fifty on the old M scale, and we ain't even
outta the street yet. The stop is comin too fast, too fast! I jam my
palms on the dash and Johnny comes this close to a fourway
lockup. *Thump!*, and Tommy rolls off the rear seat and slams into
the back of the bench. I hear a little moanin sound.

—Shit, Tommy, you okay? I call, turnin around and lookin
over. Then I see he's laughin it up, flat out on the floor.

—Where to? Where to? Johnny asks.

—Shit, I dunno, I say, thinking bout *home* but knowin they'd
cuss me up.

—Hit the highway! Hit the highway! Tommy starts chantin,
his chin propped on the bench between me'n John.

—Highway it is, John yells, then shrieks through the intersection and down to the freeway.

The air is hissin all around us, and Tom and John start remem-
berin a guy called Sean, who I hardly knew, I only once danced
with his sister. He had a Mustang which he pumped up hisself,
rebored the cylinders and I don't know what else to soup it,
maybe some mechanics out there could fill ya in on the job.

But he was on the highway, 401 east or somethin doin what the
cops said was 230 k's when he becomes intimate with a overpass
support pylon. John says he seen it, his dad heard an accident on
his police scanner and John went out to see, and there was the
Mustang, now only about three feet long, and someplace inside
a pancake named Sean. Ambulance drivers said they shoulda
brought a bucket.

I don't wanna listen to the gags those guys say, but I can't help it, I'm just hypnotized by the engine's growl, all I can think about is speed, just goin and goin. Halfa me's thinkin, "Yeh, Johnny, push it, push it," as we fling over a hill and onto the ramp, the rest is wonderin what the fuck's the other half's prob.

—Hey, this thing's got a deck, Tommy says, then flips a cassette into the front. —Pop that in!

I don't hear right away, I'm staring at the merge into busy traffic while John's foot starts plungin to the floor.

—What's it? John asks, picking up the tape and makin a novel outta the print on it.

—It's Jack DeKay, my cousin got that from a show at the Shoe. You should hear that stuff.

—Probably more crud, John mutters, then slaps it in.

The tunes commence, and it's movin music, real drivin rock'n roll. John edges us up, slips quick between a trucka chickens and a Buick, then into the zoom lane. The speedo says ninety-five and climbin.

—A-fuckin-mazing, John laughs, dodgin through traffic.

Somethin's hummin in the back of my brain, some weird feeling I can't explain. My feet and hands tingle, it prickles up my arms, legs. I heard talk before bout a thing when you go fast, like a monster or a devil. It's like high speed ain't just how fast yer goin, but really a place you get to.

We pass cars'n trucks like they're standin still, 110 MPH! That's like twice the limit, like the rest ain't movin while we go normal speed!

—Roll me hotrod, roll me some, cause I heard the Devil is about to come! Johnny and Tommy're singin with the tape.

—Roadster move, roadster move, I think, my teeth startin to ache from the grittin, when *boosh!*, I'm easy. It's like we pass a obstacle, the sound barrier or maybe the scared barrier, and now everything's cool. I lean back in the seat, stick my arm out the window and play with the air, make my hand like a plane flickin up'n down, bankin back'n forth.

—It's nothin! I shout over the howl of air.

—Huh? Johnny screams back. His eyes're glued forward, I don't blame him cause everything come up so quick.

—It's nothin. Those horses! They purrin like kittens. We're doin, what, one twenty? About two hundred in kliks?

—I'm in love, I'm in love, he chants back.

We're outta the thicker stuff now, it's light traffic and Johnny, he's good. I can hear Tommy from the back, he's poundin on the vinyl seats, crowin to the next song, called "Burnin Up!"

—Hey, whose is it? Whose wheels, huh? I ask.

Johnny grins, I know he wants to say, "She's all mine," and I think he's gonna, he'll lie sometimes if he wants to be cool and who don't? Once he got all tied up in a big one, we were at the park, chuckin a baseball around, talkin bout girls, and then we started about one girl, I think it was Shelly Osmaglen, a real knockout, "the mayor of Hummina City, Babe-a-lon," we said, the number-one best babe. So what Johnny does, he says that he fucked her, eh? But that wasn't the worst, right, he said anybody could, if you knew a secret word that he knew. All you hadta do was ring her doorbell and say the word and she'd wrap her legs around ya twice, right, he says this. Like a bull, or dogs, they know a word they get trained with, and you say the word and they attack, maybe the word is "hopscotch", and then they kill, right? Okay, we laugh some, we shove him and say har har, he's funny, but he don't lay off, he keep sayin it, One word, man, one word.

—Yeh, what's the word? Al says.

—Oh, like I just tell it, right? For free?

—Okay, how much? Al asks, he's even got his wallet out, he hates Johnny's lies.

—Oh, I never thought it's for sale. Can't have everybody wearin her out, right? Okay, so a hundred. Cash?

We roar. Now he's really gotta be shittin us. Like, a hundred for that? Bullshit.

—Jeez, Johnny, cantcha give a friend a break? All I got is eight bucks, I moan, and we all laugh cept Johnny, he's turnin red, mad. Fuck I hate tempers.

So Al, who's had enough of this shit, starts crackin balls way out in the field and we go out and catch em, try to be as crazy as we can, slidin on the grass, jumpin and landin on our faces to make the big catch, to save the inning.

I guess it's later when Tommy and Nils, at different times, gives Johnny a hundred each for the word, The Word. (Where Tommy gets a hundred, I dunno. Nils does mechanic work and makes a few bucks here'n there. Maybe John gives Tommy a break or maybe Tommy stole it from his dad or somethin.)

So bout three days later, Nils and I and Blister and Andy are at the mall, I got some overdue books and Nils is lookin for more ones on magic and Blister needs a air filter and Andy just comes along. So we're at the mall, in the glass elevator down from the third floor, and Blister spots Shelly, he starts goin *hummina hummina hummina*, and then we're all doin it, it's like a tribal thing, all these guys goin *hummina hummina hummina*, cept Nils, who's all sweaty and just starin at her. Andy says we oughtta get ice cream, so we all go, but Nils says he needs somethin at the drugstore, on the second floor.

Roxanne, this cool girl who's a totally amazing painter, is workin at Baskin-Robbins. We shoot the shit a while and she gives us all a little extra on our cones.

—Hey, we all gonna be at the beach tonight. You comin? I ask her and she kinda smiles cause it's traditional: I always ask, she never comes.

—Yeh, sure, Kyle, tonight fer sure, is what she always says, I guess she thinks we're weird, or maybe her dad or somethin never lets her go, or maybe she will be there. I always wish she would, we was both in drama last year and we did lots of scenes and everybody liked em.

So we're eatin our ice cream, just shootin the breeze, when Shelly comes down the escalator with Nils right behind, she's still, lettin it carry her, and he's movin down towards her, his jaw set hard, face real serious. We all stop and watch, Blister, Andy, Roxanne, me, a bitta sticky ice cream coilin down my hand, inside the palm.

Shelly reaches the bottom just as Nils gets behind her. He squeaks his head in close to her ear, this is bout ten metres away. You should see this place, the escalator comes down into a open space all three levels high, with the elevator beside and skylights up high, all brown tile, a supermarket there, stereo shops, hair place, bulk food, lottery booth, bank, cleaners, Baskin-Robbins 31 flavours.

Okay, so I'm takin my time tellin this, relax, kay? The point is, we don't hear the word, it's too far away, he says it softly and he never says what it is.

But Shelly hears it.

Holy shit, she hears it.

I ain't never seen a reaction like that; nothin human goes like that, so fast. That a body is able to do that, I just can't believe.

Sometimes you see somethin, like a hummingbird, fuck they're cool, like bees but okay cause they don't sting. Sometimes when I play with my cats, I got this string on a stick and they chase it. The string is all bouncin like nuts, there's no way nothin could get it, but then Mali, the black one, just snaps her little jaw and she's got it in her teeth. (The game used to be called "fish on a stick" cause of this fake catnip fish on the string, then one day it breaks off but Mali and Lashy don't even care one bit, it's the string that's the best, so now the game's called "fish on a stick" but guess what: no fish!)

Well Nils is as surprised as everybody, as Shelly even, I don't know why he's so dumb to say it in a mall, whadda dork! But maybe that saved his life.

Cause he said the word, and she fuckin *toasted* him. Her elbow come back in his ribs, and I mean it, he went flyin! Right over the railin from the escalator, on the hard tile, on his back. We don't hear the word, but we hear the noise he makes: *Ooof!* Next, she picks him up by the front of the shirt and does that thing like on TV, her forehead on his face, smack! We hear that, too. I see the blood and I'm runnin like stink, I think I dropped my ice cream, I mean I don't know where it went anyway, fuckin good ice cream too, and I just run right past Shelly, she's spinnin into some kinda kick that gets Nils in the gut, he goes: *Uh!*

Do you know when there are stories about people who get superhuman strength for a sec, like a mom whose kid is under a truck and she just picks it up like it's a feather? Maybe I had a bit of that, I get Nils under the arms and lift this guy, he's maybe forty pounds more'n me but I pick him up and *carry* him, runnin, round to the other side of the glass where the elevator is, where the doors is, they're closin and we pop in, Shelly is *right* there, the doors close and I see her eyes, like a zombie or somethin, scary anyway. Her hand lashes out towards the gap, I pull back, Nils pukes (yeh, no lie; he *barfs*) all over some guy in a green suit and the doors go *click!*, *bang!*, her hand musta hit the door.

—Jesus, the guy with slop on him says.

We're goin up. Nils hurls again, there's blood everywhere from his nose, even some blood in his puke and I am *scared*. He's shakin like a jackhammer.

Lucky the guy didn't push two, cause Shelly hits the escalator doin ninety and was waitin there, I see this through the glass, she moves like a cheetah. We get to three and hustle into the library, to the can in there, the guy with the yech wants in to clean his shoes, fuckin no way, I lock the door behind me. We wait.

Pretty soon Nils is in the stall, lettin the rest go. I start shakin too.

—Hey, Nils, you okay? Nils, you okay in there, fuck man, talk to me.

I push open the door, he's on his ass beside the bowl, leanin against the wall, eyes clenched, spew on his chin, shirt, blood from his nose, pantin like a dog.

—Hey, Nils buddy. What, you okay? I say, can't keep the tremble from my voice. Nils don't say nothin, he just pants, bleeds, drools goo from the corner of his mouth. —Nils, talk to me, say somethin. Say, "Don't fret it Kyle, I'm a-okay," willya? He still don't do nothin, his breath's slowin down, the rasp gets slower and he slides a little on the tiles. —Nils.

His eyes open a little, just two slits, just white slits and he takes a real long breath, lets it out slow, I count ten, twenty seconds. I back off a little, swallow.

—Yo, Kyle, he says softly and I move to hear him, try to listen close. —Did I come?

Well fuck, we both fell over and laughed, I almost split a gut and he's wincin and moanin with pain, broken ribs, broken nose, what the fuck else I don't care cause he really is okay, that tough stupid crazy bloody fuckin sonofabitch!

And then *bang! bang! bang!* on the door and we shut up fast, chickenshits we are, but it's Blister and Andy and they say it's safe, she's gone, and I let em in and tell them what Nils said, and we laugh some more, god it hurts, it hurts!

We get Nils to emergency and hafta wait like two hours before anyone gets a look at him, so meanwhile I call Johnny and tell him what's the deal on Shelly and his word. Johnny's awful scared then, he wants to tell me the word, like that will make it okay.

—No fuckin way, Johnny, no no no! I just wanna know where you heard it and maybe you know why she freaked.

—Christ, Kyle, I don't know. It's just a word, right, how can it do anything?

—Yeh, where'd you get it?

He goes aw shucks and everything and says he just made it up but I know it's a lie and tell him so, and finally he goes, You know

113

Shelly's little brother, Burton? It's a long pause after, so I gotta say, Yeh? until he goes on. —Well, Shelly was in a course for self-defence last year, remember, cause she was almost raped that time. It's called Fu-Muck or somethin, I don't know, the guy who made it up isn't even Chinese.

Again, he wants a "yeh" before he goes on.

—In Fu-Yuck or Muck or whatever, it's almost like hypnotizin. Lotsa people learn karate and stuff and when they need it go all frozen and can't use it. So in Fu-Kuck they hypnotize you with a secret word you say to yourself to make you go into fightin mode. Burton knew the word and told me. I thought there was no way, no fuckin way.

—So you never fucked her.

Pause. —Naw.

—Did ya tell anybody else the word?

—Shit. Tommy. My mouth goes all dry and I hang up the phone. I dial Tommy's and it's busy.

Okay, I don't wanna draw this all out cause what happened to Tommy's nothin like Nils, but it coulda been. I get Blister to drive me to Tommy's house and he goes way too slow and I'm goin, Run this yellow! and Pass this guy! so he's gettin pissed off a bit but now I don't blame him.

Blister finally tops off by layin two streaksa rubber on Tommy's street and I'm outta the door and on the front step in half a sec. *Thump! Thump! Thump!*

—Hey, yo, anybody in? I call. —Tommeeeee!

I'm just bout ready to leap back into Blister's vette when the door swings open with Tommy on the cordless, listenin real intent-like. I sigh like a dyin balloon and pull open the screen door. I go to open my mouth and he puts his hand up, he's grinnin like a fox. He puts his paw over the mouthpiece.

—Hey, Kyle, whoa, you gotta getta loada this! Now I'm kinda annoyed cause he's okay and we drove all here and I don't wanna hear any stupid phone, what if it's the joke line or some shit like that, but then he's got it on my ear. I listen for a minute, look at his shiny chops, and wanna slap him there.

I hear a girl's voice moanin and screamin and sighin and breathin, I hear the sounda stuff breakin.

—Man, she really wants it. One word and she's gotta have it! he says.

—You shitface, I say and his stupid smile is gone. I grab the phone from him and slam it on the porch, then stomp on it.

—Hey, fucker, that's my phone, he says, but he sounds scared.

—She just kicked the crap outta Nils, you know that? When he said the magic word. His head goes back a little and I think of these friends of my mum who had a dog and they would hurt her with the newspaper when she was bad. Soon they only gotta roll up a paper and she ducks and squeaks, like she was hit. That's how Tommy's head goes when I say that.

—Whaddaya mean? he says, soft now.

So I explain it to him, and I even say he shoulda found out hisself, that'd teach him.

—All that noise wasn't her all horny? he says, it dawns on him.

—She was probly kickin the hell outta her room, or maybe the kitchen, or maybe her grandpa, I don't know.

Blister's behind me, he learns real quick what Tommy was up to, he just shakes his head and says, On the phone?

Tommy is all dazed now, shakin his head, and he don't stop, he comes forward almost not seein me, sits his butt down on the top step next to the bits of the phone, his head still shakin, still shakin.

—Hey, Tommy, you okay? Blister asks.

His head still shakes, still shakes, then stops suddenly.

—Jesus Christ, he goes.

—What? Blist and me both say.

—Jesus Cheee-rist! he goes again.

—What? me and Blist say.

—I paid a hundred bucks just to get beat up, but most people would do that for free!

◑ So why was all that? Oh, I was sayin about Johnny's lyin. Okay, so I ask him whose wheels these are and he just grins.

—It's Val's, he finally says, kinda shruggin. Val's his sister from Florida, I don't know her too well but she must be cool to drive a smoker like this.

—Who done all the work? Who spooked it up?

—She did, he says, grinnin, hey, maybe he's even prouda her.

—Cool, both me'n Tommy say.

He just smiles'n smiles and Tommy starts goin, It'd sure be cool to have a sister, it sure would be nice to have a girl around, it sure'd be good, so I know it's time to turn around and give him a punch in the jaw, not really hard but just to make him shut his face. See, he's got a sister. Okay, there's more'n that, he's got a sister named Kat who I liked, maybe I was fourteen or somethin and she's not just a babe, she's totally funny, really sharp. Once I heard a story, there was this other guy who liked her and was tryin to make her go out with him, he thinks he's so great, he says, Hey, I got big hands and big feet. You know what that means? and she don't even blink, she just goes, Yeh, they had to cut back somewhere. I laughed my ass off when I heard that, I think that's when I got interested. I was thinkin what a dumb guy he is, like so many dumb guys, they say such fuckin stupid things like how great they are. I don't think a girl wantsta hear it from yer big mouth. Lotsa guys just go around sayin they're great so much, they think they can be fuckin assholes. It's like guys who think they're great in bed, once my older sister said they're the ones who're the worst cause they don't think they gotta try. If yer a guy who's readin this and think yer a sex god, guess what, yer probly crap! Don't be so fuckin selfish!

—Hey, let's get off here and getta drink, Tommy says, in perfect Tommy style cause we're almost past the ramp and in the leftmost lane.

Johnny heels the wheel over and we punch through the other two lanes, my stomach stayin way back there while we almost rear-end the cars goin slower'n us, which is every single one of em.

—Fuck lookoutlookout! I suddenly realize I'm sayin as we almost skin a pickup also goin for the lane and horns go nuts and everybody's wavin their middle fingers around and we get to the lights at the top of the ramp and the guy in the pickup goes, Hey, what-the-fuck-watch-it-you-fucks! and I'm screamin mean words back before I realize, crap! It's Al. It's big Al in his truck.

—Bejees, Kyle, he says. —What's doin? You wanna die or somethin?

—Al, Cheee-rist, it's mother-maniac here, he's drivin like, jeez, and everything I say sounds stupid cause I'm all flustered up. What's a good word . . . flummoxed. I like that, I'm flummoxed, so I say, Hey Al, sorry, I'm flummoxed, and this big grin goes on his face.

—Sorry about that, Al, Johnny says and Al makes like he's slappin him, and the light's green and people start honkin.

—You goin . . . ? He points to the donut shop and we all nod and go, Yeh. Johnny gets pissed with the horns and leaves about a kilo of rubber on the ramp. I look back and see Al shakin his head and just movin off normal, real easy, and I think that's way cooler than goin nuts. When you're cool, you're supposed to be relaxed, right? Laid back? Then why're so many guys who think they're cool such spazzes? Answer: they're not cool.

We go into the Tim Horton's parking lot and Al pulls in a second later. He backs in, like always. He's so . . . composed.

—Hey, Al, yer so composed, I say when he gets out and leans in my window.

—What's this? he asks, grabbin the shoulder of my housecoat.

—These dorks get me outta my bed and don't even let me dress. I ain't goin in.

—Oh, come on, chickenshit. Afraid someone'll see yer legs? Johnny says, and he and Tommy laugh it up, har har.

—We ain't gettin ya anything, Tommy chuckles. —You want somethin, you gotta come in.

—Well I don't want nothin!

Tommy and Johnny go in and Al says, I'll getcha a coffee, you want one? and I nod.

—Double cream, three sugar, I say, and he wrinkles his nose and smiles and goes in. He's the best.

I sit alone in the car listenin to the *tick-tick* of the coolin block, the highway behind, the bingin of the gas bar next door. It starts to heat up in here from the sun, it's a really bright day and I have a bit of a squintin headache so I close my eyes and it feels good. I only got one wish right now, if a leprechaun came and said you get one wish I'd go, "Gimme some clothes!" Not only do I feel like a dork, in the parking lot of a donut shop in my dressin gown, people pullin in for takeout coffee and lookin at me, but this thing's hot, one a those flannel things, dark blue, yikes! A little sweat drop goes down my chest and I shudder.

Johnny didn't even leave me keys so I could hear tunes. I can see those guys inside, tryin to bug Al into forgettin me, but he don't do it. He comes out, cool, hands the coffee to me, then leans against the car and cracks the lid on his.

—Be careful, he says, then climbs in his truck. I wanna call him over, whaddaya mean, Al? But he starts the engine and pulls out right when John and Tom come over.

—Kyle, yer turn, Johnny says and hands me the keys through my window. They're all sweaty and hot from his hand and I slide over and stick em in.

—Hey, it's my turn! Tommy yells, squeezin his giant Coke cup and squirtin hisself from the straw in the process.

—That's just why it ain't yer turn! Johnny jeers, gettin in and bangin a paira sunglasses onto his face. We jam our coffees on the dash against the windshield.

—Ahh jeez, is all Tommy can say. —Ahh jeez, you never lemme do nothin. Nobody lets me do nothin. I kin drive. They gave me a licence too.

—Everybody makes mistakes, Johnny says, and it's pretty funny how quick he says it, but I see Tommy's face in the mirror and feel a bit bad. He's all right, you just gotta know him. Sometimes I think he don't know how to do nothin cause nobody lets him do nothin. Course, it ain't *my* sister's car.

I twist the key and all them horses thunder up. It's really wild in the driver's seat, the vibration on the wheel all up my arms, my shoulders, into my skull. It ain't a mean shake, like it hurts or nothin. It's more like a comfort, soothing, like a rocking chair is? Boom boom boom.

I click it in gear and it lurches, clawing against the brake like some beast pullin on a chain. Rollin out, back in drive, I take it real easy, ready to stomp on the brake if she's gonna run away.

—C'mon, pyjama boy, Tommy says in his pouty tone. I think, "Yeh, well fuck you," and let er rip. She takes off like lightnin, wheels screamin as they try to bite the asphalt, Johnny and Tommy are both goin *Whoaaaaa!* as I kick the brakes and spin the wheel and suddenly it's like winter, a patcha ice with the car doin donuts, the rear end shootin sideways while the front wheels hold on. I'm tryin to remember whaddaya do . . . oh yeh! Steer into the skid, but by the time I got the wheel goin she's stopped. A little cloud of fried rubber drifts out from underneath and everybody in the parking lot is lookin at me with mouths like little circles. Some guys might feel like the best, everybody starin, but I know what they ain't thinkin. They *ain't* thinkin anything like, "What a great guy, he must work with children." They're thinkin one word, and it begins with "ass" and ends with "hole".

I take it easy gettin onto Kingston Road, head west, towards home. I know what's inside this car and I know what's inside me, and these two things are pals, right? They both want the other one to come on out, they wanna shake hands and buddy-buddy and I know just where they like it, up around eighty MPH, one hundred and thirty kilometres per hour. So I resist that hunger inside and do Kingston at five kliks over the limit, at a sweet ol seventy-five, which just happens to be the age of my grandmother on my dad's side, who is a pilot and was the second woman ever to break the sound barrier.

I can feel Johnny's eyes on me, see him from the corner of my eye, but I don't look. Tommy's all over the rearview, tryin to catch me, to push me over the edge. I avoid checkin behind. My shoulders feel like rocks I'm so rigid, holding back, my teeth clamped, restrained, sweat on the sides of my face, down my back and chest. Fuck fuck fuck fuck. Let it go, Kyle, let it go!

So I do. I relax. I take a breath, in fer six, out fer six, let my shoulders drop, unclench my teeth, lighten up on the wheel, breathe again. But the speedo creeps up. It's like the most natural position for my foot is on the floor with the pedal mushed underneath. Those horses take over fast; the car practically jumps at the chance to cruise up. I wanna slow down, but you know when you're drivin how sometimes it's hard, I mean you know you're goin too fast but lettin up is the wimp thing to do, even if you do it real carefully? Jesus.

And then I get a lucky break. The light ahead goes red and I'm quick on the brake, maybe too quick but it's okay, we cruise to the line real nice, no problem, stop, breathe. Johnny and Tommy are yackin, I hardly hear em cause it's all bullshit.

—I puked worse than that once. Once a whole lasagna came up and I hadn't had lasagna in months. . . .

As long as they're talkin like that they won't be buggin me. The opposite light goes yellow but I'm cool, I ain't gonna jump at it.

—Hey, fags, where's the homo toga party! someone shouts from beside me. It's these two guys in a brown Camaro, not one a those classy late-sixties ones but a new kind, IROC or some horseshit like that, the car for goofs who can't get a real sports car.

I'm about to tell the guy on the passenger side that he can go fuck his backwards baseball cap backwards, dig? when they shriek away like a crow, the light's green and the last thing I hear after the engine's chug is this geeky laugh.

For a second it's really quiet in the car, just the pump of the cylinders, the click of valves under the hood. Johnny and Tommy are shut up, not even breathin, I can feel them both staring at me even though I'm lookin straight ahead, watchin that shit-brown car receding down the hill over the Rouge River bridge.

The car behind us, a red punchbuggy, honks, then pulls around the left and crosses the intersection. I don't even look if the driver is glarin at me. I just sit, countin breaths, in fer six, out fer six, in fer six, out fer six.

I watch the Camaro climbin the hill on the other side.

I lift off the brake then go, nothin big on the gas, just enough to get us up to forty-five MPH. We almost coast down the hill, real smooth, and it feels like the engine complains, that it don't like runnin so slow. We start up the hill after the bridge and I just give it enough to keep her at forty-five, right on the line.

Johnny starts to say somethin but I shake my head, so little that I hardly can feel it but I know it's enough cause he don't say nothin. We're crestin the hill, past the park, the gas station, the stables on the right.

Johnny gasps and a little smile takes the corners of my mouth.

The light there is red and at the light, waitin in the left lane with a red Beetle on its right and Al's white pickup in the far lane, is one shit-brown Camaro. I jerk us into the left lane and Johnny's hands come up, he's thinkin I'm gonna rear-end those buggers or bugger those rear ends, like *I'd* be the one.

I cut the wheel left again and put us into oncoming traffic, but remember – the light's red. Cars sit across the intersection, ready to go.

Tommy's babblin somethin that sounds religious and Johnny takes up a word or two from him, like "kingdom come" and "trespass".

I lend the engine a bit more gas and she shudders with fresh power as we come around the *wrong* side of the traffic island.

The only traffic is from the left, a ramp comin off the highway. A blue Pacer or somethin comes up and runs the yellow and I gotta tug the wheel to avoid it. Our lights go green and with a little squeak I send us back into the left lane goin the right way, *in front of* the shit-brown Camaro. For a second there's nothin from Tommy and John, then they laugh like goddamn crows, I can't believe it how hard they laugh and even I smile and smile.

—It's all in the timin, boys, I say.

Now of course these fucks in the Camaro gotta try and beat us so I get liberal with speed. Johnny slams back in his seat and the coffees (hot hot!) go everywhere as we accelerate, leavin that piece of crap way behind. Forty, fifty, sixty, seventy miles per hour. I try to keep her around seventy-five, the traffic's light so it ain't bad (meanwhile the limit's down to sixty kliks, or forty MPH, so I'm lookin for cruisers). Shit if seventy-five ain't enough. The Camaro comes up doin maybe eighty-five and I gotta lay it on. It's becomin like a mosquito you gotta keep slappin. I think they're gonna come back but when I check the rearview they're gone, maybe found their turn, anyway it means I can let up again. If I can.

We're at maybe ninety now and it feels bout right. I give the gas a little headroom and we slow, but it's not good, it's too slow, we're like grandmas like that.

Kingston Road goes like a funnel from three lanes to one right after the 401 entry and exit ramps. There ain't a lotta traffic but there's some and I'm dodgin them like slalom flags but somehow I can't slow down. Maybe it sounds dumb and you won't know what I mean, but it's like if you're in the hot shower and it's so nice and comfy but it's time to get out, maybe yer sister's bitchin to yer mum that you been in too long, but you also know the bathroom's cold so you just stay in till the hot water's gone, ever done that? You know you should get out, but you can't. That's what me'n 130 kilometres per hour's like.

So while I boot between cars like a friggin maniac but all I can hear is accordion music in a minor key in my head, Johnny and Tommy are screamin, Slow down! Slow down! Cars honk, wheels shriek, and the engine keeps pumpin like a giant heart.

Suddenly, *blam! blam! blam!* and we all duck, we actually duck like we live in Miami or somethin and guns go off all the time, but this is Canada where it's nice, almost nobody's got guns cept maybe for huntin moose on fall weekends, not for shootin people. The car starts shakin bad, I let off right away, give some brakes.

—What the fuck? Johnny says, his voice bouncin with the car's shakin.

—Someone shot out our tire! Someone shot out our tire! Tommy yells, as if.

Blam! Blam! we hear, just as loud as before, the engine starts coughin but it's only one lane, no place to pull over until we reach

121

Meadowvale Road, maybe only doin twenty miles and a million cars behind us, jeez what a change. I pull over on the gravel at Meadowvale and the engine's hammerin. I shut it off.

—What you do? Johnny says quietly. —What you do to my sister's car?

—Aw, I didn't do nothin John. You're right here. Was there somethin I did? Hey, Tommy, did I do anything bad to this car?

—Maybe went too fast, Tommy mutters.

—Ah, fuck you, too fast. That's bullshit. Johnny went just as fast before.

—Yeh, but the speed limit was a hundred! This was only sixty here! Johnny cries.

—I can't believe it. I can't believe what I'm hearin! I shout. —How fuckin stupid can ya be? What the fuck does the speed limit have to do with it?

—Yeh, Tommy says. —Yeh, it was a hundred before!

—What the fuck does the speed limit have to do with it? I scream again, those dumb fucks.

—The car knows, man. It *knows*, Johnny says, he almost sounds like he's gonna cry.

—The car knows? I can't believe how kooky my voice sounds, how I'm screechin, I'm so pissed at these morons.

And suddenly shit-brown pulls up beside us. The fuckin Camaro. And this is the worst part.

—Hey, fags, had enough? the guy on the passenger side says and without a thought I get out of the Nova, slam the door hard, and pull this guy outta the window of his car. No shit. I don't know how I did it, I don't even remember where I grabbed the sonofabitch, he was just in my hands. Maybe it's like the way I carried Nils when Shelly kicked the crap outta him, maybe it's an adrenalin rush or somethin. Anyway, this guy is in my hands, he's about my size and in one quick move I've banged his face into the fender of the Nova. *Boof!* it goes, and a splat of blood bursts there on the green and the first thing I think as he dribbles to the ground, his face all pulped and his hero of a friend peelin away, is that this car is too green, that red would be nice, aren't red cars faster?

I stand there for a second, breathin, lookin around. I feel so calm all of a sudden, a little tickle of wind comes up and feels cool, nice and fresh. I smile a little, breathe the fresh August air. A whiff of cut grass rises up, and mixed with the camomile rooted in the gravel it smells real nice.

—Kyle, a voice says, and I let my eyes focus on Al. He's standin in front of me for I don't know how long. His truck's parked in front of the Nova, the guy from the Camaro's sittin on the tailgate with his face buried in a towel that was once white but is now lookin mighty patriotic. I think maybe he's bawlin, maybe not. Al's got some dark blue rag in his hand, he's handin it to me, pushin it into my chest.

—Put this on, he says.

—Why? I ask. I think how weird it is, Al givin me somethin to wear. —Is it a gift?

—Yeh, he says, not smilin. —A gift.

Then he lets it fall open, and I see it's a dressing gown, a housecoat just like mine. Then for a second the sun feels really hot on my back, like fire, and I look down and jeez I think I'm gonna die, I'm naked, buck bare naked.

—It got stuck in the car door, John says, comin out from behind Al. —And then you put a dent in. . . . Al presses his big hand on Johnny's shoulder and Johnny shuts up fast.

I put the housecoat on. It's real hot inside, I'm glazed with sweat and want a water or apple juice or beer or Scotch or somethin cause my throat's all parched.

Al goes over to the guy with the towel, talks to him quietly. The guy shakes his head, nods, nods again. Al takes him round to the truck's passenger side, lets him in, comes back.

Al goes over to Johnny. —You and Tommy wait here. I'm gonna take this guy to the hospital, then Kyle home, then I'll get you some gas. Okay?

Johnny nods and Al goes around to the truck's driver seat.

—Kyle, come on, he says.

—I'll call later, Johnny says to me, I can't tell if he's mad or not, everythin's moving so smoothly, Johnny gettin in the Nova, Al closin his door and startin the truck, me openin the passenger door, the guy with the towel slidin over, me gettin in, beltin up, us movin out.

Nobody in the truck says nothin as we ride along until we get to Centenary. We turn up the drive to the emergency and I say to the towel guy, You all right?

He lets the towel down pretty slowly, ready to snap it back if he keeps bleedin but it's mostly stopped, I think it was from his nose. The towel's all brown and crusty.

—Good thing I got a hard face, he says, and even smiles a little. We're there and I help him out, he even waves as he goes in, and we drive off. Al's quiet again and when we pull into my drive he asks, You all right?

—Yeh, I say. —I'm okay. You want some apple juice?

He shakes his head. I get out and he drives off. I watch him goin up the street, no squealin, no rushin, no heat, just smooth acceleration, clean shifts. Composed.

I gulp three glasses of frosty cold apple juice and take a long, cool shower. Halfway through, my little sister bangs on the door.

—My turn! Kyle, it's my turn! she shouts. —You're usin all the hot water!

—It's a cold shower! I yell back.

—Mom! Mommmmmm! she cries. —Kyle's in the shower and he's usin all the cold water! ●

The Machine Escapes

☾

T HE AIR IS THICK WITH HEAT as it laps against the little white building from which Hewyn emerges. Claustrophobia has driven him outside ahead of the others, but he feels no better under the incendiary sunshine, his eyelids crushed into moist slits. As he surveys the gravel compound that is entirely circumscribed by chain link and barbed wire, the sandblasted rock and scrub rolling away beyond it, he imagines with amazing clarity the slow ooze of his sunglasses down the instrument cluster of the rental car.

The rest of the group files out behind him in a cloud of arctic air with its decayed odour like the inside of an old refrigerator. An elderly woman touches his arm and he recoils. —Are you all right? she asks, her voice impossibly delicate beneath the concussion of the Arizona sun.

—Of course, he snaps, swaying. She seems impervious to the heat, the incandescent suns glaring on each lens of her sunglasses below the brim of a grey helmet on which is stencilled "Titan Missile Museum". She is wearing a cotton dress, rippled pantyhose, orthopedic sandals.

—You don't look well, the elderly man with her insists. He is thin and red, in tan slacks and a flannel shirt.

—I don't expect it gets this hot in Canada, she remarks, and they nod at one another. Hewyn can feel the arteries on the sides of his neck swell and shrink, swell and shrink. He suffers a sudden rage at these kind people, rage at the man's buttoned collar and rolled-down shirtsleeves, rage at the woman's gnarled knuckles and chapped nostrils. For days he has been congratulating himself on the success of his infiltration, the southern tincture he has applied to his accent, the swagger with which he has spiced his walk.

The man puts a cigarette between his lips and produces a box of matches on which is painted a brilliant pelican gulping fish on a pier above a shimmering harbour. From the box he takes a match. His hands are gigantic but each motion is delicate and precise. The man rehearses the strike once, twice. At this moment Hewyn feels a globe of panic expand in his gut. The staggering heat of the air: what if it is hesitating at the threshold of combustion, awaiting a spark, a sudden radiant second, to ignite the atmosphere and unleash a firestorm to engulf the planet? Hewyn's hand rises. The man strikes the match; the head flares. Hewyn completes the motion by jabbing his finger into the damp corner of his eye. The old man passes the cigarette through the invisible flame and draws its smoke indulgently into his lungs.

—The Titan II, a second-generation liquid-fuelled ballistic missile, was the largest ICBM developed by the U.S. Although the actual yield of the warhead remains classified, it was a megaton weapon. That means it could deliver a blast equivalent to several million tons of TNT.

The tour guide is Grant, a short fat man with a Texan accent. Hewyn trails the tour group, whispering Grant's phrases to himself, rehearsing the accent: Tay-ee en tay-ee. Sev-rall mee-yill-yon tuns ah tay-ee en tay-ee. Running shoes and sandals crunch on the gravel, pausing before each esoteric display: oxidizer and fuel hardstands, missile engine and nose cone, antennae and security sensors. Hewyn whispering improbable phrases over and over:

— . . . aerozene-50 and nitrogen tetroxide are *hypergolic*, meaning they ignite when mixed . . .

— . . . provided by the TPS-39 Doppler system . . .

— . . . Mark VI nose cone with its ablative shielding . . .

—Ab-lay-tive shay-alding. A-bell-*eh*-tive shay-*eel*-ding. This he says too loudly. Heads turn. Grant pauses and twitches uncomfortably. A gigantically fat man, sweating and wheezing, frowns meanly and stamps the gravel with a gigantic foot. Hewyn looks into the sun, staggers, lets the heat explain his delirium. The big man's plump daughter, a girl of fourteen with lips smeared fluorescently orange, beams at Hewyn. He gazes into her sunglasses for too long.

Hewyn pulls off his helmet and scratches his head vigorously. The girl breaks away from her titanic dad and walks beside Hewyn as the group approaches a glass case.

The enclosure overlays the top of the nuclear missile silo. Tourists cup their hands and look inside, depositing greasy Rorschach smears onto the glass. What they see is the tip of a Titan II intercontinental ballistic missile.

A wound cut into the nose cone advertises its impotence.

—Course, we won the Cold War through economics. Every hour and a half a Russian satellite overflies the museum and photographs that hole, just to make sure we're keepin' our end of the deal.

—Ow-wer end a' th' *dee*-al, Hewyn whispers. Eyes rise to the brilliant blue sky. A jet inscribes an exclamation mark into the stratosphere.

◗ Hewyn had left the motel too early and so cruised Tucson's broad strips, the windows rolled deep into the doors and evening air dry and prickly as cacti against his cheeks. The city continued to glow like red-hot iron long after the sun retreated beyond the scrub-covered hills. He passed vast lakes of mercury light, the parking lots of plazas and steak houses, Circle-Ks and Dunkin Donuts. By 8:30 it was dark. He stopped at a 7-Eleven and bought six cans of Coors and put them in the trunk.

Following a long list of directions scribbled on a piece of motel stationery, he made his way to a side street and moved slowly down it. Tucson's light-pollution legislation made the suburbs as dark as the desert and Hewyn swore loudly as the hands of his watch approached 9:00 PM.

After half an hour he finally found the house, low and wide, unimpressive among the other low, wide houses. He shut off the ignition and spent a few seconds composing his excuse, then got out and approached the entrance.

Her hair. He had dreamed about her hair, the deep coils as thick and sweet as night in a forest, the way it filled his face when she sobbed into his neck or rocked to draw him deeper. He tapped the doorbell.

—Hello, Vesna.

—Late. When you phoned and said you were in town, I was afraid to think that you hadn't changed.

—I got lost.

—I know.

She stepped back into the vestibule to admit him and as his eyes adjusted he saw the light in the halo of fuzz on her head.

—Your hair.

—Take off your shoes.

When he had done this she drew him against her, the seashell-crescent of her ear and the bristled hemisphere of her head denying familiarity, until his hands – the memory of hands – rose and recognized angles and bumps, the tectonic shoulder blades and chain-link spine.

—Still skinny, he whispered into the ear.

—You're fatter.

—What happened to your hair? he asked, stepping back.

—I cut it. The heat, she replied, taking his hand and leading him down the hall.

He watched as she moved through the halogen light of the kitchen, drawing ice, filling glasses with iced tea and tequila. The quick, clumsy motions, the static smile and tiny hummed musical phrases; his emotional self grew gradually convinced that this was Vesna.

—Carl is in Phoenix this week. He's often there. But he telephones.

Hewyn nodded. He suddenly noticed the refrigerator. Their own had displayed layer upon layer of postcards, notes, love letters, advertisements, playbills. He had often imagined her afterwards, sorting through the strata like an archaeologist, seeking the answer to the uppermost layer, the final level, the index card on which he had penned his confessions and farewell.

On this refrigerator, however, there hung one item only, an Easter bunny made from a paper plate and macaroni, fringed in coloured yarn, and spray-painted gold. She caught him gazing at it and he looked away.

—Don't you miss the snow? he wondered, drawing an ice cube out of the glass and into his mouth. And through the clack of it on his teeth: I know I'd miss the snow.

—I missed you. But don't any more.

He looked straight into the blue ponds of her eyes, stared into the obsidian pupils. She returned his gaze, and for once he was the one to look away, tried to blame defeat on grit in an eye, rubbed and rubbed it.

—Would you like to see the house? she asked, and Hewyn tried to swallow the lump of dread that slithered up his throat.

He trailed her through rooms with cream trim and Tex-Mex

decor, ponchos and spurs on the walls, sand paintings and mesa landscapes. In some he noted objects that had once decorated their own apartment, Vesna and Hewyn's apartment: an Ikea lamp or that antique globe with the brass armature, discrepant in the adobe landscape.

The tour ended in what had once been a dining room.

—A piano, Hewyn said, pressing his hand to a black gloss finish a mile deep.

—A baby grand, she replied, buffing away the smudge of his palm.

—Have you started . . . ?

—Heavens, no. But she likes to play. That's where she is right now: at her lesson.

Hewyn flipped the cover open and a look of panic clouded Vesna's features.

—Don't.

—Just a little nocturne, he said, seating himself.

—It's hers. Don't.

—Debussy?

—I said *don't!* Vesna cried, and smashed the cover down, resonating the strings.

—You have to let me play something.

—You haven't outgrown that?

—A few bars. That's all, he said, and re-opened it.

Vesna snapped the cover down again, almost crushing his fingers. From her pocket she retrieved a key which she twisted in the lock. She returned the key to her pocket.

—Vesna. You have to let me play it, he said firmly.

—No. It's hers. I don't want you to taint it.

—Taint it? You obviously don't understand. I have to play it. I have touched it and now I must play it.

—Of course you've retained your obsessive-compulsive superstitions, Hewyn, but I'm not going to help perpetuate them. It's her piano and I will let no one but her play it.

—Okay, okay, Hewyn replied, palms up. —Okay. I can do this.

—Come back to the kitchen. I'll make you coffee. Black double sugar, no doubt.

She drank herbal tea and he had black coffee with double sugar. For many minutes they slurped and said nothing. Vesna's expressions shifted and churned and Hewyn sank lower in his chair, aware of the consequences of these internal debates. But when she finally spoke, it was with surprising tenderness. Hewyn's terror deepened.

—Hewyn, why did you have to go away? Why did you go away?

Hewyn set his mug down, planted his feet on the floor as if he were about to stand, then picked them up again.

—I didn't exactly leave you.

—"Dear Vesna. I'm leaving. Signed Hewyn."

—It didn't say that.

—It did. Not in those words. Not in those words. But it did.

Hewyn drew a long breath through his nose.

—Vesna, I wonder if you remember the way we used to be. I think about it often. Do you remember when *The Globe and Mail* said: "They play together like limbs of the same body"? It was an epiphany. Do you know what I am, Vesna? I am a machine. For making music. I am the essential component that makes the piano sing. The air in its voicebox. It is my purpose.

—I've heard all this before. You said the same for me. Me and my flute. And what happened?

—You became pregnant.

—We became pregnant! We became pregnant! You and I! I didn't do it on my own. Where was this "air in the voicebox" while you were sprawled over me, except maybe in your grunts and gasps? You were an integral part of that mechanism.

—Don't yell. Just please don't yell.

—I'm not yelling. I'm raising my voice slightly because I'm upset.

—It's yelling. Please calm down. I admit it. For a moment I was part of the reproductive machinery. But the result of that union: it took you over. Like a parasite. No, let me finish. You couldn't play any more. Not as well. And I knew that even after the gestation and birth, your machinery would be switched over to being a mother, to caring for it.

Vesna bolted to her feet and hissed, For *it?* For *it?* Caring for *her!* Caring for your daughter! How can you keep talking about machinery? This is a human being we have created. That is the *purpose* of your "machinery". If you disagreed, why didn't you have it removed? It could have saved us all a lot of trouble!

She grabbed her purse and wrapped the strap around her forearm.

—I have to pick her up from her lesson. You are going to meet her. Then you'll see what your machinery can do. You stay there. You stay right there, and if you leave . . . if you leave . . .

She hammered her fist on the counter, turned, and stomped out. He heard the front door open, then her voice through sobs: Hello little one. Hello my little one. Go on in. Go on.

The door slammed.

Hewyn sat with his hands clenched around his mug. A tiny pattering came from the hallway. He stared at the doorway, his fingers tightening on the cup. He had been calm during Vesna's outbreak, but now his breath hastened, he could hear it whistling through his nostrils. The pattering stopped. A single high peep, inquisitive, puzzled, came from just around the corner. Hewyn felt an icy drop of sweat creep down his spine. An orange face appeared, enormous green eyes, a pink nose.

—*Llllow*, the cat said as its eyes met his.

Hewyn set the mug gently on the counter and backed out the opposite door, into the living room. The cat started towards him and he slammed the folding door. Its eyes appeared through the slats, staring up into his own.

—Go on! Go on! Shoo!

He backed up, then turned and reached for the upper shelves, swept his hands along the tops, sending clouds of dust into his face. He sneezed and pulled open drawers, rifled through the junk in them, wedding and baby photos. He opened the bench, ransacked the Chopin and Mozart and Debussy. No key. There was no key. Sitting on the bench, Hewyn gazed at the black shell of the piano's keyboard cover. He pressed the pedals, made all the keys ring as he stomped on the sostenuto.

He had to play a note. With his right hand. An E flat above high C. At the very least. He reached up and tried the cover. It was unlocked. He pushed it all the way open, looked at the rows of white and black, felt their potential like heat beneath his fingertips.

—Ha.

He cracked his fingers, then thought of something defiant to play. Took a breath and closed his eyes.

Brang! the piano boomed.

Even before he opened his eyes Hewyn heard the low C, D, F, B flat and B, then saw the cat standing on them, its nose coming up to sniff his face. He slapped the animal off the keyboard while rolling the opposite direction, onto the carpet.

He jumped to his feet and raced for the kitchen door. It was still closed. The cat had made its way around to the room's other entrance; Hewyn hadn't noticed the alternate doorway. He crashed the kitchen door shut behind him and raced down the hall and out the front door.

The rental car skidded and spun as he jerked the wheel. A white car veered and a horn blared; it might have been Vesna with a small blonde child in the car seat beside her. Hewyn gunned the engine and sped out to the main thoroughfares of Tucson. Soon the road passed between fields with row upon row of aircraft: B-52 Stratofortresses, F-4 Phantoms, F-15 Eagles, and countless others, their intakes sealed in plaster, awaiting war or obsolescence.

● The tourists are underground, the walls a hospital teal and thick with conduits. They have descended metal stairs, passed through foot-thick doors, noted enormous springs from which the vessel containing the underground complex is suspended. In the event of a nuclear strike. *Boing.*

They are in the control centre and their underground guide, Will, who is taller and thinner than Grant but shares his southwestern American a-okay accent, is explaining to those clustered around the consoles of 1960s instrumentation that this was a "No Lone Zone", where personnel were never permitted alone. This makes the fat fourteen-year-old girl excited; she tries to catch Hewyn's eye each time the term arises.

Hewyn's attention is shifting to the tour. Procedures ensure a correct launch under the most adverse conditions while preventing unauthorized activation. He is impressed. That madness can be so coordinated. That the blood and bone and tendons and knife of the madman are not insane.

—Here we will simulate the expected procedures at the Titan II site were the president to authorize the use of nuclear weapons. Little girl, would you like to be the Deputy Missile Combat Crew Commander? The fourteen-year-old scowls, but he is handing her a key and Hewyn, who has been aloof for most of the tour, is spellbound. She laughs shrilly and takes it from him as if accepting a car key. She pretends to listen to the description of authentication codes, time of launch data, and butterfly valve lock code (which sounds quite attractive), but she is really imagining the side of her face, the flash of her eyelashes over her big blue eyes, her open mouth and pouting lips.

—As you can see, the MCCC's launch keyhole is some distance from that of the DMCCC, our little friend there, yet the keys must be turned within two seconds of one another and held for five seconds. This means that two people are required to launch the missile.

—Like making a baby, she says, and blushes at a gasp from the group. She wonders why she has said this. Hewyn is the only one who laughs. Will's face is crimson.

—Turn your key now, he orders.

They each turn their keys.

On the Launch Control Complex Facilities panel, "Launch Enable" lights.

—The BVL has been unlocked.

The "Batteries Activated" light comes on.

—Electrolyte has flowed into the missile's onboard batteries. APS power. The missile is on internal power. Also, nine thousand gallons per minute of sound-attenuation water begins to flow around the missile. Silo Soft. The 785-ton Silo Closure Door is opening. Guidance Go: the thrust mount is locked into place. The target is now in guidance memory. Fire Engine: the propellants come together in the engine thrust chambers, and the hypergolic reaction generates immediate thrust.

Hewyn is transfixed by the progression of lights. The shudder of the complex as fire fills the silo. It's the end of the fucking world.

—Lift off.

● Hewyn's rental car pounds the dry pavement. The steering wheel is soft in the heat but stiffening under the arctic blast of the air conditioner. His hands permanently imprinted.

The car is a good machine, doing what it does. The missile rises out of the launch duct, separates from the humans in the control centre. The umbilicals cut. No known human force can stop it. It arcs over the north pole and incinerates Communists.

He passes a golf course nestled among the saguaro and cholla and sees a gardener spray-painting the grass. The tortured sod glows green. Paint the trees and the lakes and the skin of the dying. Paint Hiroshima. Paint Moscow.

He has an idea. In a small arid town of shacks and cattle, he stops at a phone booth. It accepts his calling card and he dials. —Hypergolic, he rehearses as it trills. —We were hypergolic. The ringing ceases with a click. There is silence. —Hello?

—Daddy? the voice of a little girl implores. —Daddy?

The air is rippling about him. Glass tendrils wave from the grille of the car and his lips are salty.

—Yes, he replies, and hangs up.

He drives for a long time parallel to a train. It is some distance away, running along the foot of a ridge of red rock and white sand. The train is moving at seventy-six miles per hour. There are new cars on the flatbeds. Even at this distance the sun is dazzling on the chrome. Farther back are tankers on which is stencilled "Santa Fe", a mythic land, a Narnia or Oz. Hewyn feels a twinge of sadness when after an hour the train curves away to the south.

A dark spot floats far above the highway ahead. As he gets closer he sees it is a collection of circling birds. Buzzards. Something dead or dying on the highway. He leans forward as he approaches the spot but sees nothing but a silver mirage ripple. He hammers the brake and wrenches the car off the highway. Gravel sprays into the fenders.

There was a flash of orange.

He shuts off the engine and gets out and walks back along the highway's shoulder. His ears ring in the silence. No cars come from either direction. The asphalt is grey and coarse, lines fading beneath the solar assault. He glances up a few times and the buzzards seem lower. He looks down at the dry scrub and grass that borders the gravel, thinks about snakes and scorpions.

It is a kitten. Not dead. Breathing rapidly. An orange kitten the size of his palm. His shadow sweeps over but there is no reaction. Hewyn takes a long look in the direction from which he has come, then another in the direction he is travelling. Wind rasps in the scrub. The sun burns his head.

He pulls the car back onto the blacktop and glances into the rearview mirror as the first of the buzzards touches down. ◐

Grieving Beach

☾

A<small>T FIRST</small> I <small>THOUGHT</small> it was my muffler, or perhaps a crash of thunder, but when I had shut off the engine and the noise continued it became evident that I was hearing the crashing of the sea. I had glimpsed it numerous times while meandering up the coast, caterpillars of white crawling along the undulating grey surface, but had not from that vantage grasped the violence with which it was assailing the shoreline. It was invisible to me now. I stared through the windshield out at the back of a whiteboard house, and set into the wall a white door beside which sat a basketful of tattered geraniums that twitched in the wind. I watched them for some time, then pulled the keys from the ignition and opened the door, amplifying the surf's crash. The air smelled of salt and sea and rotting fish, and it tugged at my hair and messed it in the same way it twisted and battered the flowers. I went to the rear of the car and opened the trunk and withdrew my luggage, a single hardshelled suitcase older than my own self, the only suitcase I have ever used. I shut the trunk and walked around my car and up a flagstone walk to the door and knocked. Sometime in the interval that I waited passed the moment at which it would have made sense to knock once more with greater vigour, but, as in all things, correct timing escaped me and it seemed ludicrous to knock again after such a long pause. But then the door did open and a stern-faced woman with silver hair and a stout frame stood before me unsmiling. In her hand she clutched a serving ladle to which there clung a film of broth with mushrooms that steamed in the wind. She looked at my face for several seconds before glancing down at my suitcase, which for her apparently represented some sort of passport into the building, for she stood aside and let me enter.

—This is a bad time, I said as I brushed past her and into a dark foyer with a desk on which sat a cash register, a bell, and a rack of tourist pamphlets.

—Mr. Fen? she asked as she closed the door.

—Yes.

—You are coming in a bad timing. This is dinner. You eat now.

She started to head down a narrow hallway but my voice halted her.

—Actually, I'm rather tired. I would just like to check in and get to my cottage.

She paused, her grip tight on the ladle, then came back and rounded the desk. From a wooden rack she took down a key and handed it to me.

—You are making the paperwork later. Come in later. Number six is yours.

Then she headed down the hall and disappeared through a doorway. I glanced around. Forward there was a lounge, small and lit feebly by the windows, populated by too many chairs and a small piano. Beside the hallway ascended a wooden staircase, but other than that there was nowhere to go. I started off down the hallway and pushed through the door.

A candlelit room; half-a-dozen faces looked up at me from around a huge table. The woman who had greeted me was standing at the head of the table, spooning out broth from a pot.

—How do I . . . ? I shifted my suitcase to the other hand. —Where are the cottages?

—Why don't you join us? a woman's voice, English in accent, suggested. I looked at the faces, too flustered to have noticed who had spoken.

—I guess if I go out the way I came. Then around?

—Ya. Ya, around. Go now. Go go go. Then she resumed spooning the muddy broth into upheld bowls. The sight of it nauseated me.

I turned and walked back down the dim corridor and out the door into the wind. The light had hardened, emerging as it did from roiling clouds that spat into the breeze the occasional spray of rain. I rounded the house and ascended a set of flagstone steps, then emerged onto a deep beach now being consumed by the surf. I stopped there and stared out at the thick sea, the wind not quite cold but wet with salt spray, the sky and water identical twins of slate, differentiated only by the whitecaps below and the fast moving troughs of cloud above. The surf deafened me, hollowing out a little pocket of solitude in which I felt a profound and oddly reassuring loneliness. Lost in that vast panorama, I leaned into the embrace of oblivion.

A light far out in the sea withdrew me from that trance and I saw that it was a freighter or oil tanker at first sight stationary but within a few moments showing slow northerly progress. From such a distance it appeared stable and steadfast, but I knew better, that her decks were heaving on the rough water, with the waves crashing over the bow and her crew pitched violently about.

I moved forward and the stone path intersected a narrow boardwalk that ran along the top of the beach. I made an arbitrary decision and went right, away from the house, and headed towards the cabins. Each was a small cube with a chimney and windows facing the water. Number seven came first so I continued along until the next one, which turned out to be mine. I made my way up the wooden walk to the door, inserted the key, and entered. I closed the door and flicked a switch inside the door and a lamp on the bedside table came on. I went to the bed and put my suitcase on it and sat down. The sea and wind, muted by the walls, continued to brawl outside. I got up and opened the suitcase and took out all my clothes and put them in the drawers of a dresser facing the bed, then put the suitcase under the bed and took off my jacket and hung it in the closet. I sat down on the bed. I got up and entered the bathroom and turned on the light and peed into the blue water in the toilet and looked at my eyes in the mirror, looked at the green irises fringed in red veins and wondered if they qualified as bloodshot. Then I turned off the light and exited the bathroom and sat on the bed. I took off my shoes. Then I got up and put them in the closet beneath my jacket and came back and sat on the bed. Then I got up and went to the TV atop the dresser and picked up the remote and pointed it at the TV and turned it on and with one hand in a pocket flipped through all the channels, most of which were static, then turned off the TV and put the remote down. Then I sat on the bed. I got up and picked up the remote and put it on the bedside table and sat on the bed.

The room, I estimated, was six *tatami*.

At that thought I recalled a phrase as spoken by my friend Hiro. —*Kono tabi wa domo.*

The thin light from the windows continued to dim. I looked at my watch and it was 6:45 PM. The cottage shook against the wind and rain. It was time for bed.

◑ After a thick and dreamless sleep I awoke with light filtering in through the pair of windows at the front of the cottage. I could feel right away the change in the weather, the wind diminished but still lively and the barometric pressure considerably higher. I got up and dressed quickly and went outside. Upon the wooden walk to the front of my cottage I stood and squinted out at the grey sea. It continued to pound the beach but at a point far below the line of debris, driftwood and packing foam, it had pitched onto the sand during the night. The temperature had dropped too, and I buttoned my canvas coat and pressed my hands into my pockets.

I was hungry now and headed towards the white house, then made my way around the back and entered.

—Good morning, Mr. Fen, said the old woman who had opened the door for me last night.

—Oh. Hello. I suppose I should pay up now?

—Yes please. Will you stay how long? She consulted the calendar. —Nine days?

As I filled in the paperwork I could see her from the corner of my eye, staring, a small, tight smile on her face.

—Here you can forget everything. All the bad things, they leave. They fly away like black birds, she explained as she tore off my credit card receipt and stapled it to the bill before handing it to me.

—Um. Good.

—Go in now for the breakfast that is almost eaten. Go. Go!

I headed down the corridor and into the dining room.

—Good morning.

—Oh. Good morning, I said as I sat down at the large table. I looked at the woman who had addressed me, the only one in the room.

—You're British?

—Fancy that, she replied, lighting a cigarette. —You don't

mind, do you? she asked as she took a puff. —I know that woman would bust if she saw me doing this.

She sucked on the cigarette, then scooped some scrambled eggs onto her fork and ate. She puffed again and ate more.

—You should get yourself some eggs, she said, leaning forward and lifting the lid from an electric frypan. —They're still hot and there are plenty. Watch out for the sausages. Little too much of the sodium *and* the nitrate. The waffles are fine, though, and that's real maple syrup. Probably not such a big deal for you, though. Shall I get you some?

—Mmm. Not really hungry. But I'd like one of those cigarettes, if you've got one to spare.

—Oh. Well of course, she said, and pulled out a Canadian brand I had not seen in some time and extended it across the table. I took one.

—Light? I asked with it in my lips.

—Sure. She probed for her lighter and brought it up and held it over the centre of the table, lit, so I had to stand up and lean over the eggs to put the tip of the cigarette into the flame.

In a rapid swirling wave of muted ecstasy a wall of anxiety crumbled and a world beyond it was revealed.

—Oh god, I muttered.

—Wonderful, isn't it? First one in a while? she asked, and I saw her great grey eyes which reminded me of the sea outside, and her blonde hair packed into a comb at the back of her head with wisps like fog coiling at her cheeks, and I felt breathless and light-headed and had to suppress a drunken thrill of imagining her body against mine.

—It is wonderful, I said, and drew in another cloud. I looked at the food spread before me and though a moment ago I had detected a plea for food in my gut, everything suddenly lost all appeal and became to me as unappetizing as gravel and pondwater.

—Lilian, she said.

—Purdon, I replied with an exhalation of smoke.

A song of Germanic origin, sung in a gravelly woman's voice, approached from the corridor and produced a look of panic on Lilian's face. The door swung open and the proprietor entered with a pitcher of juice and pot of coffee. She froze when she saw us.

—Hello Anna, Lilian said meekly.

—Smoking again in this house? Again?

—Sorry.

—Yes, sorry, I said, but continued to smoke.

—Go out. Go out! she cried, and shoved me.

—Sorry Anna. My fault. He didn't know. Come Purdon, we'll finish these outside.

—Yes you go outside! Now. Now!

Lilian giggled and came around the table. She took me by the arm and led me down the hall and outside.

—She's very uptight. Probably lived through the Holocaust or something, she muttered as we rounded the house and headed out onto the beach.

—That's rather insensitive, I remarked.

She was almost my height but tilted her head down to allow her to look up at me.

—We're all insensitive, Purdon. The only difference in sensitivity between individuals is in what we say, not what we feel. None of us really cares.

—I care.

—See, I'm better because I'm honest. You lie about your sensitivity and then feel good about it. But you're not telling the truth.

—You're very candid.

—It's part of the privilege of what we are. What we've gone through grants us a licence for temporary eccentricities. Ah, there's Michael. Michael! she called and we headed towards a man who was staring out at the sea.

He did not turn until we were almost upon him. He twisted to see who we were then turned his eyes back out at the sea.

—Good morning, Michael. Missed you at breakfast. Purdon and I were just chased out for smoking. The teacher was very angry with us.

—Hullo, Lilian. How was your night? Michael asked without looking away from the water. He was a tall wiry man with greying hair, wearing a jean jacket and cowboy boots and a baseball cap. He stood with his arms clenched around his chest and his feet close together. Lilian released my arm and moved ahead to stare out too, as if searching for the object of his attention. She turned around and looked back at him.

—Did you sleep last night?

—Yes. Slept right through for once. I don't think I woke up at all.

—Lucky sod, Lilian said, taking out her cigarettes and offering the pack to Michael. He ignored it and she held the pack out to me so I took one. —Not me. Don't think I've scored five minutes of sleep in the last month. Just lie there thinking. Thinking and thinking and thinking. What about you, Purdon?

—Oh, I'm a good sleeper. Haven't always been that way. But lately. It's like I go into a coma. Only thing is I still feel tired the next day. It's all so. . . . I paused and decided not to finish the sentence. It didn't seem necessary with the two of them just staring out at the sparkling sea. I started to feel warm in the sunshine and unbuttoned my jacket, removed it, and draped it over my forearm. I smoked half the cigarette then felt suddenly nauseated and tossed it into the sand. A tender light, I thought. This is a tender light. I turned and began to walk south across the beach. I got about twenty paces away before Lilian called out.

—Purdon! Purdon, wait for me. She hurried beside me and set her hand on my free arm and we walked silently for a few minutes.

—Hope I'm not being too clingy, she said after the pause. I looked at her and she smiled, closed her eyes for perhaps thirty seconds, and opened them again. —I couldn't do that without you. Keep walking with my eyes closed. So it's a good thing you're here. Mrs. Kirby! she shouted abruptly, waving vigorously up the sand at the last of the cottages where an older woman was sitting on the edge of the boardwalk with her head down. She looked up and shaded her eyes with a hand, then extended it into the air.

—Forty-eight years. Think about forty-eight years for a moment. I'm ten years below that mark in age and Mrs. Kirby was with Mr. Kirby for that long before he passed away in August. Can you imagine? Yet she seems to take it better than most. Her whole universe destroyed and she still maintains the brightest demeanour. Most of the time. Like now she seemed a little doleful but that's to be expected, don't you think? Oh. I'm sorry, am I chattering? It's what I do, I chatter. Keeps the thoughts down anyway. Dr. Mendelssohn says I should shut up and listen for a while but when I do all I hear is the thinking voice, thinking and thinking.

I had stopped walking at the mention of the name.

—Dr. Mendelssohn? Do you know Dr. Mendelssohn?

—Why Purdon. We all know Dr. Mendelssohn. All of us. Michael and Mrs. Kirby and Randall and Bess and that friend of hers Caroline too, oh I bet they're lesbians. You can tell by the way they look at each other. There's a look people get when they've touched each other while naked. Sorry, I'm still babbling, aren't I? Dr. Mendelssohn says shut up. Shut up and listen. Not in those words, mind you, she's far too polite for that kind of talk.

—But how is it . . . ? I mean, how does everyone know her?

—As you do, Purdon. She's the grief counsellor.

—Then how is it we all ended up here together?

—How did you end up here? Why did you come?

Now I looked out at the sea, as if something had formed there, some ship perhaps, with grand sails of white rippling in the breeze. Something we could all see, all of us on the beach, except for Anna of course, she was just the Belgian or German or Danish innkeeper. The rest of us were patients. Clients I mean. That's the right word. All clients of Dr. Mendelssohn. Of the grief counsellor.

Lilian nodded. —She's been telling me for months to come down here. I don't think she really figured that we would all listen to her advice. I'm sure it's not the ideal situation, having eight grieving souls occupying the same stretch of sand here on the Atlantic seaboard, but I'm noting the good in it too, the sense that we all understand one another, that we can all truly empathize with the other's plight. It pisses me off the way people look at you when they hear about your situation, the snottiness of them, as if they could give a shit that there's nothing to go home to, and nothing to go out to, the way that every which way you go is not a way to those we've lost, that they are nowhere now and something like that is so very very hard to grasp, we are totally unprepared for it and it's a wonder it doesn't drive everyone completely mad. When have we ever been conditioned to lose something and have no way of retrieving or replacing it? When? When? How can we be expected to cope with that? It's like . . . it's like a black hole or something beyond our grasp. It defies the laws of physics and logic. Yet every single one of us will have to deal with it. That something . . . that somebody . . . some *body* essential to the integrity of your existence can be so irretrievably eliminated. How can it be, Purdon? How can it be?

She delivered only the last sentence to my face, and then was against me, crying softly and still the talking went on, incomprehensible streams of syllables against my shoulder.

By the time we returned to her cabin (number seven, next door to my own) she had stopped and regained most of her composure. She apologized just once but added, I'm sure you'll get your revenge in a similar fashion.

—Well. I'm not much of a crier. Kind of wish I was, it might make it easier to swallow. I have this tightness here. I passed a palm across the front of my chest.

—You have to cry, Purdon. It's the only thing that gets me through it. You have to do it. I have wonderful cries. Full blustering wails. It's the only respite, temporary though it may be. I'm a mammoth bawler, always have been. You know, not just teary at the romantic bit in a film. The least stress can turn me into an infant. Used to be the only thing that would make Gabriella shut up. She'd be wailing and there was nothing I could do to make her stop so I'd give up and start in myself and she'd quit right away. Just gaze up at my face hanging over the crib like a big weepy planet. And that would make me laugh, you know the gap between laughing and crying is so slim, boo-hoo and ha-ha just a lick apart, that's how Arthur put it. From boo-hoo to ha-ha. You can still laugh, can't you Purdon?

—I don't know. Got something to laugh at?

By then we had arrived at her door. She stood with her arms crossed, shivering as the sun had slid behind a cloud, a mean-looking shape with a dark belly that hovered above us like some menacing spacecraft.

—There's always yourself. To laugh at I mean. I laugh at myself constantly. Really I'm quite hilarious. Keep posted and you'll laugh at me soon too. I'll commit some atrocious faux pas and you'll be grasping your belly and howling. Would you like to come in for some tea?

—No. No thank you. I might just lie down for a while. I'm next door, I said, nodding towards my cabin.

—All right. I mean it's no wonder you're weak. All you had for breakfast was two cigarettes. That's not even a food group. Maybe later? Tea later? I've also got some cookies. Shortbread I believe. They're very good. Come in a fancy tin and all.

—Okay, I said and turned towards my cottage, feeling the energy draining rapidly from my limbs and becoming abruptly panicked that I would collapse on the boardwalk. I got into the room and pitched myself onto the bed and within moments was fast asleep.

◗ All that blood. The sirens were growing louder but they were the wrong kind, not the high, rapid twitter of emergency vehicles rushing through the narrow streets of Kobe but North American sirens, and so I clutched Kanako's hand and waited for the arrival of the non-Asian firemen, burly Hollywood-style paramedics who would come bursting through the door and have to squeeze down the narrow hallway to Kanako on the blood-soaked futon.

My eyes were open before I awoke, detecting the flashes of red and yellow lights that penetrated the windows. I tumbled off the bed and moved to the window and looked out. A fire truck and an ambulance were parked on the beach almost in front of my cabin, and the crews were milling about in post-emergency languor, filling in paperwork or putting away equipment. Bad timing again. I had missed it. I opened the door and leaned in the doorframe, watched as the doors to the ambulance were clapped shut and a fireman banged on the side of the vehicle. Lights still flashing but siren silent, it pulled away. A police officer was talking to Lilian and Mrs Kirby. Lilian was pointing out to sea. I moved forward on the boardwalk and watched the activity. The fire truck started up and moved away to reveal an RCMP cruiser. Lilian turned around and spotted me and I raised an arm but she turned back to the officer as if she didn't see me. He closed his report book, nodded, and got into his car. Lilian and Mrs. Kirby watched him follow the tracks of the other emergency vehicles, past the white house and over a small ramp out to the road. Arm in arm, the two women approached me.

—Mrs. Kirby this is Purdon.

—Good afternoon Purdon, Mrs. Kirby said. She was a small woman of seventy or eighty. She wore a pleated skirt with a beige blouse and pearls and straw hat.

—What happened? I asked, nodding towards the sea.

Lilian, surprisingly silent, looked at Mrs. Kirby.

—Michael decided to go for a swim, Mrs. Kirby said with a quick nod. —With his clothes and boots on.

—Oh god, I said. —Is he all right?

—It depends on what you mean, Mrs. Kirby said, looking straight at me. —He's alive. He wasn't ready to come out here. Dr. Mendelssohn should have known better than to suggest it. Not everyone here should have come. And again she gave that tight nod before turning and walking off towards her cabin.

Lilian had wrapped her arms around her shoulders and was shivering.

—I could use a really hot cup of tea about now. You?

—I guess so.

—Well, come on, she said, and entered her cabin. I paused and looked out at the calm sea and followed her inside.

As I entered she emerged from the bathroom with an electric kettle. She set it on the bedside table and plugged it in.

The layout was identical to my own. A crowd of photographs on the dresser. I moved there and looked them over.

—We always end up with so much less than we ever expected, she said, standing beside me. —Not unlike photos of an exotic vacation. The way they are astonishingly inferior to the experience and always will be. Almost makes you feel contempt for these meek representations.

I looked over the photos. They were of an older man with large teeth, a balding head, and thick spectacles, and a little girl of perhaps three, with round cheeks and eyes as grey and metallic as Lilian's. The hair was thick and white. A few photographs showed the man and the child together, and two also included Lilian.

—Arthur and Gabriella, she whispered.

I picked up a photo showing the pair of them and gazed at it closely.

149

—What happened?

—Oh, are we going to do that? Describe each others' tragedies? Dr. Mendelssohn does say we need to talk about it. Although in a literal sense they're not exactly tragedies. Always meant to correct her on that. "Tragedy" is a word both overused and used incorrectly. "Tragedy" in the Shakespearean sense is disaster coming as a consequence of some tragic flaw or moral weakness. Macbeth and his quest for power. King Lear and his misinterpretation of Cordelia's love. And a tragedy is usually meaningful. The meaning in this, and here she nodded at the pictures. —The meaning in this seems to have escaped me. Car accident. That's all. No great dramatic gesture. No bizarre circumstance. An "accident". Such a harmless word. And what about you, Purdon? What's your "tragedy"?

—I'm afraid that in my case it was a moral weakness. Or really a moral flaw, if there's such a thing. I suffer from terrible timing. Doesn't sound like much but think about it. *When* you do something is as important, if not more so, than *how* you do it. Take for example when you're –

At that point the kettle began to shriek and we both smiled. She sat on the bed and prepared the tea and I pulled a chair from against the wall and set it before her. She offered the tin of cookies and although I had no appetite I accepted one and ate it very slowly. For several minutes there was silence between us as we sipped our tea and stared into our own universes.

—I suppose they'll take Michael to a hospital?

—Mmm. Yes. Observation, they call it. They watch you. You get watched.

—Poor man. You seem to know everyone here. What's his story?

—His lover. AIDS I think.

—Oh. Oh I suppose that means . . .

—What's your story, Purdon?

For a moment I feigned confusion at the change in topic, but then found myself talking.

—I went to Japan to teach English. Not just for that though. For the adventure. Oh yes, also for the women. I think a lot of guys go there for the women. To conquer the Asian woman. To occupy. To plant the Western flag. We have this idea that they're crazy about us there just because they worship America. North America. But we are confused, we North Americans. They don't worship us. They worship our culture, and that's entirely different. Still, Western men do have success there, perhaps for the novelty, perhaps because – though many of us can be sexist pigs about the whole thing – our expectations about the behaviour of Japanese women are in some ways less sexist than the Japanese culture's own expectations. Mind you I'm just trying to set the scene. Of what I was when I arrived and how I changed. I am a Western man and Kanako was a Japanese woman. Have you got a cigarette?

Lilian passed me one along with her lighter.

—She was one of my students. I still remember my first impression. Sadness. Even when she smiled, which was often, she still looked sad. She drained all the bluster of sexual conquest out of me. Three months later we were married.

I lit the cigarette and took a few puffs.

—I don't know if I was a lousy teacher or what, but she never gained more than a rudimentary understanding of English. So I started to learn Japanese. Most people were very amused when I started learning. I had a vendor applaud me when I successfully ordered and paid for some *gioza* entirely in Japanese. But then as my competence with the language increased the reactions changed from delighted encouragement to suspicion.

—What's Japan like?

—What's it like? It's like nothing else. It's industry and neon and chrome and gardens and temples and tradition. The urban region from Osaka to Kobe is a narrow band wedged between the ocean and the Rokko Mountains. On summer days those mountains look like an ink-wash backdrop. Cloud churning between their peaks. And then it descends, it navigates the channels of the rivers. It rolls over the city in a blanket of humidity. The city sidewalks are a sea of Asian faces where no one speaks English. They're taught in school but never get the opportunity to try it out in any practical way. People will approach the unsuspecting *gaijin* in the street or on trains to practise their English.

—It's amazing but I can with absolute clarity recall every step of the trip home from the school. I would come from Sannomiya, the downtown district of Kobe where the language school was located. My stop was Ashiya station on the Hanshin line, partway between Sannomiya and Osaka. It was easy to get on the wrong train – a special express, for instance – and go speeding through the station. I did it frequently. So did many of my students who had been riding the trains all their lives. But I didn't take the wrong train. Walk down the steps, drop my ticket into the gate. Pass the ticket machine and several vending machines selling coffee and tea and beer and cigarettes. Down a ramp past a bicycle parking area under the tracks. Then down onto the street and under the bridge beneath the tracks. South past the post office and over a pedestrian bridge that not only crosses a highway, but at the same time runs beneath an elevated highway, still under construction, as it was destroyed in the earthquake in 1995. Then a sidewalk beside the highways. Shielded in parts by plexiglass. Past rebuilt structures, a few empty lots where buildings once stood. Past a sukiyaki restaurant and a dog that barks at you every time you walk by. Past a vending machine selling Coca-Cola and Pocari Sweat. And right after that the entrance to our building. Recently rebuilt, made of grey concrete. I went up the stairs and unlocked the door and went inside.

The cigarette had burned down and I took a draw, then stubbed it out in the ashtray. Kanako didn't like it when I smoked.

—Would you like another? Lilian asked, holding the pack out.

—*Iie kekko desu. Watashi wa yamemashita.* No thanks. Where was I?

—You just entered the apartment.

—Yes. Not a large place. We were poor, Kanako and I. Her parents had died as a result of the earthquake and she had had to take a job in the office of an importer. That's why she was taking the classes. Once we were married a few people expected her to quit the job, but she was very untraditional and I doubt we could have afforded it if she had. So I opened the door to the apartment. I opened the door and entered the apartment.

I paused for a long time.

—Purdon, have you told this story before?

—Hmm? Yes. But only in Japanese. My parents back in Hamilton. They didn't even know about Kanako. They think I just got fed up with Japan. What really happened is that I lost my connection. Kanako. And when I lost her I lost Japan. I miss it. This. This place is foreign. Now I don't belong anywhere. A place is never home. An empty house? That can never be home. Kanako was home to me.

—The rest of this story is a tale of bad timing and a man cracking under pressure. If I had been home ten minutes sooner, if I had not stopped for a pastry with the other *gaijin* teachers who had collected in the lobby to celebrate Emily's birthday, I would have made it home in time to save her. She was still alive when I came in, lying on the futon. She had lost so much blood into the mattress that it had thickened. That was my first thought, can you believe it? How like a sponge the futon had become, how it looked a good five centimetres thicker. And then I felt for her pulse and it was there but very weak. Kanako's cellphone was on the table beside her. I don't know if she had made a call or tried to, but I fell apart. The new language abandoned me completely. I couldn't remember a word of Japanese, and the operator knew only one phrase. "So sorry sir. So sorry sir."

—I ran down the steps and into the street. Deserted. Then I saw the display case of plastic food outside the sukiyaki place, ducked under the *noren* and hurried inside. I had seen the old man who ran the place several times. He had always seemed intimidated when I walked past. I shouted at him in English, don't know what I said. He backed away from me with both hands up. Then the phrase flashed through my head. *Tasukete kudasai. Tasukete kudasai.* Please help me. Please help me. That's all I could say. Kanako was dying and I couldn't find the phrases to save her life. *Sugu ni tasuke o yonde kudasai.* Please get help quickly. *Kyukyusha onegaishimasu.* An ambulance, I beg of you. *Shukketsu shite imasu.* She is bleeding. *Ninshin shite imasu.* She is pregnant.

Lilian, who had settled sideways onto her pillow, bolted upright, her eyes wide. She started to speak, cut herself off, and instead leapt off the bed and dashed into the bathroom, where she locked the door. I sat there in the chair for a few minutes, looking around the room. I finally got up and went outside.

Shining from behind me, the sun cast itself onto a lone cloud that was hanging over the sea. The colour reddened even as I watched and the salt air felt refreshing on my face. I looked up and down the beach where footprints and bumps stood out in sharp relief, forming shadows that crept slowly down to the rolling surf.

Mrs. Kirby was approaching along the boardwalk. She looked uncertainly from me to Lilian's cabin. Just as I thought she was going to walk past, she stopped.

—Good evening, Purdon. Are you also heading to the dining room?

I felt suddenly very hungry and indicated that I thought that to be an excellent idea.

—Then perhaps I can accompany you there, she said, and hooked her arm through my own.

I socialized tenderly with Mrs. Kirby and a freckled girl named Bess and her suspicious friend Caroline and the nervous Randall. Anna came in with a pot of steaming corn on the cob followed by a procession of other dishes, and I ate ravenously and chatted with the others before getting up and retiring to my room. The sleepiness was coming on fast, exacerbated by my full belly, and as I approached the cabin I felt the panic of weakness overtake me. Within ten minutes I was in bed and within eleven I was asleep.

◗ I was awakened deep in the night by a staccato knocking on my door. At first I just lay there with the covers pulled up to my chin, hoping the intruder would go away. For no rational reason I thought it must be Anna demanding more money, perhaps she had miscalculated the cabin's fee, and it seem exceptionally rude that she would employ this tactic to retrieve it. But the knocking continued and I got up and put on my *yukata* and turned on the lamp and opened the door. It was Lilian.

—So sorry, Purdon. This is somewhat uncivilized of me to intrude, but I feel awful for abandoning you like that at the hardest point of your story.

—It's all right.

—No, it's not all right. May I come in?

I paused to indicate a negative, but she stood there waiting for my answer. I had acquired the Japanese habit of never saying no. She pushed past me and dragged a chair from against the wall and sat down in it. She was wearing a short silk bathrobe. She crossed her legs and lifted a pack of cigarettes from her pocket and lit one. She held the pack out and I waved it off and sat down on the bed.

—Did I say I'm sorry?

—You did.

—I really and truly am. I mean it Purdon. It was very rude. It was very insensitive. It's just that when you said that last part. When you said that last part.

—*Ninshin shite imasu.*

—Yes. You should have warned me that that was coming.

She tilted her head forward and began to cry. I watched her as the cigarette burned down. I went to the bathroom and got a glass and put some water in it and sat down again and took the cigarette from her and put it in the glass. She hadn't moved. Her face remained angled down and tears fell from her eyes onto her thigh. I reached out and put my finger under her chin and lifted her face but she kept her eyes turned away. When I kissed her she kept her lips taut until my tongue pushed between them and then hers emerged to greet it. I pulled her out of the chair and on top of me and she did not resist. Abruptly she was all there, kissing me hard in return, pressing against my body with hers. Kanako had bought me this *yukata*, and I had to let desire push the sense of betrayal from my mind as Lilian unbound the sash and parted it. I was naked underneath. She did not hesitate to take me in her hand. For a moment she seemed mesmerized as she stared at my cock in her palm, her face inches away. Then she pressed it to her warm cheek and caressed it gently as she unbuttoned her robe with the other hand and shook it off her shoulders. Remembering Kanako's tiny brown body made Lilian's skin seem terribly pale, her breasts almost too large. She was of average height and build, but naked she appeared to me to be hulking, a presence too much for my own body. Then she took me in her mouth, just once to make me wet, and moved her hips forward so she was poised over me. I looked at her face but she was oblivious of everything else about me. She watched as she lowered herself down, she felt terribly hot inside and let out a long moan as she closed around me. From then on she shut her eyes as she moved up and down with almost indifferent attention. It took me a long time to come and at one point this appeared to frustrate her. She sped up her rhythm to the point that I started to feel numb. I finally had to close my eyes and concentrate. When at last I started to orgasm Lilian pressed herself down on me hard and let out a loud, animal wail and collapsed on top of me, her hair obscuring my face. She seemed to be unconscious or asleep. Her breathing slowed and her body went limp. I lay there for perhaps half an hour, still inside her, as she began to snore lightly. I wanted to get up. I needed to use the bathroom.

Finally I started to turn sideways until her body slid off me. She didn't wake, and I pulled the *yukata* closed but couldn't find the sash so just held it over my body as I went into the bathroom. There I stripped down and stepped into a very hot shower where I soaped myself excessively from head to foot. Without a condom, I kept thinking. Without a condom.

When I returned to the bedroom she was still there, asleep. I sat on the bed and contemplated the situation. My travel alarm clock showed 4:40 AM and I was not tired. I put on some clothes and went out onto the beach. It was a clear night and stars saturated the entire sky except in the east, where a half moon was rising, radiating a stream of yellow light onto the sea. The wind was mild but very, very cold, perhaps a few degrees above freezing. Within minutes my eyes modulated to the darkness and I began to walk south along the waterline. The sound of the low tide drowned out my thoughts and I walked for a long time, until ahead I saw lights on a dock and fishermen preparing their nets for the day. I stopped and surveyed them from a distance and they did not see me. When at last the little trawler departed from the pier and headed towards the blushing horizon, I turned around and headed back. Colour proliferated over the sea, and I laboured along the sand, expecting the cottages and the white house to appear at any moment, but dunegrass and sand seemed to be the only features of the landscape. My legs were exhausted and I was cold and shivering and weak and could think only of my bed in Ashiya with warm Kanako beside me, her little arms clinging to my body, her black hair against my nose. I finally had to stop and rest. I sat on the sand facing the rising sun as it illuminated the steam of my breath.

When it had cleared the horizon and started to warm my face, I stood and continued north. I had not far to go. Another five minutes of walking brought the first of the cottages into view and within ten minutes I was before the door to my own. I waited there, listening, wondering if she was still inside. Should I knock before entering? I decided not to and entered. The light on the bedside table was on, but the tangled bed lay vacant. I felt relieved and insulted. I stripped off my clothes and pulled myself deep under the covers and lay there trembling for a long time before falling asleep.

156

◑ A knock again awakened me and when I went to the door it was Lilian and the sun was high in the sky and she gave no recognition of the events of the previous night.

—I was getting worried. Wondering if you wanted to go into town and have lunch.

I stared at her and she stared back. —Give me ten minutes.

I shaved and dressed and rapped on her door. She opened it immediately and we went to the parking area behind the house. We debated which car to take and finally decided on mine. I drove slowly north along the highway and was passed by several vehicles travelling at high speed. We saw a few derelict homes before coming into a fishing village. Many stores and buildings were boarded up and people stared at us as we emerged from the car. We began to head for a small seafood diner.

—Oh, wait. There's a chemist's there and I need a few things. I'll meet you at the diner?

I ordered tea for both of us but hers was cold by the time she arrived carrying a pair of plastic bags. She kissed me on the mouth and sat down across from me in the booth. I ordered more tea.

—Is it just me or does everyone seem dreadfully depressed here? she wondered as she gazed out the window.

—It's a depressed economy. They've run out of fish.

—Well, it certainly makes them dreary. They're worse than our lot back at the inn. Oh, I want to show you something.

She kept the bags beneath the table away from my view as she dug into one and then the other. She withdrew a lipstick and got out a compact and applied some.

—Well? What do you think?

—It's your colour.

—Not too peachy, is it?

—It's lovely.

—Then kiss me.

I leaned across the table and kissed her for several seconds, then sat back and wiped my lips with a napkin.

—You don't need to do that. It's the kind that doesn't kiss off.

Lilian fussed with the bags and finally tied a knot in the top of each and placed them beside her seat. Our server, a small girl in her early teens with dark rings under her eyes, arrived to take our orders. As I pointed to items on the ragged card that served as a menu she frowned and wrote them out in longhand. Two orders of fish and chips with coleslaw. Beer, but also ice water for me.

We spoke little while we ate, just looked out the window at the meagre traffic in the street. I paid and we returned to the car and drove holding hands across the gearshift. Lilian kept the bags at her feet and would not allow me to carry them.

We spent the afternoon driving about on the coastal highway, stopping a few times to examine scenery which to me appeared identical wherever we went, then returned to our beach. Lilian went back to her cabin to drop off the bags, was gone for half an hour before meeting me at the inn's parlour, where we played childhood card games like Fish and Snap and Concentration.

We spent the rest of the day that way, performing the domestic tasks of a couple on holiday. Tea in the late afternoon. A hand-in-hand promenade along the beach where I sought and found my footsteps from the night before. Later we retired to our rooms to prepare for dinner. She wore a pearl necklace and matching earrings and we sat beside each other with our legs pressed beneath the table and in conversation behaved as if we had been together for years. And at last when dessert arrived and we declined coffees, we went outside where Lilian smoked two cigarettes and we examined the stars.

—Well, I finally said.

—Yes. Let's go to bed.

She emerged from the bathroom wearing a long flannel nightgown. We made love with the lights out and no mention of condoms. I kept tracking a distant horror that skirted the horizon of my consciousness, ready to bank my way to unleash its weapons. But most of all I was puzzled. That this was so easy and natural and offered such comfort. Wondering how it could be wrong, yet knowing that it was.

For six days it went on like this. Drives along the coast. Picnics. Meals in various fishing villages. A jaunt into Halifax for some tourist purchases. Together in the parlour reading magazines and novels, playing Scrabble, writing letters. Watching television in my room. Making love like an old married couple. Wondering if she was faking her orgasms.

She brought a few of her photos to my cottage and set them up on my dresser. I thought about posting some of the tiny print club stickers of Kanako and me (and whatever *kawaii* cartoon character was featured at that particular *pricla* photobooth), but they seemed so small and pathetic beside Lilian's ornate frames.

Lilian had a curious habit of disappearing at dawn. I awoke every morning in an empty bed and I would not see her again until breakfast. I wondered if she was trying to avoid a scandal, yet she certainly made no secret out of our relationship, kissing me at the dining table, holding hands on the beach, adding affectations to her speech, calling me her "darling" or her "man". Playing house.

On our one-week anniversary I awoke and it was sunny again, with warm beams of sunlight penetrating the room. I woke up slowly and saw first the minute cracks in the ceiling and then turned over to gaze at the empty shape of the sheets where Lilian's body had lain. I leaned over to her pillow and smelled it and found her scent there. For a few minutes I breathed that scent, asking my instincts if it was good or bad, if it was something I could live with more or less permanently. The verdict was a cautious maybe.

The pictures were gone from the dresser. The bathroom light was on and the door open so I called, Lilian?

No reply came so I got up and looked inside. My things – razor, soap, toothbrush – were as I had left them. I brushed my teeth and looked at myself in the mirror. My eyes seemed clearer than they had in months. The veined patterns the whites had developed were diminished. I took a deep breath and noted that some of the tightness had lifted from my chest. My throat and especially my voicebox felt less constricted. I hummed a few notes and they emerged with soothing richness.

I put on my clothes and went outside. The day felt unusually warm. The sea was blue and sent a steady progression of waves rolling up the beach, while the light had a delicate quality to it, as if the sun were posted in the sky to set a mood rather than illuminate the planet.

I knocked gently on Lilian's door and waited quite some time before I decided that there would be no reply. The door was unlocked, and when I entered the first thing I noticed was that all the photographs were gone. I did not spend a long time looking through the room. I felt confident that she had forgotten nothing.

I went into the bathroom and splashed my face with cold water. The room was full of her scent. I sat down on the closed toilet. I needed to think, but about what? I sat there for ten or fifteen minutes and nothing of significance crossed my mind. Nothing at all. Just superficial thoughts. Events. No insights. No depth.

I put my chin in my hands. The garbage can sat before me. At the top lay the tube of lipstick she had bought the week before. I picked it up and opened it and looked at the waxy nub, sniffed it. There were other packages in the garbage and I leaned far forward, my chest resting on my thighs, and gazed at the contents. I retrieved a plastic wand, held it delicately between two fingers as I did not know its function. I placed it next to the lipstick on the edge of the bathtub and dug deeper into the garbage. There were some cartons to which I did not give close inspection as they appeared to be associated with feminine hygiene. At the bottom of the can was another plastic strip, identical to the first. I placed it adjacent to the other and restored the rubbish to the can, except for the lipstick, which I tucked into my shirt pocket. I got up from the toilet and looked into the medicine cabinet. Aside from a depleted Advil bubblepack it was empty.

I opened the doors beneath the sink and inside was a plastic bag on which I recognized the logo of the drugstore. In it were more cartons. I retrieved them one at a time and put them on the countertop. I dug the other two out of the garbage can and put them there too. I counted them. There were eight. Their function was spelled out clearly on eight cartons, eight times, and yet I still could not make sense of it. I went back to the plastic bag and found six sets of literature from the cartons, and six more of the plastic strips. I put them with the others on the edge of the bathtub and sat again on the toilet seat and examined them. They were each identical. Except for the first one I had encountered.

Whereas all showed two windows, one blank and the other displaying a red vertical stripe, the final also showed a blue stripe in the first window.

I felt a warmth on my cheeks and stood up to look in the mirror. Curious, I thought. I was crying. ◗

Trees Witnessed This

☾

T HE RENOVATED FARMHOUSE that had became my parents' new home hooted softly when the wind blew. This noise, generated by a churn of air between the living room and kitchen staircases, was a long, slow moan, like that of a ghost in pain: *Hooooooooooo.* I heard it the first time I stepped through the side door into the mud room. The carpet there was mushy with melting snow and ice. I continued through the little entrance room, past the overcoats and parkas dangling from wooden pegs, and entered a hot and fragrant kitchen.

My mother was standing at a countertopped island wearing a blue summer dress and a white apron, an arm submerged to the elbow in a can of flour. Her eyes were vacant as she stared at the stove and I watched her for several seconds, noting the augmenting curve of her back, the new grey in her hair. She was still a beautiful woman, tall, with an expression of complacent strength, a little squint in her eye as if she were heading into a strong wind but bearing it bravely.

I dropped back into the doorway, scuttled off my boots, and re-entered. The earthenware tile felt cool through my socks. —Well, I think you have all gone quietly insane, I announced. —This new house is miles from civilization. It's miles above the treeline!

—Rad! she called, consciousness returning to her face. —What are you saying? There are plenty of trees! You're just in time to help me. I dropped my ring in here. Her eyes narrowed with concentration as she burrowed for it. She withdrew, then peered inside. —Help me find it before Papa comes down.

I slunk off my black coat and let it fall in a heap behind me. —Better wash my hands first. I soaped and rinsed while she set the canister down and dragged a palm across her forehead, leaving a smudge beneath her grey bangs. She handed me a towel and squeezed my shoulder.

—How are you, son?

—Despite my concern for the state of your mental health, I'm excellent, I replied, drying my hands before plunging them into the deep can. Flour is strange stuff, liquid in a state of transformation, a kind of fine, dry slush. It is almost silent. I dug at it, squeezed it, slid it through my fingers, glancing up once with a grin of optimism but she was looking away, blue eyes clear, fingertips resting on the island. I scanned the kitchen. It was big, freshly rebuilt, with a cavernous sink, glass-doored cupboards, a giant commercial gas range, acres of counter space. She had always dreamed of counter space. We used to tease her about it; if she exclaimed, You know what I want? about something unrelated, the whole family chimed in with, Counter space! Many pots were clustered on the stovetop, a little industrial complex of billowing steam and quivering lids.

My father entered from the living room, a stocky man, balding, flushed, dressed in jeans and a green sweater. He truncated a yawn when he saw me.

—Hey, Rad. Just get in? he asked cordially. His voice was deeper than I remembered it. And I had never seen him wear jeans before.

—Hello . . . Dad, is it? I questioned, doing an exaggerated double-take. —No, obviously an impostor who doesn't that know my father has a tie surgically attached to his neck. How's retirement?

—Oh, rough, very rough. Just spent the last hour taking a vigorous nap. You know, I'm actually starting to think I was wrong about my earlier doubts. Leaving the city was the best idea of all. The best.

—George, Rad was complaining that there aren't enough trees here.

—There are plenty of trees, he replied, frowning and heading for the panoramic window as if to confirm that they stood where he had left them. —It's the trees I like most. They are so friendly. You know the thing about trees? They don't judge. That's what I like; not being judged all the time. Feels like I've been judged my whole life in one way or another. But look at me now. Who cares what people think? Who cares?

My father had never cared about what people thought. He had worked for Canadian National Railways for thirty-three years, buying locomotives to pull mile-long trains across the country. Because he was not a salesman he was free to cultivate opinions and express them to those around him, commonly people who were trying to sell him locomotives.

—What I meant was, it's like this place is above the treeline, I explained. —A joke about how far north you've moved. You know, a joke?

—A joke. Mmmm. Judith, where is your wedding ring? he said, grasping her hand and examining it as if searching for a lost digit.

—It's in the flour. Rad is finding it.

Their eyes turned expectantly to me just as my fingers encountered it. I felt the roughness of the inscription inside: "You are. Love George", a maxim that puzzled everyone. Debate had raged over its meaning, debate to which my father remained indifferent. Was it a declaration of her Zen-like contentment – something she had not possessed in her younger years? Or had he been unable to afford an adjective (*great, terrific, enthusiastic, vertebrate*)? The latter theory predominated; their relationship had germinated in poverty. I preferred the first hypothesis; it implied a minimalist philosophy to which my father had never subscribed. Yet Mum had never questioned the inscription and I enjoyed the speculation that it had transformed her in some way, made her calm and deep.

—Here's the fugitive, I said, holding it up and peering at her through the hole.

—How could it possibly slide off, Jude? You're always complaining that it's as tight as a noose, my father said as he took the band from me and pushed it onto her finger.

Then my sisters entered, all in their twenties, golden-haired, laughing, Mary shaking snow from her tresses, wiping her ear and cheek, Janet slapping a woollen mitten against her thigh, Audrey with a hand on each of them as she kicked off her boots. —You were too close. No one's allowed to throw from three feet away. —You need ducking lessons, I thought you saw it coming. —Don't let Mum know; she'll say something about losing an eye. A shriek as Janet stepped into a snow puddle, then another as she pushed Audrey into it. Mary's smiling eyes, ice-blue like Mum's, met mine, then fell to her coat sleeve where her hand emerged, clutching a snowball.

—Jan, let me help you with your coat, Mary said, tugging Janet's zipper down and slapping the snowball against the bare skin below Janet's throat. Janet screeched, her renowned temper coming to bear for an instant, and swung a mitten against Mary's cheek.

—A challenge! Mary cried, striking with her own mitten and hurling it to the floor. —I throw down my gage!

I began applauding, dispersing flour into the air.

—Dust! Rad, the flour! Mum lamented, raising her arms into the lazy cloud as if to collect it. I put my own arms up.

—We worship thee, oh great farinaceous cloud, I said, and Mary and Audrey joined me, their hands in the air, and we danced through it.

Mum began to herd us out of the kitchen. —Go get ready for dinner. Twenty-five minutes. Oh, where's Adrian? Rad, isn't your brother here yet?

◗ Dinner was the traditional feast, an extravagant collection of textures and colours and flavours served in stoneware pots, on silver-rimmed platters, in china bowls, and on porcelain servers. Mum prepared each dish in myriad fashions to appeal to every taste: potatoes mashed for my father and me, boiled for Mary, roasted for Jan and Audrey, baked for herself, Adrian, and his wife, Lily. Carrots cooked for Adrian, raw for everyone else. Sourdough bread, croissants, butter and margarine (regular and low-fat); corn on the cob, creamed, and from a can. Turkey and roast beef and fried tofu for me. Homemade applesauce, cranberry, thin and thick gravy.

—My Judith, master of compromise, my father announced as he headed a train of us, each carrying a dish or more to deliver like freight to the table.

With everything in place we stood each behind a chair, waiting for Mum to fetch the applesauce and declare the meal open. I glanced around the long dining room. The pre-dinner ebullience had faded and a querulous air filled the room. I hallucinated filaments of tension entering each person through the base of the spine, emerging through the shoulders and neck.

Lily had been replaced.

◑ Twenty minutes before the meal had commenced, Adrian and little Wayne began knocking on the bevelled glass of the front doors. Many minutes had passed before Janet walked by and heard the noise and directed them to the side entrance.

—They're coming around now, she said as she entered the kitchen.

—Did Lily bring a salad? my mother asked.

—I didn't see.

Adrian, Wayne, and a lanky woman with black hair entered next.

—What the hell's going on with the front door? Adrian demanded, struggling out of his parka.

—We're not using it in the winter, Mary said, tugging Mum's apronstring. —Right?

Mum replaced a lid on a pot and turned to answer, but froze when she saw the unfamiliar woman at Adrian's side.

Adrian's anger dissolved. —Hello Mum, he mumbled, face flushing. —This is Chantal. No one breathed.

When the moment passed there came an exaggerated expression of hospitality as welcoming voices drew the newcomers inside. Mary moved to take Chantal's silver fox fur but Adrian intervened, insisting on hanging it up himself. Wayne and I shook hands; he was more solemn than usual, and his eyes darted about nervously. Everyone nodded and smiled at Chantal and we led her to the living room, where she took a seat on the big chesterfield.

We regarded her like a rare gem; she exceeded six feet in height but her face and hands and feet were tiny. Sable hair fell below her waist and was streaked with silver. She smiled self-consciously and gripped the cushions with both hands.

Mary darted to the rocking chair opposite. —I'm Mary. Hmm. Let's see. Let's see. Fashion model? Chantal ignored the inquiry and searched for Adrian, who had remained in the kitchen.

—My name is Rad, I said, taking her little hand in my own and sitting beside her. —Did you have a good drive up?

She nodded, her gaze fixed on the kitchen door.

—Well, Mary said impatiently. —What do you do?

—I, she said, then cleared her throat. —I am a schoolteacher. She spoke deliberately, each word articulated, enunciating the French accent instead of defeating it. Janet and Audrey responded hastily, as if she had just described a bodily function.

167

—A schoolteacher, oh, that's . . .

—What grade are you . . . I mean what level do you . . .

—This year I am teaching grade four. I prefer kindergarten or grade one, but it is hard to have a choice. Can you tell me where is the toilet, the bathroom? she asked, standing, smoothing her dress.

—I'll show you, Mary said, leaping up and going to the staircase. Chantal hesitated, looked at each of us, and followed her up.

—Hmm, what street corner did she come from? Janet wondered, straightening the trinkets on the piano.

—Well, I guess that little interview was enough for her to prove her worth. I mean she's been in the building all of six minutes, I said, standing up and barking my shin on the coffee table.

—Looks like the table has chosen our side, Janet said with a smirk.

I limped into the kitchen. The scene was no better in there.

—She has as much a right as Lily! Adrian was insisting.

—What's the matter with you? my father demanded. He was standing by the door to the dining room with a stack of plates gripped in oven mitts, and he had suddenly acquired a sunburn.

—Janet kicked me, I moaned, rubbing my shin.

Mum stood before the fridge, staring into it as if searching for the reason she had opened it.

—Should I, you know, open the wine? So it can respire? I asked.

—Respire? she inquired, her distant gaze meeting mine. I reached past her into the fridge and plucked out a bottle of white wine. I set it on the tile countertop beside a bottle of red, then started knocking through the cupboards and drawers muttering, Corkscrew, corkscrew.

—Here, she said, selecting the third drawer down and retrieving a porcelain-handled corkscrew. I picked up the bottle of Merlot and drilled into the cork. With a pop it emerged; I lifted the bottle up to my lips and took a long drink.

My mother, for whom this display had been performed, was oblivious of all but the potatoes, which she began to pulverize with a small rake.

◗ Clink and clank of crisscrossing dishes, voices requesting *cooked* carrots or *baked* potatoes, scrape of chairs. No one said anything while meals developed from the palette of dishes. Beyond my father at the head of the table, the blue in the arched window thickened as if the house were sinking into a deep sea; reflected candles glinted on the glass like the eyes of bioluminescent fish.

I completed my plate with a dab of red cabbage and appreciated the completeness of the meal, the aroma of each dish, the perfect framing of napkin and silverware, placemat, china.

My father grunted to attract our attention, then raised his glass and proclaimed with some reluctance, A toast! He looked up and down the table, at the ceiling, and finally at the wine lapping the sides of his glass. —To the family, which at last, after failed coordination of Thanksgiving and Christmas, blesses our new house and makes it *home*.

A carillon of clinking, followed by the silence of drink. Even Wayne had a few sips of white. He had disappeared just before the meal, and Adrian had searched for ten minutes before finding him upstairs in my father's study, his nose in a book about the railway.

—Although it's not really the family, Mary said slowly, swaying her glass almost imperceptibly towards Chantal.

We attempted to disregard the comment. There had always been a sense of brittleness in Adrian and Lily's relationship. I recalled the day Adrian had introduced the lanky blonde to the family. That time we were celebrating my mother's fiftieth birthday and the venue was a restaurant in the city. —This is Lily, whom I'm going to marry. And we're also having a baby. That had been ten years ago.

We ate silently. Surprisingly, my father attempted to soothe the tension: Well, Rad, how's your little theatre group?

For once I didn't hear the sarcasm in his voice. I sat up in my chair and answered with enthusiasm, Oh, good. It's going very well. We're doing a medieval piece next, from the fifteenth century. A morality play about youth and corruption and getting saved. There are some new people in it, all with big families, of course.

Everyone continued to savour the food. I looked up and saw that Chantal had stopped eating and was staring at me. My eyebrows rose and she asked, Why do they, of course, have big families?

Now others at the table paused and looked at her. She flushed immediately so I began to speak rapidly. —That's a good question. Very good. You see, we are a small theatre company, not well known, I mean we advertise with posters and all but people just don't come out to see the independent plays, especially the stuff we do, you know, experimental, revolutionary, so the best way to get a big audience is to employ a cast and crew with large families and groups of friends who will come and fill the house.

—Is this a big family? she asked.

—No, Mary said. —The company uses Rad strictly for his talent. Do you have a big family, Chantal?

—Well, there is a brother and he has –

—Or does Adrian use you for your talent?

At first I thought my ears had popped or an important blood vessel had exploded in my head. Mary is a sweet girl and she is my sister. I love her. But she thrives on conflict.

—Does anyone want to hear about the new show? When we're on? Who's playing which parts?

Chantal was upset. She began tossing mashed potatoes onto her plate and they struck like wet snowballs. I looked around the table at my mother, who stared down at her plate, toying with the meal's remnants. Mary and Audrey commenced a blitz of sour looks at Chantal, while Jan had become fixated on the way candle-light refracted through the wine swirling in her glass. Adrian was eating, taking more helpings when his plate was depleted, chewing aggressively. Wayne had slipped so far in his chair that only his eyes appeared above the tabletop.

—Tension, I said, with the idea that by announcing it I could defeat it. No one spoke and the room's stress rose with each mouthful. My plate was empty. I toyed with a roll, buttered a small piece, swallowed it. I felt terribly full and the room wavered in a drowsy haze. Chantal gulped her wine and Adrian refilled her glass. Wayne's plate appeared untouched, but a nearby dish of pickles was clean. He slurped loudly from a Coke can.

—It's empty, Chantal said sharply.

—I'm going out for a cigarette, I announced, pushing my chair back.

—I'll come, Chantal said, and stood and crumpled her napkin and tossed it beside her plate. As we both exited I evaded the dumbfounded stare of my father.

● The night was cold but windless. Snow, blue and deep, rolled away to a low hill behind the barn where moonlight silhouetted the skeleton of a tree, made it look craggy and mean. We smoked for a long time without speaking.

—You are very kind to me, Chantal said. —And your sisters are not. I always have a problem with women. They do not like me.

I sucked on the cigarette. It was one of hers, a Marlboro which filled my lungs like oil and compounded the intoxication of wine and food.

—They're all mixed up. Mary hates being a secretary. She didn't finish nursing because it made her sick. And Audrey wants to marry a fellow who won't marry her. And Jan's dog is old and sick and there's nothing she can do.

—Aren't you mixed up?

—I'm the worst of all.

She turned her head to the sky and her throat was pale, almost blue like the snow. —The sky is so big and clear. When I was a little girl I lived on a farm. I almost forget that away from the city you can see so many stars and planets. Look at them! Like they are gems pressed into crystal globes surrounding the Earth. She spread her arms and through the quick clouds of her breath the stars expanded and merged. I stomped out my cigarette and put my arms around her and kissed her for a long time. She crushed me, pressing against me so firmly that I had to dig into the snow to keep from toppling backwards. I could taste the smoke and wine and food on her breath.

I pushed her away but she resisted, held on. I unwrapped her arms from my torso and backed away.

—Don't do that. Your brother is inside defending me even though he hates me, she whispered.

—I think it's the fur. I can't stand that fur. I must've caught a whiff of it, the smell, it's like death.

—But it is not real! she cried, laughing.

—What?

—It's *faux* fur. Look! She unbuttoned it and held it open like a flasher. I approached, looking. Inside the left breast was a tag, black and gold, *Fait de matériel artificiel.* She laughed again and enveloped me in the coat, kissing my cheeks and nose. —I've never heard of the name "Rad". It is part of a car, right?

—It's short for Radisson. It's a dumb name.

—It is! she cried.

I tried to glance over her shoulder at the door.

—Let me go, I hissed, and she liberated me.

—Let's run to that tree! she said, pointing at the lone maple in the field, then stepped into the deep snow. Three strides later she was on her back, laughing, gazing upwards.

I followed and fell beside her. —That's Jupiter, I said, pointing at a steady luminary near the zenith.

—Saturn, she replied. —Jupiter is there. You can see the moons.

—You can? No you can't.

—Look. The little specks around it. Callisto. Io. Ganymede. Europa.

I squinted but that only made it worse. —I'll have to trust you.

We lay there for ten minutes. The storm door opened and Adrian, coatless, came out.

—What are you doing out here? he asked, his voice uncertain.

—Stargazing, I said.

—Planetgazing, Chantal added.

—Mmmm. He crossed his arms and examined the sky, checking the validity of our claims. His head eclipsed the porchlight, illuminating the corona of curly black hair but casting his face in shadow. —I think we'll go, he announced.

—All right, she said, rising to a seating position, shaking out her hair and then standing up. She turned and offered me a hand but I waved it off. —Get your coat and your son, she ordered without turning back to him.

Adrian re-entered the house.

—You can phone me, she whispered.

—But I won't.

—But you can. She crouched then, lifted my right foot out of the snow, put her hand around my ankle, and slid it over my sock until she touched skin. Her hand was warm. She held on for five seconds. Then she let the foot drop into the snow, stood, and waded back to the porch. There she lit a cigarette. A minute later Adrian came out with Wayne.

—Should I say goodbye to your family? she asked.

—I did it for you. See you, Rad.

—Bye, Adrian, Wayne. Goodbye, Chantal. I did not look as they crunched away to their car. I heard the doors open and slam.

The engine churned for too long and finally kicked over. White light washed over me. My breath glowed in the headlamp beams. Gears clicked and shadows slid and drifted as the car backed away. The light swept over the house's red brick; the transmission clunked into drive. Then the car faded into the night. From inside the house I heard the clatter of dishes and the gush of running water.

I moved my head a little until I could see the lonely maple. I turned to the dark mound of the barn. I swivelled again to see the black figures of pines against a speckled sky. ◑

The Selenographer's Child

Fig 2.4 ~ *The lunascope's anterior manifold, with the primary retaining plate removed to reveal the gas diffusers. Brass pipes conduct liquid nitrogen through the upper baffle, where it is split into four streams by the Wislow centrifuge. The tertiary speculum is secured in a web of Dacron fibre, reducing vibration through antithesis field rigging. Wave harmonics are computed by the circuit cluster at top* (CIRCLED).

T HE MOON is a chalk-white clock in the sky, describing not hours and minutes but the phase of the month and the calendar of our bodies. Tonight she shines her brightest, so brilliantly that at first gaze Adso squints, feeling the cool light on his face. A moment later his eyes are stretched wide to collect every photon of the precious light. Detail is obscured by the blast of sunlight across her face. It is a shadowless noon on her surface. He presses an eye to the eyepiece and touches a knob. The primary oil lens shifts in its mount, refining the focus.

Adso hallucinates a noise, a tiny *snick*, when the first nibble begins. The perfect circle seems to shudder under this initial assault of darkness and Adso keys the shutter over the first plate. He suffers a moment of panic as the shadow advances faster than he expected. He has prepared only thirty-eight plates and imagines a computational error that will leave him with less than the necessary frame count. He draws away from the eyepiece and rolls the tall chair to his desk where the scrolls and charts are neatly stacked. He leafs through the charts, A6, A8, A9, draws out the statistic bars from A13 and transcribes them onto a fresh sheet of paper, the pencil thick and black on pale parchment. When the data have been entered, a fine pepper of graphite between the thick characters, he touches his thumbnail to a digit on the edge of the ivory sliderule. He adjusts the cursor, the red hairline rolling into position over engraved numbers. For many minutes the only sound in the observatory, aside from the constant *tick-tick* of the sidereal motor, is the hiss of the cursor over the markings, and the subsequent swill of pencil across vellum.

He compares the original computations with these recent ones, tapping the pencil to his chin, and nods.

He rolls back to the eyepiece. Above the cylindrical shell of the lunascope a giant clock, its hands fashioned from fine wires of bronze, advances towards the second marker. Adso touches a stud and the second plate shifts into place. His index finger grazes the focus knob and the oil lens thickens, hardening the moon's edges once again. The bite is bigger. Adso feels a distant ache. Moon sorrow, Jessa calls it. She is standing at the observatory's door with a blue poppy in a vase and two lead-crystal tumblers of hot brandy on a tray. As he turns away from the eyepiece she sees his frown and says it aloud.

—Moon sorrow.

At first it deepens his sadness, but then he is smiling. She sets the tray down on the table beside the couch and sits on the edge of the cushion, her hands resting in her lap atop the rich green fabric of her dress. He looks into her vast green eyes and sees himself reflected there. His smile sharpens. Then he is gone from her, his eyes seduced away by the eyepiece, and *click*, he exposes the next plate. The hands on the clock sweep silently over serifed digits handpainted on its ceramic face.

—It's a cookie, Jessa says as she looks up past the muzzle of the lunascope. —A great white cookie.

—Hush, he says without looking up, his finger grazing the knob that bends the oil lens.

—I managed to produce an orange sepal on this *Papaveraceae* specimen. See, she says, and holds up the flower.

—Hush! he demands.

She sips her brandy. She can hear his breath through his nose. *Click.* The bite deepens. *Click.* Adso continues to adjust the focus after each frame, the shutter-release cylinder moistening in his palm as he records the progress of the eclipse. *Click.* His ears twitch like a cat's at the tiny *plip* from behind him. He does not take his eye away from the eyepiece, still manipulating the lens, exposing the plates. A tear on wood.

Another tear falls, strikes, and he turns. When he sees her, head cocked forward, the pale shell of her hand over her eyes, his first thought is for the images, for the plates with their obscuring moon, his disappointment that the next thirty will be bereft of the sharpness of the first eight. He turns a dial and sets a switch to automate the image capture. *Click.* He rises from the chair and moves to the couch.

—Jessa, he whispers, and her tear-soaked eyes rise to his own.
—Jessa.

Click.

Her scent is of green grass and leaves. She bites his lip too hard, he wonders if there might be blood and he is amused at the thought that it doesn't matter that he is injured by her, as his hands roam beneath the weave of her sweater, feeling the smoothness of her hot flesh. The pinnacles of her nipples under his palms.

Click.

And now the lace of her panties is bunched in his palm, he is tugging them down from beneath the heavy fabric of her skirt, her legs kicking free. Opening beneath the clumsy wandering of his digits. Until they meet the wetness. The intake of her breath.

Click.

Her hands moving too quickly, fumbling over the fasteners. They find his skin, pressing here and caressing there.

Click.

Then the silent hot moment of her poised above him, the view of this potential action hidden beneath the warm rough of her skirt, and finally, he thinking how like two carefully oiled parts, each machined to precise compatibility, they slide together and become one, the second of penetration recorded as tiny spikes on the scrolls of the hygrometer and barometer.

◗ Jessa lies in a lunate curl on the sofa, her breath slow and even. Adso clucks his tongue during the rollout of the plates from the developer fluid. He balances a plate against his hip, light from the moon which has re-emerged from the Earth's shadow casting upon the emulsion. Imperfect focus.

Fig 3.9 ~ *The lunascope's upper lens muzzle, as seen through the ventral access port. The oil lens is fixed in a shock-protected liquid mount and is adjustable remotely through compression of argon gas (to prevent oleo-oxidization) delivered through titanium-wrap tubing.*

INSET: *Exploded view of focus cylinder showing Carpel rings which, when rotated, affect lens depth.*

● The cool pond of sleep boils away, leaving Adso panting and gasping in a crater of tangled sheets and blankets. The shells of his eyelids glow like heated metal, and when he opens them the walls and the ceiling are incandescent. Through the open curtains a ram of sunlight hammers against him. He tries to rise from the bed, but his arms and legs are weak and leaden and he slowly slumps back against the burning pillow. His ears are full of rolling liquid, as if the fluid of his head is aboil, and he retreats into a frantic slumber.

In the dream the light is moon-cool, he is standing in a field of grass. The wind is a river, it hisses through the blades, the moon floats above telegraph lines and scraps of cloud twist past her face, giving the illusion that she is moving across the sky in contrary motion, from west to east. But then he sees that she is moving against the wires too, and is getting smaller, retreating. He reaches up and feels her cheek, it is rough like unfired clay, and the powder of it falls into his eyes, he must blink them clear. He looks away to the ground, to the moonlit grass that moves and hisses like some billion-footed insect inverted against the traction of the sky, and when his vision has cleared the moon is half-size, she has subsided this much, moving away from the Earth, from him. Suddenly he is on the moon, his feet submerged in her liquid dust, the pulverized detritus of an eternity of crashed satellites. He glances up and sees the blue-green crystal of the Earth above him and himself standing on it, looking up – at himself – on the moon. His hands are stretched above his head, they are straining for his own self which is diminishing. Diminishing.

He contracts on the bed, held in place by her hand on his forehead, he presses against her and struggles because it is she who has chased the moon and himself away, but she is strong and she holds him in place until he ceases his resistance, panting.

—My moon, he whispers to her.

—You have a fever. I will get you something.

—No, he moans, rising against her. —No, leave me alone. But she does not.

Fig 8.7 ~ *Lunascope sidereal motor, disassembled for servicing. Clockwork mechanism is pictured at* UPPER RIGHT, *with breach in the cesium pendulum container open to show detector array. Dynamos are powered by Lynchfield capacitors (set of four, at* LEFT) *which are charged in alternating sequence, phasing manipulated by a brass camshaft,* BELOW.

◑ Adso streams numbers down his charts, lunar subtends, lunation quotients, uranometric conjectures, having not yet looked tonight at the object of his calculations as she hasn't drifted into view of the great slot above the lunascope's barrel. She is twenty-one hours past full.

He has stopped writing, stopped computing, is staring into the candle that suddenly flickers in the rippling fabric of wind that tumbles through that opening, swirls through the observatory like an invisible curtain. His forehead glistens with sweat. The fever continues to ride through his bloodstream like liquid metal, his throat is dry, and as he hunches deeper into the fabric of his cloak, he thinks about the dream, which is vivid in his mind, the images, his breaking heart at seeing his own self cut adrift in the sky.

Setting down his teacup he moves to the door and opens it, stands looking out at the field, at the grass higher than his head bobbing and shifting in the skirts of the wind, the chill warns him but he pushes on and walks out, hearing the chiff and chatter of grass around his body, his eyes lowered to the earth before his feet. He steps out from the shadow of the greenhouse and the dome of the observatory and finds the moonlight upon him, as cool as the night air, and thinks with relief that he has made a mistake in his notion of some lunar ailment, and here he stops and already smiling gazes up at her, this sphere now riding out towards Earth's flanks, turning her darkened cheek to him, and when he sees her he knows that something is wrong, it is impossible to determine what, perhaps the colour is a dozen angstroms off, or maybe her shape isn't precisely what it should be at this moment after a full moon and eclipse, but in his stomach he feels the pang, the roll of nausea, and he sinks into the grass. The crickets, unperturbed by his collapse, continue singing to each other and the night.

—Adso? Jessa's voice carries softly out of the open door and into the giant grass and moonlight. Adso does not look up, and for a moment Jessa thinks that he is prostrating himself before the sky, that he is praying. And she is correct.

She moves slowly to him through the stalks that whisper around her about the broken man in their midst. And she gazes up at the moon and can see nothing wrong, but knows by the shape of Adso's sorrow, by the arch of his back which now she presses with her hands, that there is something terribly wrong. She can feel his fever through the cloak and she slides her hands past his shoulders, falls into him with her face and breasts and stomach, tries to wrap her tiny form around his wearied bulk, wanting to take him inside her entirely, into the heat of her body and the bath of her womb.

Then he rises, Jessa still clinging to his back like a little monkey, and returns to the observatory, and there shuts down the equipment, closes switches and subtracts power from vacuum tubes, and carries her out, turning off the lights, leaving tiny eyes of orange neon scattered through the space, of machines left in standby for his return. It will be many days.

He climbs the stairs to their bedroom, and shuts out the light of the poisoned moon with opaque blinds and curtains of dense silk, and falls slowly forward into the vast bed with its frame of polished copper, and once he is down Jessa skitters from his back and undresses him and then brings the warmth of quilts and comforters and soft pillows to his body, and finally her naked skin, around which he closes his fevered heat.

Fig 11.2 ~ *Analysis engine,* EXTREME DETAIL. *Silicon fabric weavework overlaid with pyrite gauze, suspended in a mercury syrup which is baked at 1100 degrees centigrade for nineteen hours, then compressed into wafers. Scintocks are soldered with quantum wire made from a superconducting yttrium-doped compound.*

◗ The sickness lasts six more days, until the moon is cleft in half, dark and light hemispheres in equal measure. He has not watched her progress, has always turned down the blinds to obscure her. He lies awake for most of the sixth night and at a breath before dawn, when he knows that she lies in the dense blue cushion of the western horizon, when the opposite side of the sky glows like forged gold, he ventures out again into the grass, gulping cool dawn air into his convalescing body, and looks. The theory he has been harbouring is crushed. He is well, but the moon is worse.

Across the continent there are a dozen moon women and men like himself. That day he intends to telephone each and ask about their theories of the diminishing satellite. The first is his dearest friend, Disa, a thousand kilometres away. Disa is delighted to hear from his colleague and friend, and they plough through the formalities until Adso can ask him,

—Disa. What of the moon?

—There is much of it, Adso. You and I both know that.

—But why is our beloved ill?

Disa pauses as if he thinks this is some sort of riddle. Adso's frustration mounts.

—Have you not been looking at the moon, my friend? he demands.

—So long as we do not live beneath a dome of perpetual smoke, while my eyes remain unplucked from my head, and as long as she calls the sky her home, I will always gaze upon her.

—But Disa, if you have seen her then her illness should be obvious. Do you not detect her sallow complexion? Can you not perceive the corruption of her shape?

From the opposite end of the phone there is silence. Then:

—Adso, this illness. Are you sure it does not persist? That the impurity you detect is not a film or custard of this sickness that glazes the glass of your eyeballs?

Adso attempts to reply, but fury constricts his throat, and instead he hurls the phone into its cradle. He snatches it up again and dials another number, that of Belina. But she also responds with surprise and ridicule, and it is not long before Adso is phoning Bettl. But Bettl has already heard from Disa, and refuses to allow the discussion to begin. And by the time Adso has moved to Creedon, all the selenographers – petty, gossiping fools – know of his observations, and have dismissed them as hoax or madness.

183

Fig 14.9 ~ *The moon, twenty-four days, seventeen hours, fifty minutes old. Note the increased darkness of Mare Copernicus, plus the visual distortion of the* UPPER PORTION *of the arc, suggesting compression or diminution of mass at the lunar core. Image has been enhanced through quantum photonic sampling.*

◗ Seven days later the moon fades behind her own shadow. Adso thinks with remorse as he observes the place where he knows she is hiding that he will never see a new moon, that a new moon is invisible, like a babe in a womb. Each day following offers her slow emergence from the uterus of the heavens, but in growing visible she becomes the waxing moon, and is no longer new.

He watches this birth cycle with trepidation. The exact moment of her appearance is computed, and upon this spot in the sky he has trained the lunascope. A plate lies in wait in the dark cavity beneath the camera's shutter. Thirty-one others lie behind it, ready to roll into place. Hour and minute hands shuttle across the face of the ceramic clock. Adso sits upright in the chair, a freshly-sharpened pencil in his grip.

The moment arrives.

A sliver of light opens up, an incision in the darkness.

Click.

A prism dissects the image, spreading these viscera of light into a thick rainbow.

Click.

Numbers reveal the light's chemistry. The displays shudder and shift as the energy intensifies. Adso records these numbers. Within moments he knows that they are amiss. A mortified wail escapes his lips and he slumps forward onto the desk. Jessa, who has been waiting outside, hears it and knows, moves away from the door and back to the greenhouse, to her virescent roses and sable irises. She takes up her speculum and begins to harvest grains of pollen from the anther of an alabaster orchid, the delicate work sabotaged by her tears.

As the month progresses and the moon broadens, Adso carefully records the results. He sends them to his colleagues, who do not respond. When the moon is full he watches her with his naked eyes and knows that the numbers, collected by the impassive machines, do not lie. The moon is plagued. And getting worse. Why can no one see it?

The third moon is more yellow than the second, and her shape has compressed into a shimmering oval. By the fourth month the yellow is tinted by green, not a fresh foliage green of verdant hills, but rather the green of putrefaction.

Adso continues to collect data, recording them on long strips of paper, on film plates, in his head. And he is writing about the changes too, an essay with references to the past and present moon, a paper of conviction and clarity that will prove to his colleagues, who should all know better, that the moon is deliriously ill and – according to his observations – will be dead within five months. Unfortunately, the Lunar Congress does not meet until the final night of this predicted tragedy. Adso inhales the thick botanical air of the greenhouse with his hands dangling loosely at his sides, as Jessa incises the pedicel of a carnation, one hand resting on the robust curve of her belly. She asks, What could the delegates do to save her?

—Nothing. Nothing, he sighs. —But it demands acknowledgement. Acknowledgement and tribute, before she is gone for all eternity.

The fifth moon is half as bright as her predecessor. The sixth moon is half as bright again. Adso searches desperately for comfort, almost finds it in the idea that if each successive moon is only half as bright as the one before her, then she will never truly fade from the sky. He also knows, however, that were this hypothesis true, it would mean that soon she would be invisible without the most sensitive of instruments, wafers of silicon as thin as photons, examining the same spot of sky throughout the night and on nights following, until all the observation time could be compiled into one faint photograph. For his own eyes, she would be dead.

He forges ahead with his paper, convinced perhaps that this labour will serve as penance for whatever sin has sentenced her to this fate.

Jessa's condition requires more effort from him. The household chores, once shared between them, have become virtually a full-time effort, and he cannot help but feel contempt for her, especially when she continues the delicate engineering of her plants. She weeps too, for his rage and sorrow, for the gulf that continues to widen between them. But she is strong, and she accepts this.

The next moon is not only dimmer, but smaller, with an anomalous shape. On some nights she is oval, on others her edges are indistinct, sometimes ragged. Her colour is a deep violet, and Adso thinks as he looks up at her of a bruise in the sky, a trauma that can never heal.

Fig 23.7 ~ *Northwestern sky, photographed from 55°51'22" N at 102°66'57" w, 24 September, 21:25:33z, 18° above ecliptic. The full moon is the faint patch at* UPPER RIGHT, CIRCLED.

◗ Before the emergence of the following moon, Adso goes to Jessa in the greenhouse, from where she rarely emerges now.

—Adso, she whispers when she sees his grim face.

—Jessa. Oh, Jessa, I don't want to be alone. Don't let me be alone.

—You are not, my love. And she strokes his hair, which has thinned and become more grey in the past month.

—Will you come with me to the observatory? This may be her last revelation.

—I will come, she whispers, and he helps her to her feet.

They sit one against another on the couch beneath the lunascope. Adso looks at the sky and Jessa watches the side of his upturned face. She wants to touch it but does not, is moved by the childlike expectation on his features. Still hopeful. He does not look at her, remains focused on the sky, his eyes growing wider by the minute. He consults the clock, looks up, returns to the clock. Then he looks at the night sky. A faint smudge of deep blue rises into view. He slowly lowers his head into Jessa's lap. She looks too. The moon appears to her as she has always looked. Jessa presses her hands to his head, feeling hot tears soaking through her skirt.

A month later Adso is setting a table in the observatory with small plates and wine glasses. There are twelve places, each with a name card. Jessa watches him from the couch. She is as big as a caboose. Adso opens bottles of wine, places a plate stacked with a pyramid of cheese.

Disa and Creedon are the first to arrive. When Adso opens the door they both stare at his expression, his crushed features, the wires of grey in his hair, and then look at one another. They follow Jessa to the table in the observatory as more of the selenographers arrive, Belina and Bettl and Gyren and Fadleda. The good cheer they were hoping to share around the table is darkened by Adso's sorrow. When they have all assembled, the moon's appearance is minutes away. Adso fills the wineglasses, stands at the head of the table, and speaks.

—Tonight, my friends, our lives are over. You have denied my observations. You have ignored my warnings. But on this night we will see the last of the moon. In a few moments the full moon will rise into view of the lunascope. In something less than a minute after that, she will disappear.

He moves to the eyepiece, touches a stud, and a view of the black sky, dotted with stars, appears on a broad screen he has patched to the lunascope. He moves in front of the screen before continuing.

—These are what my calculations have told me. This is what you deny. Tonight, sadly, I will prove that it's true. That soon we will live in a world without a moon. This world that has always had one. I do not know where she has gone, or why. But I wish to toast her one last time before this farewell.

Adso raises his glass. The selenographers stare at him, stunned, but he is not looking at them, he has turned to stare at the screen. A few pick up their glasses and look to the screen as well. Jessa, her glass with just a splash of wine painting the bottom, looks intently between the display and her husband.

A dim glow fills the bottom left. It grows slowly, thickening, spreading towards the opposite corner. Then a ragged edge comes into view, it is barely visible, a few tones lighter than the sky behind it. It slides into full frame, this dark broken object, this traumatized satellite that is little more now than a crumbling out-line of darkness. It continues to drift towards the upper right cor-ner of the screen. Adso's breath is laboured, as if he is trying to push it there, as if her success in touching the screen's edge will prove him wrong. It is what he wants, what he hopes for with all his heart.

And suddenly, she is gone. The screen is black. The party, as a collective, gasps. Adso inhales, the words on his lips are "you see," but they never emerge, they are displaced by a shriek from Jessa's lips. Adso rushes to her, helps her from her chair to the couch, where she sprawls.

—Time, she whispers.

There is a moment of panic as the selenographers scramble up from the table, rush about in a frenzy of indecision, but it is Bettl, who is now a selenographer but was once a midwife, who comes to the rescue. As the night rolls on, oblivious to the death and the life commuting beneath it, the death of a satellite and the life emerging with the stench of blood and viscera and the shrieking that for hours fills the inverted bowl of the inside of the observatory, most of the selenographers depart, but Disa stays with his friend Adso, who holds Jessa's hand, who urges her on and for the first time in many months thinks not of the moon, which is now dead, surely dead, but of his wife, who has cared for him and loved him always. He holds her little digits in his fingers and coos in her ear, as the sweat streams from her body and her belly contracts like a fist. Bettl's voice is sharp and clear as she shouts, Push! Push!, and Adso's teeth ache with the effort of trying to help with the birth, the tendons of his neck stand out as Jessa's do, she is blind to him, blind to all but the pain, the unbearable pressure within her that is seeking escape.

And just when Adso thinks that Jessa can take no more, when he feels her body resigning from the tremendous effort, there is a sudden gush, Bettl's face illuminates with victory, and the observatory is filled with a cresting wail. A moment later Bettl holds up the screaming prize, a tiny girl slick with slime and blood, eyes clenched shut and hands balled into fists the size of marbles, mouth wide to release the plaintive voice. Bettl clutches the child to her body, moves around to Jessa's side where Jessa, Adso, and Disa look down at the wriggling babe.

Bettl moves a sponge over her face and head, clearing away the mucus. And where the skin is clear, Adso detects a beautiful light. The skin seems to incandesce, he steps back because he cannot believe it, but where the muck is cleared away this child seems to glow from within. He recognizes the light immediately, it is moonlight, the purest light on earth, light he thought he would never again behold. Light he thought dead. Radiant child. She shines brilliantly.

—Like the moon, he whispers.

—The what? Disa asks, and for a moment Adso's forehead wrinkles like the skin of the bawling child.

—I'm not sure, he says. —But I don't think it's important.

Jessa at last looks away from the baby, past the little head, and catches the look in her husband's eyes. A light luminesces there, a unique refulgence, only she thinks that she has seen it reflected in his eyes a thousand times before. ◗

Marshmallows and Jawbreakers

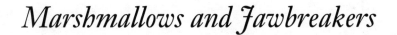

THE BUS IS HOT and naturally the fuckin window is closed and in front of the window is a old lady who looks like she would never ever let me open it so I just stand with all the other hot people around me and read my book, it's *A Passage to India* which takes place in India where it's hot too, maybe hotter'n here, who knows, so I just keep readin and sweatin until I can't fuckin take it any more and pull the dinger and the bus stops and I get out and guess what: it's even hotter outside and now I have to walk through this heat along a sidewalk maybe one million and if not then one *billion* degrees but I am still readin and walkin and likin the readin so who cares? When you're hot then you just gotta think that one day you'll be cold, one day in a few months if you live in Canada, so enjoy cookin yer butt off cause in six months or less (probably less) you'll be freezin it off instead. In fact, I think I got a sayin now, it's this: "In Canada you are at most five months from either freezin or boilin." Say it to people a lot; just member it was Kyle who made it up.

Crossin the parkin lot of Highland Farms, which was just paved and is like walkin on a griddle, I hear a whoop and look up from the book and the heat in India to the heat in Canada and there's Blister comin outta the store and in his hand he's got a bag of just one thing, marshmallows, I hate the fuckin things but I think Blister is actually addicted to that crap so I try not to look at it cause I'm gonna say somethin about those fake little pillows made in some chemical factory.

—Hey Kyle, what shit you readin now?

—Hey Blister, what shit you eatin now? I says, forgettin that I wasn't gonna say nothin about it.

—These are for Tommy's thing.

—Thing? What thing?

—On the creek tonight. Member? He wanted to be a party guru for once. Member how he was all "Everybody makes parties but me. I don't want to be a goin-to-party guy all the time, I want to make a party and then everybody will say 'great fuckin party, Tommy.'" I dunno, maybe it's just a way to try and get laid or something. You know Tommy's never been fucked, right?

—Right, I says, but feel my face goin hot because the thing that's true about Tommy is also true about *moi*. What's the big deal about it? But it is a big deal, that's why my face is red.

—You okay, bud?

—Yeh, just this heat ya know. So are you gonna roast those at the party?

—They taste great right after one of these, and then Blister pulls outta his satchel a plastic bag full of red balls about a centimetre across each, shiny. —Jawbreakers.

—Fuck Blister, I think your teeth must be like plaster with all the sugar you eat. I mean, I'd have diabetes by now if I was like you.

—Well you ain't, and neither is nobody, and that's the truth of the world. Anyway, these ain't sweet, they're hot and in the middle a surprise.

—What, it squirts or somethin?

—Naw. Scary surprise.

—What, some gum?

—Nope, no gum.

—Does it make your mouth blue?

—No. It don't make your mouth blue.

—Does it make a popping feeling?

—Look Kyle, you just gotta eat one to find out. Later. Then you'll want one of these, and he holds up the marshmallows.

—Yeh, and then it'll rain blueberries. I'd rather stick one up my ass.

—You might do that too. Stand in a rain of blueberries stickin marshmallows up your butt.

—So that party's tonight. Where again? Fuck, am I even invited?

—Course. Unless you've given up your membership in the clan of "everybody". You think Tommy knows enough people that he could leave someone out? He looks at his watch. —It starts in like an hour. And it might be tricky to find. Come on, it's down from your house, I'll walk with ya.

Don't get me wrong, Blister is a swell guy, but I just wasn't in the mood to be footin it home with him. Mostly I just wanted to read the book. But what can ya do?

So we start walkin and not much to say so then I'm glad when somebody else shows, it's Nils and he's just comin outta his house and down the walk with a monster bag of chips and a tubba dip too.

—Hey Nils, good to see ya. What's with the chips'n dip?

—For Tommy's party. Hey Blist, you get the jawbreakers?

—Got em right here in my satchel. Plus some mallows of the marsh variety.

—Good stuff. Hey, the party's near Kyle's house, we'll walk down together.

—What the fuck does everyone want with marshmallows'n jawbreakers? How bout some beer?

—Tommy's gonna bring the beer. He just wanted us all to bring somethin for with it.

—Well I ain't got shit. What am I gonna bring?

—Fuck if I know, Nils says. —Maybe your ma's got something. He thinks for a sec, then says, Hey, maybe she could make some of those tuna sandwiches. They're the best. Say, Blist, you ever have one of Kyle's ma's tuna sandwiches?

—Naw.

—You should. They're better than gettin stabbed in the head. Your mum could be Mrs. Tuna Sandwich if she wanted.

—Yeh, if she married Mr. Tuna Sandwich. Hey, it's Johnny.

And it's true, there's Johnny on his skateboard pumpin his leg for speed, zippin down the street towards us with a big plastic can hooked in one hand. He pulls up beside us and nearly falls off the board.

—How do ya stop these goddamn things anyway? he says, then grins. —Hey, everybody ready for Tommy's lame party. Blist, you get the jawbreakers?

—Got em!

—What's in that thing? I ask, pointin to the plastic drum.

—Just a load of cucumber soup I made. Hey, stop snickerin, this is some good shit! Figure it's good cause it's hot out. For the party. Hey Kyle, what you got?

—His mum's makin those great tuna sandwiches.

—Awesome! Best tuna sandwiches on the planet.

We move again then start down my street and see Andy up ahead, he's got a big paper bag fulla somethin.

—Yo Andy! Blister calls, and Andy turns.

—Hey, fellas! I thought I was the only guy goin to this thing.

—Hey Andy, what you got in the bag?

—Dogs and buns. Figure we could do em on the fire. You think?

—Great idea, Johnny says. Go great with my soup. And Kyle's mum's tuna sandwiches.

—Tuna sandwiches? Super!

I'm wonderin what the fuck is goin on, feel completely clued out about tuna sandwiches and jawbreakers and Tommy's a virgin and who the hell is comin to the party on the beach, maybe I'm sick from the heat or maybe I'm just right outta the loop all of a sudden, not sure why or when it happened, maybe while I was in India, in my book in India and the world just kept turnin and flowin without me. What the hell, here we are at my house and the procession of me and my friends is wanderin up the walk to the door.

—Hiya Mrs. Klee, everybody goes, and she hi's everyone back and then Johnny's askin about how the tunafish sandwiches for Tommy's party are goin.

—Tuna sandwiches? I've never made a tuna sandwich in my life! And crap, those guys are all laughin and har-harrin me, when exactly did I fall outta the loop? So now I don't even have the fictional amazing super tuna sandwiches my fictional mum, Mrs. Tuna Sandwich, would make for the party.

—By the way, she says, Alan called. He said to call him back soon, it's important.

—Yeh, he wants to tell me about how he wishes he had his fat mouth full of your tuna sandwiches, I say, and there's more har-har and I start to laugh too cause those guys really know how to fuck someone up. Then I think they must also be gaggin me about Tommy's party but then I look how they're all carryin somethin and think that no, can't be, cause pranks always gotta be free for these poor losers and they spent some cash on all that shit. So the party's real but I'm screwed cause I don't have nothin to bring. Maybe I won't even go.

—I ain't goin, I say, and start up the stairs to my room and they're all like, come on, Kyle, you gotta go, it won't be nothin without you there.

—Yeh Kyle, Johnny says. —You're principal. You're the chief and the man and I haven't never been to a party you weren't at and had a good time. So fuck Tommy and come to the party.

—Okay, enough with your dirty mouths, Mum says. —Go to your party, go go go!

So I run up to my room and flip the book onto the bed and put on a clean T-shirt cause this one's a stinkbomb from the bus and the walkin, and off we go.

Nobody's really sure where it is, not at his house because Tommy's dad is a freakin butt weasel (or so Tommy says) so he's found some special spot that everyone knows where it is and the place each guy knows about is a different place.

One thing they do agree on is that you gotta cross the bridge and step over the guardrail and head down into the valley of mosquitoes and poison ivy, now I find out, when I coulda got some bug spray before goin down there, thanks so much fellas! So we descend the slope and I'm beatin back the bugs cause it seems whenever we go anywhere that there's insects I'm the one who gets em all.

—Hey man, here's what you do for everybody instead of bringin food to Tommy's party, Johnny says through a fat grin. —You're the buglight.

—Yeh, says Blister. —Everybody, new nickname for Kyle. Buglight. Hey, Buglight! Buglight!

—Hey, here comes Buglight. Hey everyone, here comes Buglight! Johnny calls.

We get down to the path beside the creek. It's about seven now and the sun is gone which means the bugs are worse than ever for poor ol Buglight. I look up at the bridge, it's a big three-lane jobber, you can hear the thunder of cars'n trucks boomin over it and into the ravine. I've never noticed what a monster it is, big fat concrete pillars among the trees. Highland Creek is five metres wide here, and for the first time I wonder why it's a creek and not a river. I mean, what's the diff? Are there books, or maybe specialists, who go, "This one's a river. But that one's a creek." I think of the Ganges River in India, it's in the book. It's got crocs in it and sometimes dead bodies float down it. I think this creek, which is a river, has some fish in it, I've seen em before, big thick fish with bubbles of guck on their faces, like scars or some kind of chemical burns, man this world is fucked up that puts poison in the water. What could be more important than water?

Now we're standin here and I'm swattin the bugs because no one can agree which way we go, under the bridge and up north up the creek or the other way around towards the lake. I don't even know one thing about where the party is so I have nothin to contribute and just stand there whackin and cursin.

—Okay, can we flip a coin or somethin? I finally yell.

—Maybe you have a opinion on the matter, Buglight, Blister says, pullin on a cig.

—My opinion is let's go the fuck one way or go the fuck the other way and get outta this swarm of mosquitoes. There's a sandbar about half a klik that way which is probably the only place here for a party.

—Not that you could expect Tommy to pick the best place, Blister says and everyone cackles.

Nils whacks a mosquito on my back and hands me a cig. —Keeps the bugs off, he says, lightin it for me. I suck on it and spit the smoke around me, suck and spit, and guess what, it kinda works. Nils is overdue for some kind words. Good ol Nils.

So we head south, away from the bridge and movin along the narrow path through the weeds and shit and I know, I just know that every other plant is poison ivy and I am goin to be so itchy tomorrow you'll need to throw me in a pit full of epileptic porcupines before I feel better.

The path begins to widen and then suddenly we're out on that sandbar and there's Tommy all right, on his knees in the sand in front of a huge pile of wood, he's flickin a lighter against a giant thick log tryin to get the thing goin.

—Hey Tommy, fart on that thing, it's faster, Johnny says, and Tom turns around. I see his face and know that he's stressed, man, this is like the most important goddamn thing in his life and here it is already gettin screwed up.

—Hey guys, he says, sittin back in the sand. —Got a cigarette somebody? Nils gives him one and he uses the lighter to get it goin, and he mutters with it in his mouth, At least this thing burns.

—Tommy, let me explain to you the concept of kindling, Blister says, and starts haulin branches and twigs outta the woods.

—What you bring? Tommy asks me, and I already feel my face goin hot again.

—He brought hisself, Johnny says. He's a buglight.

—What, you mean so bugs can see what they're doin?

—Duh! Tommy, you must have gone to idiot school because that kind of stupidity can only come with years of trainin.

—Everybody was supposed to bring a thing. I got like fifty bottles of beer in the creek there gettin all cool and everybody is supposed to have brung somethin to eat.

—Lay off, Tom. Kyle's presence brings more to a party than any caterer could do. So lay off before he leaves and this party is the disaster you're afraid it's already become.

—Hiya Kyle.

I look past Tommy and comin outta the forest with some wood in her arms is Tommy's sister Katrina, who I ain't seen in about two years and it's obvious to me that she's spent that two years just gettin prettier and prettier.

Then a mosquito lands on the back of my head and starts to bite me so like a goof I'm standin there in front of Katrina bustin myself on the skull.

—Sorry Kat. I'm a buglight.

—Me too, she says, and shoos away some of her own gang of mosquitoes.

—Kyle's already got the name Buglight so you gotta come up with somethin else, Johnny says, now suckin on a beer.

Suddenly there's the whiff of woodsmoke and Blister's standin beside a fire that is just startin to take hold.

Now outta the woods comes about six other girls all with pieces of wood. Kat starts to help them so I go over too and we bring it over to the fire, and Kat starts introducin them all as if I can remember while doin all this who is who, there's Joanne and Kayla and Marci and Lisa and Jessica, those are just the names, on whose head each one belongs I have no idea, I think Jessica is a skinny girl with red hair who mostly stands with her arms crossed, bumpin up and down on the balls of her feet. Oh, and Joanne's a big girl with a loud laugh. I think she's just Johnny's type and go to tell him but he's already boogle-eyed and watchin every move she makes, and then he goes over and starts to be Mr. Charming with his "Hey can I help you with that, Miss?" and it sounds like the purest crap and I can't believe that she's gigglin and eatin it all up.

Blister has fine-tuned the fire into a beautiful tower of burnin wood, as high as my chin and sendin light up to the trees which look fine against the sweet blue of the evenin sky. I see the first star and think about makin a wish. What hogwash, I think, and make one anyways.

—Hey, Buglight, Tommy calls.

—What? I say, then realize that the best way to make a stupid nickname stick is by actually respondin to it.

—Whyn't you bring some of yer mum's super salmon sandwiches, and then he laughs so hard at himself that I don't even have the heart to tell him that he's fucked up again.

—You got me, Tommy, says I.

Somebody passes a beer into my hand and there are dogs on sticks hangin over the big fire so I sit down on a log and start suckin on this beer and it tastes fine and the fire has even started to keep the bugs away.

Then we're eatin dogs and there are bowls of cold cucumber soup and chips'n dip and it's all really fine except I have this funny thought which I don't say, I just think it, but I wish that I also had one of those great tuna sandwiches that my mum doesn't even make.

I'm on my second beer but what's the big deal, it's lite beer so Tommy fucked up again.

—What is this shit, Tommy? I call out.

—Hey man, it works. If you order lite they don't ID.

Which happens to be true. Even though Tommy looks about twelve.

It's actually a good party. I think about tellin Tommy but he's way over there with his sister eatin a dog and drinkin a beer. I mean it's way over there, I'm just relaxed here full of dogs and lite beer, why should I get up just to tell Tom that he didn't, for once, fuck up.

—Hey Tom. Good job with the party, I'm sayin, and he's grinnin like a skeleton, the bastard. But Kat is touchin my arm now to tell me she likes my T-shirt, it's a green one from Arizona with four kindsa cactus on it, so she is pointin to each one on my chest and I get to tell her what each one is, saguaro, ocotillo, paloverde, cholla. I even say them with the Spanish accent and she laughs.

—Everyone ready for dessert? Blist calls, shakin the bag of jawbreakers over his head.

—What the fuck is with those jawbreakers? I say.

But Blister is handin them out, one per person, everybody takes one and I'm gonna say no because bein like everybody is just fucked up but then Kat's got one and she's poppin it in her mouth and the next thing I know I got one of the things and at first I try to chew it and then the name jawbreaker makes more sense than I like to admit.

—Don't chew it, dummy, Kat says, but she is laughin and pushin on my shoulder at the same time.

—Crap! Tommy yells. It's burnin my mouth! And then he spits the thing into the fire.

—It's supposed to, jerkoff! Blister yells. —You fucked up man. That's it for you.

I'm thinkin the same thing, though, this fucker is *hot* and spittin it into the fire is probably the only thing in the universe I want to do, but Tommy has sinned first and been branded the fuckup and that means you can just forget about anyone else doin the same thing, even though I can tell by Johnny's face that he would like to do nothin more than launch the hot little fucker outta his chops and to the moon. We all just keep suckin the things.

—Hey, where's Al? I say through the clack of that hard little ball against my teeth.

Everyone looks around, shruggin. Not like Al to miss a function, specially a party. He usually just sits quietly in the corner but you can see by his face, by the relaxed smile on it, that he's havin fun just watchin our antics. I try to think and worry and wonder about where Al is just to keep the heat of that little ball outta my mind, and suddenly I'm through the worst of it and the ball is just the size of a ballbearing. Trouble is, that ballbearing is the most bitter thing in creation. I double over, about to retch it onto the sand, when it's gone. I grope for my beer and sluice the horrible taste down my throat.

—What the fuck is with those things? I cry out.

But abruptly I want a marshmallow. Maybe it's just the sweet I need, to counteract the horror of that taste.

—Marshmallow, I say.

The bag is in Blister's hand now and my god if everyone isn't just crowdin around the guy, palms out for their marshmallows. Nils practically knocks me to the sand to get to it, stuffin it into his mouth and chewin. Nobody's botherin to roast the things. I

199

get mine into my jaw and think, yeh baby, this is totally different than that evil jawbreaker, it's all soft and cool and sweet and gimme another I've just chomped this one down. So I get another, and then another, until there are three or four in my mouth and slowly, slowly the craving is subsidin.

—Mammemmmow, I say to Kat, and she answers with the same word, and we're all of us gigglin, swallowin marshmallows and wonderin why the hell we put ourselves through that.

That's when the closed-captioning starts. I first notice it on Johnny, he's sayin somethin about yesterday's Jays game, about a play at third, and when I look right under his chin there are these faint white lines, blurry but becomin clearer, letters takin shape, I see the word "umpire" and then "freaking out" and then "cocksucker" and finally a sentence resolves itself, somethin about the umpire freakin out after bein called a cocksucker by the baserunner. But a second later the words change, they change totally to say, instead, "I don't like baseball but you guys do so that's why I talk about it." I blink my eyes really fast to make it go away, then look at Blister and he's talkin about the jawbreakers, sayin that they were pretty cheap cause his dealer fucked him around last time with some bad weed so he was makin it up to him, and these words start to form under his face but suddenly change, they say, "I'm not really sure what these things will do, and I'm frightened." Then he's sayin that the hot taste is to dull your tongues so you don't taste the actual drug in the core, which is about as yummy as eatin the gallbladder outta a putrefyin skunk. But the words under him say, "I hope these things don't kill anybody."

—Hey, I call out, but nobody turns to me. My head suddenly feels like a balloon, light and airy, and from the pit of my belly I feel a warmth, but more than that, a flow of deadly colour, floodin me from within. Euphoria. I gasp and stagger a little, the feelin is wild, it feels totally fuckin pure and perfect.

I reel and get caught in Kat's arms.

—Hey, Kat, I says. Can you see the captionin too? The words? She is lookin down at my chin, so I know she can see it, lookin down and readin and she says, Oh Kyle, I want to too. Why don't you kiss me? I look down and those are the same words that write themselves beneath her chin, just what she said, so I grab her in my arms and press my open mouth against hers and her tongue is there against mine, the shape of her body, her breasts and hips pressin against me, into me, and for a second I get the sense that she is becomin part of me, enterin me, fusin with me.

We're thrashin through the underbrush, I'm mutterin and she's readin it, says, Don't worry. There's no poison ivy down here. Come on, and she's pullin me down to the ground pressin her mouth hard against me, hands roamin over my body, tracin the cacti on my chest, then pushin my shirt up and her mouth movin across my chest, suckin my nipples. I'm lookin up into the sky where the stars have started to chase each other around, formin long, sparklin lines of energy there, swirlin and spinnin in brilliant electric textures of white and blue and green and red, and the trees around us are swayin back and forth in hula-hula dancin beach pattern, shakin twigs and branches out this way and that and tremblin to boomin musical drums played on the giant congas that are floatin above us in yoga bumpin twist and flip swordfish songs of cucumber whisper chantin, while the wigs of a puppet dream curtsy their gooey sea-salt ballads to the moon beacon grinnin a grin of sin and joy.

◑ It's mornin, early early mornin just before the sun, and it's birds that wake me up, I hear em now in their gentle twitterin, my head feels like a ball of glass, not broken but cracked and if it touches anything too hard, or even vibrates from the sound of those birds, those sweet little goddammit shut-that-noise-up birds, it will explode into a billion glitterin bits of nothin. The inside of my mouth tastes like a rug, an old rug that beer got spilled on and maybe sand too. I lift my head to find out what gives. Quiet forest. Lyin on my arm a girl, whosit? Her face buried in my armpit, lyin on her stomach, look down her back and see her skirt hiked up and her bare ass. I reach down and push the skirt back into place and she stirs and raises her head and tries to smile but I can see it hurts too fuckin much so she puts her head down again and goes back to sleep.

Katrina. Tommy's sister.

I look up at the sky and it's fadin stars and hangin on the branch of a shrub over my head is a pair of Mr. Briefs underwear, which is the kind I got on.

Except I don't got em on. In fact, my shorts is unbuttoned and a piece of the private part of me is showin to the sky. I reach down and set things straight best that I can with one hand only.

Holy shit, I think. Did we? Did we, did we? Am I still? Did we?

I wanna ask Kat but she's snorin a little now and fuck does it hurt my head. Do I ever need a cuppa coffee. And a donut.

—Kat, I whisper. —Hey, Kat!

—Lemme sleep. My head hurts.

—Mine too. Mine hurts too, fuck does it ever hurt.

—Then shut up and let me sleep.

—Kat, I got a question for ya.

—Go to sleep Kyle. Just go to sleep.

—No, but I got a question. A yes or no.

—Just go to sleep.

—Okay, I will. But first a question. It's important.

—More important than the brick that keeps fallin on my head?

—Yeh. More important than that.

—Okay. Shit Kyle, what's the question?

—Did we fuck last night?

Okay, I lie. I shoulda asked that question, in fact that was the question that my brain sent to my mouth and was supposed to come out, but somewhere along the way it got changed into somethin totally different. Somewhere on the way to my jaw and throat and tongue it got changed to:

—You wanna find some coffee?

She lifts her head fast now and winces at the pain.

—I've never wanted anything more in my life. You're right, Kyle. We gotta get some coffees in us now, and she struggles to her feet, hands on both sides of her head like tryin to keep it from blowin apart, and I'm standin too and doin the same thing except when she looks the other way I snag my underpants off the branch and stuff em in my pocket but then from the corner of my eye I see Kat grab somethin small and white off the ground and stick it in her pocket and we start to move slowly through the forest, which is still pretty dark under a sky black and pink. We get to the clearin and the firepit is red and smokin and Tommy is sittin there with a marshmallow on a stick hangin over the coals, while all around are people sleepin, Blister and Johnny and Kat's friends and Nils propped against a tree and Andy face down on the sand.

I squat next to Tommy and Kat sits on the other side.

—You guys got a smoke? he asks, all glum.

Kat hands him one. The warm coals feel nice on my face.

—Kyle, why I always gotta fuck up, huh?

—You don't always fuck up, buddy, I say.

—Look at this. My party all fucked up cause everybody got screwed up by those goofballs Blister handed out, and I even missed the fun of that cause I spit mine out.

—You're not a fuckup, little brother, Kat says softly. —You're just unique. You do things different and to people who do things always the same you look like a fuckup. But you're not.

—Now yer just makin fun of me.

—Naw, she's right Tommy. Maybe you're a little awkward is all. It's no big deal. You'll probably make a million bucks with bein different. Don't sweat it.

—That's all bullshit and you know it.

I put my arm over his shoulder. —It ain't bullshit. The worst is that you try to fight bein who you are. Just be it. That's easier. If you think you're a fuckup, just play the part. You know, if you try to be a fuckup you might fuck it up and be perfect.

—A perfect fuckup.

—Yer a downer, I sigh.

—I guess that's what fuckups do. He pauses and smokes and throws the butt into the fire and misses, then sighs, his head down. —Kyle, sometimes the thing I fuck up the most is not tellin the guys who take me for what I am that I appreciate it. You don't screw me around like them other guys always do.

—Tom, we all love ya. We express it in different ways.

—Don't let none of em hear that "love" shit or we'll get beat up. Thanks. Buglamp! Then he grins.

—Tommy, we're gonna get some coffee. You wanna come?

—Thanks Sis, but I'm gonna stay here make sure everybody wakes up okay. I think it's the host's obligation to make sure nobody dies at your party.

—Kay, brudduh. Love ya.

She kisses him on the cheek and we get up and start to make our way along the path towards the bridge. The climb up the embankment is murder on my head and my knees are pretty weak and it don't help none that I ain't got underwear on and my willie keeps rubbin on my zipper. Before we climb Kat steps into her knickers and smiles at me and I think maybe now's the time to ask but before I can we're already climbin.

We head down the main strip, then cut off to a side street and over the highway bridge to where there's an all-nite donut shop.

The sun comes up and it's warm and nice this early in the mornin and the smell of everything is sweet and good. Not many cars out either and when we get to the shop there's only one guy in there and he's readin the paper and the girl behind the counter is cranky and makes no smile as she gets our coffee and a donut each. We sit at a little round wooden table at the front of the shop where the sun is comin in.

—This is the best fuckin thing I have ever tasted, Kat says after takin a dose of the black stuff. I agree. The headache is fadin fast.

We talk about junk and she starts drawin on a napkin, big ornate weaves of lines and dots and stars, and then she holds it up and says, I saw this last night.

I take it and look at it and she's right, it captures the texture and whirls of the stars and the trees. Then she starts to draw somethin else but she covers it with her hand and works fast and I try to pull her hand away but she don't let me see and it takes maybe five minutes. Then she puts both hands over it and looks up at me, looks right in my eyes, and her eyes are so blue and deep I feel all weak and maybe a little sick, and she says, I saw this too.

She moves her hand for one second and then puts it back and I see that it's a picture of a naked guy. Then she closes her hand and crumples the napkin up and stuffs it in her pocket and moves her leg so it's touchin mine. I look down into my coffee and drink from it for a minute, then look up.

—Are you a virgin? I suddenly ask.

She laughs, then covers her mouth.

—Well?

—I don't know.

—Me neither, I say, laughin too.

We're quiet for a second.

—I mean I've done other stuff. . . .

—Me too, I say.

—Like what? she asks, smilin.

—This'n that. Kissin. Feelin.

—Yeh, me too. You ever been to a feel party?

—Huh?

—A feel party. Ever been?

—What is that? I ask.

—I only gone to a couple. I mean they weren't meant to be a

special kinda party, just everybody got so drunk it just kinda happened.

—But what's it mean? What happened?

—Well okay, so it's best if there's a single bed. You gotta have one that's not against the wall, at least the sides aren't against a wall. Basically you get felt. Or you feel.

—By who?

—By everybody.

—Everybody?

—Yeh. It's best if the lights are off. What you do is you get under the blankets in the bed and you take off all your clothes. So then you're lyin under the blankets and you're naked and then everybody is around the bed on their knees. All around you. Then they stick their hands under the blankets.

I swallow.

—Then they feel you. They run their hands over you.

—Where?

—Everywhere. It can really suck, like if some fuckin goof starts stickin his fingers in you. It's actually better if it's mostly girls.

I swallow again. Kat looks right in my eyes and presses her leg harder against me.

—Just touch you. Slide their hands over you. The second time it happened it was the best, everyone was really good. There were some guys there but they were older, like in their twenties I think, so less idiotic.

—Did it feel good?

—Oh yeh! I got so horny with the touchin on the insides of my legs, I just kept spreadin them wider, and then on my tits too it was really nice but also especially on the bottoms of my feet which somebody was squeezin.

—Did you come?

—Naw. But that was okay, it wasn't that kind of feelin. It wasn't like I needed that. One guy did, someone started jerkin him off and he shot his load in like three seconds. He freaked out when he found out it was a guy who jerked him! Went and took a hot shower and came out totally red, I don't know if it was from the shower or embarrassment.

I look down at the wooden table, at my empty cup. I feel like I've been left out of somethin, somethin amazing and important.

I want to go to one of those parties, I want to be touched like that or touch someone like that. I shift in my chair, hard as a rock and feelin my cock pressed against the cold zipper. Then I look up quick.

—Kat, you wanna go to a movie?

—A movie, she cried. —What, now?

—No. I mean later, I say, my ears getting hot.

—What made you ask that now?

—I dunno. Fuck, nevermind.

—I'm sorry Kyle, it just seemed to come outta the blue. Sure I'll go to a movie with you. I'd love to. I've been waitin for you to ask.

I wonder if she means just waitin this morning or waitin like weeks or months or years. It don't really matter and I don't question it.

◑ When I get home my younger sis Isabelle is all, "Mom's mad at you cause you didn't come home last night" and I'm all, "Shut the fuck up it's nonna yer beeswax," but mostly I'm like that because I'm dead-tired and just wanna get a few hours shut-eye. I crawl into my bed but can't sleep right away, just lyin there thinkin about Kat and all. On Friday we're goin to a movie, don't know which one yet and don't care none either, it's after the movie that I'm thinkin about. Just when I'm almost asleep Isabelle busts in and says that Al is on the phone you wanna talk to Al he wants to talk to you but I'm just, "Fuck right off and lemme sleep take a message and leave me alone!" And she slams my door and then I'm out for like nine hours.

When I wake up Mum is standin over me with a tray with food on it.

—You really sick? she asks.

—Yeh, I say, even though it's not true, after all the sleep I feel a-okay, but if I tell her that I'd get in trouble.

—What's wrong?

—Head, stomach, I mumble, but I really wanna get up so here comes the soup and I can tell ya it's gonna be a miracle cure!

When I'm finally up there are four phone messages but especially one from Katrina. At first I'm scared that it's one of those "It was a bad idea, honey" kinda calls but then we yack for three hours until my ear feels like it's mushed on my head and my eyes are all buggy. Pretty soon it's time for bed and off I go but I slept all day so of course I'm just lyin there thinkin Friday Friday Friday Friday Friday Friday Friday Friday. . . .

◑ When I get up the next day I think, what am I gonna do for the three days till Friday night? I mean it's three days away so what do I do? I ask Mum if she wants anything done. She's seriously squir-relled by the idea that I'm askin for some job, then thinks for a few minutes with a this-is-a-dream-come-true look on her face, like I'm some genie and here are yer three wishes.

—There is that shed I was going to put up in the backyard. I'm so busy at the bank that I get home exhausted and haven't had a chance. What if you did it?

At first I'm thinkin of all that lumber I saw stacked on the patio that there's no damn way, I mean what do I know about buildin a shed, then I think what the fuck? Why refuse to do somethin just cause it might be hard or make ya tired? If Einstein or Martin Luther King thought what they were gonna do was too hard and instead just sat on their fat butts where would we be?

—Okay, I'll do it, I say. —Where do I start?

—Well, I've sketched everything out. Have a seat at the kitch-en table and I'll get the plans.

◑ And it's hard work. Sun pumpin down and me wearin a soaked undershirt while measurin and sawin and hammerin. At first there's nothin much to look at, sittin on the flagstone wall suckin from a jugga iced tea, lookin at cut two-by-fours or part of one wall nailed together, thinkin that don't look like nearly enough for the backbreak I'm puttin into this thing but then gettin back to it anyway, seein how this one part is half a inch too long and sawin then raspin it down so it fits exactly and perfectly, it almost starts to feel good.

I get a call while out there, my little sister comin out and shriekin, Kyle, yo Kyle, phone! Phone! Phone! over my hammerin.

—What? What?

—Phone! Don't be too long cause I'm talkin to Lia.

—A girl?

—Duh. You know Lia's a girl.

—No, you dork. Is it a girl who wants to talk to me?

—Nope. It's not a girl. It's a guy.

207

—Take a message.

I get back to work. Sometime in the afternoon I go to the can and ask her (still on the phone) who it was.

—Didn't leave a message. Said he'd call on the telephone later.

—Why do you always feel a need to state the obvious?

—Cause it's not always obvious to *me*.

—I ain't even gonna touch that one, I reply.

◗ It's 8:30 and gettin dark when I have to stop workin. I take a long, cool shower and eat some dinner with Mum sittin there at the table and all, "My boy's growin up!" and me all scared for a sec that she knows about what's supposed to happen on Friday and I'm all, "No, no, no. I ain't growin up. I'm just a little boy." And she gets mushy and wants a hug so I give her one. I'm so dead-tired that I watch TV for an hour and fall asleep on the couch at somethin like ten.

◗ The next day is the same, hot and me workin, but bit by bit the walls go up, the door, sides, and some paint. One call from Kat and we talk for half an hour but then her dad says she gotta get off the phone, but just before she goes she whispers, My mom and dad and Tommy gotta do some kinda Scouts thing tomorrow night. So my house is gonna be empty till late! Be here at seven.

I'm standin by the phone and I go for the kitchen chair but miss and *wump!* My ass is on the floor. I get up real quick before Sis sees me and I say goodbye and go back to the shed where I'm a total workdog tryin to keep all those thoughts from pilin up in my mind.

That evenin Johnny comes by to see what's up and sees the work I'm doin and makes fun of me some but I can tell as we sit on the cool patio stones and smoke that he's impressed and even thinks it's kinda cool that I can do this. We steal a couple beers from my mum's bar fridge in the basement and watch the night comin on, all the shadows creepin up and thickenin. I think about tellin him about Kat and tomorrow night but mostly don't want to jinx it, so keep my mouth shut and just say I'm gonna be down at the beach tomorrow night, don't you worry.

Then I'm off to bed and thank god I'm dog-tired which mixes with the beer or I'd be up all night twistin and clawin through my sheets.

Then it's Friday.

I wake up old-man early, 5:40, and am out and workin by 6:20. It's pretty good now cause it's cool and the work goes good. I get another layer of paint on the sides and then Mum comes out in her business clothes but still helps me get the roof (which I had to build on the ground) on top. She gimme a little lipstick peck on the cheek and goes off with a huge grin on her face. Then I put some paint on the door too and while it dries put the brackets and nails in place to hold the roof on. There are some joints that poke out a bit too far so I shave em down. By then the door is dry and I put the hinges on, then sight the hinges in the frame into place and drive the screws in there too, then am amazed at how easy the oiled pins drop in, it makes me feel good cause it means the frame and the door and everything is just right and bang on in size and shape. I open and close the door a buncha times and it swings just right. It's past noon and I drink some orange juice and sit on the garden wall and just look at this thing, this shed, and sigh. I mean it looks tops. Listen, I know yer thinkin, yo Kyle buddy, it's a god-damn garden shed not the statue of David, but unless you ever done some really hard work to get somethin made you won't understand, so don't even bother.

I clean up then, which takes a long time because I used about a thousand different tools and there's sawdust and wood shavings everywhere, plus oil paint to clean, brushes and all that crap, and by the time I'm all done I'm totally wiped out and go in to nap for a while.

Once I wake up to hear the phone ring ring ring, but then fall asleep before somebody gets it or it stops. I think as I drift off that maybe it's Kat but better not to get it in case the thing is off. I don't wanna know that yet. If that's gonna happen let me live as long as possible in this world where we do get together tonight, and let it only get wrecked at the last second.

When I wake up it's after six, which is later than I expected, so it's a rush that I gotta take a shower and wash my hair then try a blue T-shirt that says "Funky" on it but then take it off and try a green T-shirt that says "Swanky" on it and where the fuck did I get all these crap T-shirts? Finally I put on a buttonup shirt that I didn't even buy, Mum bought it for me and I always thought I hated it and have never even worn it before, but I try it on and it looks okay. Then I think I should put on some cologne, right, some smelly crap. Don't girls love that kinda thing? But I remember my older sister, she once said guys have no goddamn nose the way they swim through a pond of cologne whenever they go for a date so you almost gotta breathe through a hanky the whole time. So okay, I'm not gonna be one of those guys. I actually got one of those cologne tester things from the mall and I take off the lid and touch it twice on my neck. That's it. You can only smell it if your nose is right there. Here's hopin she puts her nose right there.

With the shirt and the cologne my hair dried too much without combin and now it's a funny shape and I gotta make it all wet again. Then guess who comes home? Isabelle. Crap. And she's all makin fun of me and I'm just "Fuck off!" with everything she says until she gets bored and calls Lia and says mean crap about me lookin like shit and goin on a date.

When I finally get the fuck outta the house it's about three minutes to seven. Mum is not home yet so no car. My bike has a flat (for the last three months) so it's walkin, and it's a half-hour walk at least and I'm gonna hurry so fast I'm gonna be sweatin like a pig. Great. Just fuckin great.

So what can you do but just go? So I go. I jog a little then walk, then jog. Then I think I forgot flowers. How can you go on a date without flowers, you dumbshit? What's she gonna do when you walk up to the door empty-handed? Think you're just some schmo come to get laid, that's what. Ain't that what I am? I stop dead on the sidewalk, just stop and stand there and think that I am a schmo. Just another fuckin guy, that's all. Just another fuckin guy, except I went easy on the cologne.

Except. Hmmm, except. Except she wants me too. Right? She asked me to her place, didn't she? Don't that make her a schmo too? No, it don't. But why not? Cause she's a girl? Well . . . yeh! But that don't seem right. And I mean, I like her too. She's cool. I've always thought so.

Crap, I think, leapin into the flowerbed of the house I'm standin before, yankin out some of the impatiens and chrysanthemums. Then a horn honks. I stop but don't look up. I just wait, thinkin, aw shit. Here we go. Then it honks again and I turn around, ready to say aw shucks, and I see it's Al in his pickup.

—Shit, I say, grabbin my chest. Al is grinnin at me out the window. He waves me over.

—Bejees, Kyle. You gettin married or somethin?

—Aw Al, what kinda loser you must think I am. I got a date.
With Kat.

—What doin?

—Well, we were goin to see a movie, but then she called yesterday and Tommy and his parents have some kind of Scouts
thing, so I'm just goin to her house.

—Alone at her house?

—Uh-huh.

—Sounds pretty important. What time are you supposed to be
there?

—Like fifteen minutes ago.

—One thing you never do, Kyle, is leave a date in a big ol
empty house just waitin for ya. Hop in.

Is there a better friend I got? A better friend anywhere on the
fuckin planet? I round the front of the truck and jump into the
passenger side, gotta squeeze in cause there's all this junk on the
front seat, boxes and crates and bags and whatnot. Al steps on it
and we're on our way.

I just look forward out the cab, my teeth chatterin a bit and my
belly fulla butterflies. He glances at me.

—Nervous?

—Naw. Yeh.

—First time?

—What? I say, turnin.

—"Naw, I bin nervous before." That's what yer supposed to say.

—But whaddaya mean by "first time"?

—You know what I mean.

—How'd you know?

—You might as well be sportin a t-shirt, "Ain't laid yet."

—Chee-rist, Al. You got any suggestions?

—If you need suggestions you sure ain't ready.

—Naw. I mean for the nervousness.

He's racin along now, drivin unusually fast for his style. The
other thing he taught me about speed is this: do it only when you
gotta. We squeal around a corner.

—Yeh, I got a suggestion. Be nervous.

—That's it?

—That's it. Anything else I tell ya would be horseshit.

He starts to slow down, then pulls into the driveway of Tommy
and Kat's house.

211

—I can't hardly breathe.

I look down at all the shit on the seat and the floor.

—Hey Al, what's all this crap?

—You don't need to know. Not right now.

There's somethin in his voice and suddenly everything about Kat is gone. Well, not gone, but pushed aside.

—Hey, you called me a few times. Look, I'm sorry I never got back to you.

—S'okay. You had things on your mind. Then he's quiet for a while, just the engine goin, he lookin straight ahead. Then he turns to me. —Kyle, I've gotta go. Tonight.

—Go?

—Yeh. Can't stand it in this city no more. Too many cars. Too many people. Too much crap.

—Where you gonna go?

—Home. Gonna go home.

—Back to Timmins?

—Yep.

—When?

—Now. These're all my things. I just was comin by your house to say goodbye.

—Then when you comin back?

—Never, Kyle. I'm never comin back here. I can't stand it. I mean, maybe I'll visit, but . . .

—But that's like a six-hour drive!

—More or less. Less the way you drive.

I look forward at the lights of Al's truck on the garage door.

—But I need you, I say too softly for him to hear.

—What's that?

I turn to him.

—I need you, Al. You're my best friend.

—I know. You're my best friend, too.

—Then stay here.

—Can't. Won't. Look.

He points through the windshield. Kat is standin at the screen door, squintin into the lights of Al's truck. She's wearin a miniskirt and a shirt that shows her midriff.

—Shit.

—Not the normal response to something like that, buddy.

—You know what I mean.

212

—Well, I hate to kick you out, but this truck leaves for Sudbury in thirty seconds. All visitors ashore.

Next thing I know I've got my arms around him and he's huggin me back and I'm bawlin and we just hold each other for about twenty seconds and then let go and he looks away for a second and wipes his eye. Kat opens the screen door and starts walkin down the driveway, her arms crossed.

—You got rubbers? he asks.

—Huh?

—Rubbers. Condoms. You got em?

—Oh shit.

He reaches across to the glove compartment and opens it, then pulls out a handful of condoms and tosses em in my lap. I shovel em into my pockets.

Kat reaches the truck and I open the window.

—Hi Kat.

—It *is* you! I was wonderin. Startin to worry you chickened out. Hey Al.

—Hi Katrina. You look nice.

—Thanks Al. What's up?

—I'm kinda late for an appointment. Just thought I'd taxi Kyle over, make sure he got here okay. Right Kyle, out you get.

I open the door and step onto the driveway and shut the door. Kat takes my hand in hers.

—Have a pleasant evening, he says, then puts the truck in gear and backs out. A quick wave and off he goes. I watch his taillights until they round a bend, and still stand there lookin.

—Are these for me? Kat asks.

—Huh? Oh, yeh.

She takes the flowers but I'm still looking up the street.

—Kyle. Are you gonna come inside now?

I turn and gaze at her face and for a minute it hurts so much to look at it, this beautiful smiling face just gazing at me in the failing light, that I think I might bawl some more. She tugs my hand, backing towards the entranceway, and I stand still for a moment, just watching her back away, and then our arms stretch and our locked hands rise and I take one step forward, and then another as we move together towards the door. ◗

Acknowledgements

I am grateful for the support and inspiration of my family: John and Arina Panhuyzen, Amber and Larry Pierson and kids, John Michael Panhuyzen, Natalie Panhuyzen and Jeff Pervanas, Neal Panhuyzen and Laura May Samakese; Kathleen Sandusky, Margaret Booth, John Buddo, James Sandusky; and my friends: Darren Wershler-Henry, Steve Venright, Alan Tomassini, Michael Stubitsch, Sasha Snickerdoodle, Lesje Serengeti, Mali Lol, Kristine Hackett, Karyn Greer, Ian Evans, Valerie Copeland, Katy Chan, Natalee Caple, Ollie B. Bommel, and Christian Bök.

Special thanks goes to Bonnie Halvorson for information about Persian carpets and museum attire. Thanks also to my uncle, Aat Veldhoen, for the beautiful cover image.

I also wish to express my gratitude to publisher Jan Geddes and assistant-to-the-publisher Barbara Glen.

The staff of Coach House Books provided technical assistance on design issues.

This book was written with the financial support of The Canada Council, The Ontario Arts Council, and The Toronto Arts Council. The grant system is absolutely essential to maintain and promote Canada's worldwide literary stature.

About the Author

Brian Panhuyzen is a writer of literary fiction, science fiction, avant-garde poetry, and screenplays. His work has appeared in *B after C, B+A New Fiction, ink magazine, The Malahat Review, On Spec, Open Letter, Oversion, Prairie Fire, Queen Street Quarterly, Rampike, Smoke, Torque,* and in a chapbook from fingerprinting inkoperated. He is a graphic designer and co-founder, with Natalee Caple, of TORTOISESHELL & BLACK, a Toronto-based small press that has published work by John Barlow, Natalee Caple, Nancy Dembowski, Lise Downe, Brian Panhuyzen, Stan Rogal, RM Vaughan, Steve Venright, Death Waits, and Darren Wershler-Henry. He is also a co-editor at *Descant* magazine. He has worked as an usher for the Toronto Blue Jays baseball club, managed one of the world's largest email servers, and written for several popular comedians at Montreal's *Just For Laughs* comedy festival. He has acted on both stage and screen and is also a musician and a pilot. He lives in Toronto.

Visit him on the Web at http://www.brianpanhuyzen.com.

About the Artist

Aatje Veldhoen is a renowned artist in the Netherlands. He attended the Federal Teachers' College in the garden of the Rijksmuseum in Amsterdam, and from 1956–1958 received a Royal Subsidy for liberal arts painting. His paintings, drawings, etchings, and sculptures can be found in, among others, the City Museum of Amsterdam, the Amsterdam Historical Museum, the Singer Museum in Laren, and in many private collections. He lives in Amsterdam.